TO KYLE

from the author

[signature]

NOV-15-2007

THE TERRORIST CREED

by Obi Orakwue

THE TERRORIST CREED

by Obi Orakwue

Obrake
Books
OBRAKE CANADA INC.
TORONTO, ONTARIO

Book designed by Leigh Beadon.

Library and Archives Canada Cataloguing in Publication

Orakwue, Obi
        The terrorist creed / Obi Orakwue.

ISBN 978-0-9782703-6-0

        I. Title.

PS8629.R35T47 2007   C813'.6   C2007-900837-2

Printed in Canada by Webcom Inc., Toronto, ON

**First Published in Canada in 2007
by Obrake Books.**
Obrake Canada Inc.
Toronto, Ontario Canada.
www.obrake.com/books

Author's Note

This is a work of fiction, all mention of real names, places, governments, organizations, people, race, episodes and events are used fictitiously to spice the fiction with a flavour of reality, authenticity and an entertaining edge.

This book is not meant to abate and explain reasons for terrorism and Islamic fundamentalism, let alone humanize terrorists, though humans they are.

"It is a sin to hate and terror to curse
All races are indispensable members of the human
community and civilization
And should respect our differences and honour our
common humanity"

Nothing is worth more saving than the mother earth.
Earth will outlive all sins and terror
It was here when we arrived
Offering us oxygen to breath
Harbouring the exhaust we exhale
Offering us water to hydrate,
Soil to cultivate and a chance to evolve
Transforming us as it offers us all
That's needed to become part of it
When we physically die and decay.
Demonstrating that nobody comes into earth
And leaves it with physical life
Let the mother earth remain forever young
For it's always been a divine and implied dream of all
human endeavour
The ever dominant earth
The immortal earth

The Creed

Shake up the world oh Allah and bring the infidel to her knees, for the Islamic kingdom to reign.

Oh Allah, let the Infidel grow old, let her memories engulf her dreams and let her wither so that the children of Islam can celebrate the future.

And on behalf of the Palestinian people and their cause, I thank thee omnipotent Allah of Mohamed and Islam for having created the courageous soul of blessed memory who dished out vengeance in advance against the incursors, though he didn't do it on a large enough scale, because it was the meagre and incomplete nature of the attempt that precipitated the displacement of the Palestinian people. However, I hail thee oh merciful Allah for having authorized the noble attempt.

Allah, in thy tender and abundant mercy, do bless the movement, because it is the only independent Arab front with enough revolutionary ardour to wage a vigorous war and bring the infidel to her knees for the Islamic renaissance to come. A terrorist movement they call it, but Allah, imperialism, capitalism and hegemony is terrorism, even more terrifying than terror itself 'cause it entails economic, political, cultural and military terrorism. An imperialist, an infidel is a terrorist: a white collar terrorist, but terror is terror and terror we must forever use against the infidel, because terror is the only language the infidel uses and dread and only terror can retard and grow the infidel old. So help me Allah.

Allahu Akbar!

Allahu Akbar!

Chapter 1
Cairo, Egypt
May 15, 2002

American front yards and gardens blossomed with brightly coloured flowers and plants in the orchards twinkled with fresh leaves and Americans were full of joy of the spring. But it was full blown summer in Cairo Egypt, the African sun scorching the earth.

No sirens sounded in Cairo in the morning of this catastrophe day anniversary – the date Palestinians remember as the displacement day, when the state of Israel was founded and carved out in 1948. Abdul, a Palestinian residing in Egypt, woke up in his three-bedroom house in a Cairo neighbourhood. He observed a three minutes of silence, facing east to Mecca, and knelt down on the mat spread on the uncarpeted floor to pray, lauding Allah:

Shake up the world oh Allah

And bring the Infidel to her knees

For the Islamic kingdom to reign

Oh Allah, let the infidel grow old

Let her memories engulf her dreams

And let her wither

So that the children of Islam can celebrate the future

And on behalf of the Palestinian people and their cause

I hail thee oh Allah

For authorizing the great attempt

And in thy abundant mercy

Bless the movement

'Cause, it is the only independent Arabic front

With enough revolutionary ardour

To wage a vigorous war

And bring the Infidel to her knees

Silence.

Though the Supreme Disciple betrayed hugely the trust I have for his judgement when he believed that I sabotaged the movement for having failed in the attempt to deliver on an assassination mission. The Supreme Disciple gaffed at that. Yes, he gaffed. But gaffing is part of leading, so bless him Allah.

Allahu Akbar!

Allahu Akbar!

Prayed Abdul and rose.

The neighbourhood was very quiet as Abdul took his horse to the neighbourhood livery yard, except for the children reciting verses from the Koran at an Islamic school nearby. He came back from the livery yard and dressed up in a traditional Arab Kaffiyah headdress and, with a briefcase in hand, he bid adieus to his three-bedroom house that sat on a rise on the edge of the neighbourhood. And in the company of Omar his five–year-old son, he left in a taxi for the Cairo international airport to board the 1980 built Boeing airplane of Egypt Air, to Canada via Washington, USA.

As the taxi drove to the airport, Abdul took stock of his membership in the Islamic renaissance movement. A membership that began in Kabul, Afghanistan. Abdul was recruited by an Islamic scholar named Mamud. Mamud was dressed in traditional Islamic warrior attire while he administered the oath of indoctrination to Abdul and other new recruits on the swearing-in day.

"Do you agree to shoot, knife, set off bombs, explosives and kill as many infidels as possible?" said Mamud.

"Yes, I do," replied Abdul.

"And if necessary to kill innocent people within the vicinity of the target?" asked Mamud.

"Yes, I do," answered Abdul.

"Do you accept failure to carry out the orders of the movement as treachery punishable by death?"

"Yes, I do," replied Abdul.

"Do you agree that trusting an infidel with the secrets of the movement is a sin punishable by death?"

"Yes, I do," replied Abdul.

"Do you accept death and an eventual place in paradise with the holy prophet of Allah as the reward for furthering the establishment of the Islamic kingdom here on earth?"

"Yes, I do," said Abdul.

"So help me Allah," said the scholar.

"So help me Allah," echoed Abdul.

"Allahhu Akbar!" intoned the scholar.

"Allahu Akbar!" chorused Abdul.

Abdul became a sworn and full member of the Islamic renaissance movement, a trained jihad soldier ready to kill the infidels.

"Over here," said the scholar, waving Abdul to a nearby table where another scholar gave Abdul a document, 'The Boyat', to sign. The Boyat is an agreement of loyalty signed by all Islamic renaissance movement trainees and militants, agreeing to go to any country in the world for the purpose of Jihad and wait to be called upon to carry out a task of terror.

Eight years crawled by before Abdul was sent on a mission to Saudi Arabia to assassinate an American government Goodwill Ambassador on Middle East matters.

CHAPTER 2
The Mission
Riyahd, Saudi Arabia.

Abdul arrived in Riyahd aboard a Royal Jordanian airways plane on a windy Sunday evening. He brandished a fake Afghanistan diplomatic passport to the Saudi Immigration and was shown the diplomatic exit route. Sadiq, the movement's permanent plant in Riyahd, smiled broadly on seeing Abdul alight from the airport's arrivals hall.

"Welcome to Riyahd," he said.

"Did you have a good flight?" he added as they greeted.

"Yeah," replied Abdul, as they walked to the parking lot where they climbed into the back of a cloned Afghanistan diplomatic Mercedes jeep. The chauffeur fired the engine and they rolled out of the airport park-ing lot. The thirty-minute drive from the airport to the Saudi Royal Guest Hotel in uptown Riyahd was done in complete silence. The car pulled up in front of the guest hotel where Sadiq had made a reservation two days earlier in the name of Dr. Sadiq Adamu. They stepped out of the car and climbed the front steps into the re-ception as the chauffeur proceeded to the hotel park-ing lot. A bellhop attired in the Saudi national colours hurried towards them and collected their bags and they marched to the reception counter.

"Sadiq Adamu," said Sadiq to the receptionist who wore a headgear in Saudi national colours. He handed the keys to the bellhop and they made towards the el-evators. In the suite, Sadiq tipped the bellhop $100.

He bowed his thanks and left. Quickly Sadiq and Abdul unpacked his bag and went to work. They recon-nected the security gadgets – bomb detectors, wiretap detectors and anti-bomb detectors, and the recep-tor. They scanned the room for the next 15 minutes for bombs, wiretaps and other listening devices.

"I think it is clean here," said Sadiq.

"I hope so," replied Abdul.

"What is the latest assessment?' asked Abdul.

"He will be arriving here in the next eight days and will occupy the penthouse of the hotel. The state dinner to welcome him to Riyahd will be a day after his arrival, and it will be held in the Royal palace. From the experts' assessment, it will be almost impossible to access the pent house," said Sadiq, looking upwards.

"And the parking lot is laden with cameras and bomb detectors. But I think we have a chance in the Royal palace during the state dinner," he added.

"What a goddamn place to do the deed," Abdul said quietly but thoughtfully.

"It will be the greatest insult on the Saudi plutocracy that an American government Goodwill Ambassador was slain right inside the Royal Palace," said Sadiq, nodding indulgently.

"I hope it works out well," said Abdul.

"And the bomber?" he asked.

"He's well psyched up, almost at the peak, ready to do his deed as a devout Fadeyin. He will be making the Fadeyin suicide video recording a day before the deed," said Sadiq.

Hours later, when Sadiq and the driver left the government guest hotel on their way home, they pulled up somewhere on a deserted street and replaced the fake diplomatic plate number with the car's original and normal plate number, and disappeared into the starry moonlit Riyahd night.

CHAPTER 3
Royal Palace, Riyahd

Abdul and Sadiq spent the next few days fitting the prosthesis with pounds of explosive, wires and other doings of plastic bomb making, enough to wipe out any living thing within an area of ten meters square.

"Yes!" said Sadiq, pounding his right fist into his left palm, and sat back as he connected the last pair of wires.

"Ready," he added.

"Slot in the fuse now and the whole building will be buzzing with alarms and sirens," said Abdul. "The whole place is wired with bomb and explosive detectors."

"And that will be our funeral," added Sadiq.

"As it is now, no bomb detector can detect it because the circuit is open and can only become closed by inserting the fuse. Good stuff," he said, and bent to kiss the ensemble.

* * *

Abdul and Sadiq, in the company of the suicide bomber, arrived at the royal palace and proceeded to the banqueting hall, priding themselves as Bahrian invitees of the house of Saud. Five minutes later, the American government Goodwill Ambassador arrived at the royal palace.

Abdul looked around the fabulously beautiful and grand palace with great relish for the lavish exhibition of Arabic architecture. He scooped a glass of non-alcoholic wine from the waiter's tray and his gaze made an arc across the hall in search of Sadiq, the bomber and their target.

Sadiq was busy chatting with a Turkish-looking woman in her 50's in the middle of the hall. The Suicide bomber was somewhere about forty meters from the target as he talked and beamed with the royals. The hall contained an elite assembly of Saudi Arabia's rich and powerful. Some of them were members of the high council of the Ulema, a twenty-member religious group. The Ulema act as the Supreme Court, guiding the government on sensitive matters. The Ulema was particularly designed to spice the government's decisions with a religious flavour and deflate any potential public criticisms.

It was the Ulema that issued the go ahead order supporting the house of Saud's decision to host the USA military presence on the land of Mohamed.

The Suicide bomber sipped his juice from the glass he was holding and limped closer on his bomb laden prosthesis towards the target. His slight limp and prosthesis were camouflaged and covered by his flowing immaculate white robe made from high quality Saudi jacade. He paused and cast a searching glance; his gaze found Abdul at his corner. Abdul scratched his head to clue him in to retreat.

"A lot of casualties" thought Abdul.

Minutes later Abdul saw a man walk up to the target, shake his hand and embrace him heartily, then both walked off down the hall to a balcony. The suicide bomber followed the two and approached them on the balcony, dipping his hand into the pocket of his robe, and glanced around to find Abdul. Abdul blinked, clueing him to reach his knee and slot in the fuse. Abdul glance at his wrist watch – truly, the bomb detonator – and was seconds short of pressing the tiny knob when, on a second and harder look, he realised that the man chatting and smiling with the American Goodwill Ambassador was the Pakistani Ambassador to Riyahd, and five meters to their left was the Emir of Mecca, chatting with a famous Arab singer and composer. Abdul restrained.

"There could be casualties, but not the Emir of Mecca, the Pakistani Ambassador and an Arab musical icon. Too much to lose," he thought.

The suicide bomber waited to be blown to pieces and be received in the kingdom of Allah as a martyr, but nothing happened. He looked towards Abdul for a response but Abdul looked nervously away, he knew that the bomb detectors and alarms must've been set off in some quarters of royal palace, and soon, security men with tracers would swarm the banquet hall.

"It would be suicidal. Nobody kills the Emir of Mecca and remains alive and popular in the Arab world. It would mean achieving an aim and destroying it at the same time, and it's not worth it," thought Abdul.

He saw three royal guards approach the suicide bomber and drag him further down the balcony. When they were about 12 meters away from the Emir, the singer and the Pakistani Ambassador, he pressed the tiny knob on his wrist watch - the detonator. A loud explosion ensued. Red lights and alarms began to whirl in the palace. Confusion ensued as people ran back and forth between the banquet hall and the palace. Abdul and Sadiq made their way to the parking lot as planned, and screeched out of the palace, as dazed, wounded and mostly frightened and disoriented guests emerged from the smouldering banquet hall. The suicide bomber and the royal guards died instantly, and their remains were scattered in the immediate vicinity.

The explosion in the royal palace banquet hall made headlines in the Saudi and international newspapers and media. Abdul called the military commander of the movement to explain what happened and asked for more time to deliver. The military commander understood and encouraged him.

"A wasted opportunity though, but all hope is not lost. It could've served our purpose to the letter had you guys succeeded inside the palace. It could've been a knockout blow. Anywhere you hit him inside Riyahd is equally good, less heavy and devastating, but a blow nonetheless. But this time, get it done," said the military commander.

Chapter 4
Saudi Royal Guest Hotel

"It's alright here, we can do it here in the hotel," Abdul said to Sadiq as they deliberated on where to hit the Goodwill Ambassador, having failed the original, scripted plot.

"Here in the hotel premises," echoed Sadiq in deep thought.

"Good idea," he said as he began pacing the room.

On the fifteenth day as a guest in the hotel, Abdul met Nathan, an employee. They met in the hotel service elevator. Sadiq had done the underground investigation through the Riyahd investigative arm of the movement. Nathan worked in the security sector, in the computer and camera room of the guest hotel.

Nathan looked askance at Abdul as he stepped into

the elevator. Askance because the service elevator is strictly for the staff of the hotel, and Abdul wasn't wearing any service badge.

"Service elevator, eh?" Abdul said to Nathan in response to his unspoken question.

"Yes," replied Nathan.

"I am Saif, and you?" asked Abdul.

"Nathan," he replied.

"I am a guest in the hotel and I wonder if you could do me a little favour Nathan," said Abdul.

"At your service, sir" replied Nathan promptly.

"Could you arrange for me 100g of the south American stuff, cocaine, and a bottle of brandy, Remi Martin VSOP?" asked Abdul, his hoarse Yemeni accent shaping his request.

Nathan froze.

Drugs and alcohol are grave crimes in Saudi Arabia, and this stranger was pleading for him to commit a crime.

"Is he setting me up?" thought Nathan.

"Can't be, any person staying in the royal guest hotel is somebody who could afford to spend $3000 a night on accommodation, people who have so much money, power and connections that just the amount that leaks out in drinking sprees, hotel bills and tips, pleasure trips, telephone bills, parties, drugs and gifts is enough to make hundreds of poor people like you an average man in any modern society in the global village. And nobody investigates their habits. This hotel is way off the limits of petty investigations. He can't be setting you up. People like him are not out to hunt men like you. They have no time for people of your social and economic status, and besides he is a foreigner. You've never heard of foreigners in the Saudi Royal secret service. Besides, whatever happens now, whether you agree to do him the favour or reject him,, you are involved in this drug and alcohol purchase conspiracy," said an inner voice to Nathan.

"Ehmm, sure, but I don't think it will be ready today," replied Nathan nervously.

"When do you think it will be ready?' asked Abdul.

"Probably tomorrow evening or the next. You know how it is here in the Kingdom,"

"Alright tomorrow," agreed Abdul. "How much will it cost me?"

"$12,000 or so, I'm not sure. I've never bought or

sold either of the items you want, I'm only guessing," said Nathan.

"I pay upfront eh?" said Abdul.

That's more like it here, upfront," replied Nathan.

"Good," said Abdul, reaching into the deep pocket in his brown robe. He handed Nathan a bundle of crisp US dollar bills.

"Here is $15,000," he said, and dipped a hand into another pocket and pulled out another bundle and handed to Nathan.

"I don't know, but it will be about $3,000."

The button size digital camera and tape recorder at his robe's collar were filming and recording every move and response.

"Tell me when you fetch the stuff. I am in suite 15," he said as the elevator stopped and he stepped out into the corridor.

At home that evening, Nathan counted and recounted the money. He had $20,000 in his palms. He kept it on the table and stared at it for hours as thoughts fleeted through his mind. He'd never had that kind of money in his palms before.

"You can pack your belongings and move to Israel, to

Ethiopia, to the USA, South Africa, Brazil or Argentina and start a new life. You've wanted to own a little business of your own, and the money on the table can move you and start a little business for you. You can still get a bus to Manaman, Bahrian tonight. But what if you are being monitored?" the thought goes.

That evening, Nathan found his way to a house in a relatively clean and affluent neighbourhood in Riyahd. Three men sat on the mat sipping cognac and smoking cigars in the living room of the house as Nathan stepped in.

"I need some stuff," said Nathan confidently to a bare footed, tall and lanky man in a simple white smock.

"A hundred grams," he added.

"It's $10,000 now, hope you know it," said the man.

"Since when? And why?" asked Nathan.

"The city is dry," replied the man.

"Truly, it's dry now," agreed Nathan.

Nathan gave him a bundle of $10,000 and received a large capsule of a hundred grams of pure Columbian cocaine.

"And a bottle of Remi Martin VSOP," said Nathan, accepting the capsule from the man.

"$500," said the man.

Nathan counted out five bills and gave them to the man. He had $9,500 left on him.

"Thank God that there are rich men who indulge in drugs and alcohol and will pay poor people like me to fetch it for them," thought Nathan.

$9,500 was almost Nathan's yearly salary. That night, Nathan cooked a healthy, mouth-watering kosher meal, but could hardly eat it or contain his joy at the sudden income. He slept late, woke early and set off to work.

Abdul was navigating through history, politics, and current world affairs as they related to the Arab world and the Islamic fold.

He went through the history of Yemen in the fifties, when the death rate was high and the birth rate low in the province of Hodeidah, so Governor Khalidi Ashashml decreed that all bachelors and spinsters must get married immediately or be thrown in jail. Parents were also promised jail terms should they reject would be in-laws. Lots of peasants got married to daughters of the rich and famous. Abdul wished it could happen in this present day, and he knew whose hand he would ask in marriage. He thought of the 1967 Arab-Israeli war that lasted for only six days and ended with the defeat of the Arab nations and subsequent seizure and annexation of Palestinian and Jordanian lands. Just six days! Incredible. The Palestinian refugees, Haram al Sharif, the Gulf war, Operation tin cup, Iraq, Iran. It's all bent against the Islamic fold, he thought as the doorbell rang. He got up and went to the door, peeped through the security peephole and saw Nathan. He went back into the bedroom to fetch the micro video camera. He opened the door, and Nathan stepped into the suite.

"Good day," said Nathan.

"Did you get the stuff?" asked Abdul, ignoring his morning wishes.

"Yes, here," said Nathan, handing him the wrapped bottle of brandy and the capsule of cocaine.

"Good lad," said Abdul, patting Nathan on the shoulder, his camera recording the scene.

Two days later, Sadiq met Nathan in the elevator and the scene with Abdul was repeated. This time Nathan earned $8,000 in profits.

CHAPTER 5
Two Days Later
Manaman, Baharian Island

Abdul invited Nathan for an evening outing the next day. They knew Nathan would have that day off. Though Nathan was growing afraid of the approach, thinking it may be a homosexual invitation, but he accepted the invitation. He met Abdul in a street 400 meters from the hotel. Nathan seated himself comfortably in the front seat of the 1996 Honda civic coupe and fastened his seat belt.

"You are welcome aboard," said Abdul.

"Thank you" replied Nathan smiling shyly. He'd never hob-nobbed with the guests of the hotel. Abdul turned left at the end of the long wide avenue into the road leading to the motorway, heading to the Gulf port of Damman.

"We are driving out of town," Abdul said. "You know how it is here in the kingdom, everything is forbidden, from attending musical concerts or basking with friends at a resort swimming pool to open association with unveiled woman."

"Yeah,, I know" replied Nathan

At Damman, they joined the King Fahd causeway that was constructed in 1987 and connects Saudi Arabia with the Nation of Bahrain. They cruised down the 26km motorway to Manama, a border town of Bahrain, and found their way to Exhibition Avenue, the most lively avenue in Manama and one of the most lively in the Arab world. Nathan was surprised at the number of cars with Riyahd plate numbers on the avenue. They parked and went into a bar filled with mainly Saudis gulping down glasses of beer and spirits and flirting with unveiled and half naked local crumpets, while Arabic highlife music played loudly.

They joined the razzle.

After two hours of relishing the bar, they retreated to a hotel suite behind Exhibition Avenue, where Sadiq had been lodging since the previous day.

"Welcome pals," said Sadiq as Abdul and Nathan came into the hotel suite.

"Have your seats," he added, waving them towards the chairs.

"I was about to watch a documentary before you came in. And I hope you will find it interesting," he said, after they were seated.

"Pay attention Nathan," he added.

They watched in silence as Abdul stepped into the elevator in the royal guest Hotel in Riyahd and began a conversation with Nathan and eventually handed him bundles of US dollars. And as Nathan entered suite number 15 and handed Abdul a capsule and a bottle of brandy. As Abdul prised the capsule open and shook out some grains of white powder on his tongue and tasted. The audio was excellent.

The screen went grey for a moment and came on normal again. Sadiq went into the elevator and the whole scene was repeated.

"Bastards," thought Nathan.

"You never trust the sons of bitches. Never trust an Arab," his father of blessed memory would always tell him.

"Do you like it?" asked Abdul, looking at Nathan.

"It is interesting. Serious joke eh?" replied Nathan.

"No, it's fact, not fiction," replied Abdul.

Silence.

They studied themselves while murderous rage welled up inside Nathan, but he kept his cool and waited for the terms of the blackmail, the ransom.

"Nathan, Saudi Arabia is a holy land, the guardian of Islamic faith, and it adheres strictly to alcohol ban. Defiling the holy land by selling alcohol could earn you five years in jail and about one thousand lashes of the cane. Drug dealing is banned, not only in Saudi Arabia but in all countries of the world. Dealing drugs in Saudi Arabia is punishable by death at most and a life sentence in the minimum," said Abdul

"I'm aware of that," replied Nathan.

"Where are you from Nathan?" asked Abdul.

"I'm an Ethiopian," replied Nathan.

"Even in Ethiopia, nobody walks out scot-free from a court for dealing drugs, am I right?"

Nathan looked him over, his eyes burning with hate.

Silence reigned as the two waited and studied each

other.

"So what do you want from me?" Nathan asked.

"Good!" said Abdul, sitting up. "Let's talk business."

"You work in the security room of the guest hotel, don't you?" asked Abdul.

"Vey I do" replied Nathan.

Abdul looked at him on hearing the Yiddish word 'vey'.

"Are you Jewish?" Abdul asked.

"No, but I've lived and worked in Jerusalem. I worked in a farm owned by a Yiddish speaking Jew," Nathan said, half lying.

Half lying because truly Nathan was an Ethiopian Jew, a Falash Mura as they are referred to. His great grandparents had converted to Christianity in the thirties at the height of anti-Semitism in Ethiopia and Europe. Nathan's family was an Orthodox Jewish family that settled in Ogaden, South-eastern Ethiopia in late 1880's.

One dry, sunny Saturday afternoon, his great grandfather, his granny and his father, then a toddler, were in the synagogue observing the Sabbath. His grand uncle had stayed home in the old family compound, observing his own Sabbath. There was a great drought in the perennially dry Ogaden region, and there was no grazing land for the herds. A truck descending a steep hilly road in the neighbourhood galloped, ungoverned, into a dry patched field where camels, a few cattle and a donkey owned by the local evangelical priest were grazing on the scanty dry grass. The truck knocked down two lactating camels, and four others. The rest of the animals in the field had stopped lactating, and the milk from the herd was the staple for the neighbours and the faithful of the evangelical church. In anger, some of the neighbours and the faithful chased the motorist in a mob. The man ran into Nathan's ancestral compound, crossed the fairly large patio and jumped over the compound fence into the next compound and continued the flight for his life. Some of the mob chased after the motorist, but others stayed behind in the compound, vandalising it. They seized Nathan's intense brown-eyed, then young grand uncle. The intense brown eyes were inherent to Nathan's family, and the locals called them the evil eyes. The mob beat and killed his grand uncle in their ignorance and hate.

Months later, the family converted to Christianity out of fear for their lives. But they never attended church services regularly, and they still seriously observed the Sabbath and all Jewish traditions in the secrecy of their home.

"We are Jews. We converted to Christianity for convenience of existence and safety for our lives. Tell the children and your children's children. And do not marry the gentiles, observe the Sabbath and all the Jewish rules and read the Torah in the secrecy of your household," Nathan's father would remember his granny saying to his father, though Nathan's father later married a black Ethiopian woman.

In the late forties, after the holocaust and the eventual establishment of the state of Israel, when anti-Semitism seemed to be on decline in the world, the family reconverted to Judaism.

In the early 60's the family that was then comprised of Nathan's father, his toddling self and his brothers, contemplated migrating to Israel in response to the law that guaranteed Israeli citizenship to Jews from anywhere in the world.

"Every Jew has the right to come to Israel" said the

law.

But Nathan's father died in the fall of that year, impeding their emigration plan. In the 80's, when Nathan was in his teens and the Jewish Immigration law had been amended, in 1970, to reflect the Nazi definition of Judaism:

"Every person with Jewish roots and connections, non-Jewish spouses, children and grandchildren of Jews, have the right to come to Israel"

Nathan immigrated to Israel after spending two years at the Beta Israel community in Addis Ababa.

On his arrival to Jerusalem, Nathan perceived tension in the Israeli atmosphere. The tension was almost tangible, or so it seemed to him, having come from a completely different society. In Ethiopia, Nathan's problems had been low income and low budget, but in Jerusalem, his problem was being a black person, a 'fake Jew' who's come to live in the Israeli economy and not in the nation and community of Israel, he was made to understand.

However, Nathan enrolled and did the compulsory three years of Israeli military service, and later got a job in a farm owned by a Yiddish speaking Jew. The farm grew tomatoes, Jerusalem artichokes and other vegetables from the cruciferous family, including broccoli, cabbage, cauliflower and all produce that help in the protection against prostate cancer and general health of the heart. Twice Nathan tried to marry Jewish girls in Jerusalem, and twice he was refused for not being a real Jew. First it was by an Ashkenazi Jewish family – eastern European Jewish descendants who are referred to as the 'whites' and elite Jews.

"Sorry, but we, I, my wife and the entire Ebehl family, wants to marry our daughter to a real Jew, so that our grand children will not have a problem of Jewishness,' Mr Ebehl had told Nathan.

The second time it was by a Sephardic Jewish family – the Jewish immigrants from North Africa and the Middle East who are regarded as the 'blacks' of the Jewish fold. The Hezik family didn't mention names or reasons, but refused to give their daughter's hand in marriage to Nathan. But Nathan knew without a doubt it was because he was black skinned and a falash mura. However, Nathan went on with his life, working diligently in the farm, observing the Sabbath and reading the Torah. One Rosh Hashanah – the Jewish New Year that begins at the end of September – a group of Orthodox Jews decided that Schimita should be reintroduced and observed. Schimita is a sabbatical year observed every seven years when the land of Israel is supposed to lie fallow. It had been in serious observance for centuries, and Israeli farmers were allowed to cultivate their lands, all they needed to do was obtain a deed of sale from the chief rabbinate that arranged the sale, and normally the land was sold to a non-Jew, usually Palestinians. Then fruit and vegetable farms were exempted from Schimita years as they are considered kosher and also because Israel's economy was strictly agricultural. But in the present day and the knowledge-based economy, the Orthodox Jews had argued that the deed of sale would no longer stand valid and the farms must lie fallow during which period the Orthodox Jews eat only fruit and vegetables grown outside Israeli soil.

"The Torah commandments demand Schimita and it must be observed. Besides, selling lands to the Palestinians is un-Jewish," argued the splint of Orthodox Jews who wanted Schimita reinstated.

But to Nathan, they were a fruit and vegetable import cartel, exploiting Schimita to make their racket.

Well, that's a whole lot of Jewish stuff. The Jews, like many other groups of people, always want to anchor themselves closer to their own culture and religion. Nathan was most concerned because the vast farm land he worked lay fallow and he lost his job. He tried but failed to find a new job. Jobless, Nathan fled his one room flat in a run down Jerusalem neighbourhood to Riyahd, Saudi Arabia and obtained his present job, and he loved it.

In Riyahd, Nathan cooked and ate kosher, traveled near, kept his Judaic identity top secret, read the Torah and practices Judaism in the secrecy of his home. And generally kept to himself and enjoyed the life that an Arabic capital city can offer a man of his age, means and race.

"I don't like that language, you know," said Abdul.

"Now listen," he continued.

A pause.

"You know how a bomb detector and security alarms functions, don't you?" asked Abdul.

"Yes I do," replied Nathan.

"I want you to disconnect the bomb detecting device, the alarms and the surveillance camera that covers presidential parking lot, between 9.30am and 9.45 am on Saturday morning," said Abdul.

"Disconnect the security camera and the bomb detector in the parking lot for some fifteen minutes on Saturday morning, eh?" Nathan repeated.

"Correct," said Abdul, smiling cruelly, a smile that contained all the irony of Nathan's situation.

"And when I do that?" asked Nathan thoughtfully.

"We will destroy the tapes," said Abdul.

"Together?"

"Yes, together," confirmed Abdul.

"How will I know you don't have extra copies?" asked Nathan.

"My word, besides, I wouldn't want to see you anymore after that," said Abdul.

"Alright," said Nathan.

"But if I may ask, ehm…" began Nathan, then stopped mid-sentence.

"Don't ask questions. It's better you were not told and you don't know anything. Find out for yourself what they are up to, if you must. These are very dangerous people as you can see. Rich and dangerous," an inner voice told Nathan.

"If you may ask…"

"Go ahead, ask your questions," urged Abdul.

"No, No. It's alright. I've nothing to ask," assured Nathan.

Abdul looked him in the eyes for a moment and noticed the thoughtfulness in the tiny, shiny brown eyes of Nathan.

"Remember, do not get smart. Do as you obliged. And make no mistakes, I'm not afraid of your getting smart, but rather I'm trying to make you understand that you are better-off complying. Remember you've been paid for this job," said Abdul

Nathan looked askance at him.

"$17,500, you made from selling the drugs and alcohol to us might not quite be your price if you were allowed to negotiate, but we think it's good a sum for a computer and security room hotel worker to disconnect some screen and alarms system for a period of fifteen minutes on a Saturday morning," said Abdul.

"And what does a Yiddish speaking Ethiopian, former farm worker say to that?" said Sadiq, who'd been taciturn all the time.

"Nothing," replied Nathan in a deep low voice.

"They even know how much I made from the transaction. But how? They must have been following me, or rather they know where and how much the stuff costs. Son of bitches," thought Nathan.

"Don't you think that I will be held responsible if anything happens within that period, responsible for the fifteen minute security lapse? Why the bomb detector was deactivated and why no video recording was made during the same period?' Nathan asked, hoping that they might have a good and reasonable idea and alibi for him, so as to prevent comebacks.

"You're right, but ehm, I'm sorry, but we ain't thinking of providing an alibi for you now. You can come up with any alibi, or rather you can say anything to anybody after the whole thing is done," said Abdul.

Chapter 6

The journey from Manama, Baharian Island to Riyahd, Saudi Arabia was done in absolute silence. Nathan never stopped wondering what the two Arabs were up to. A million and one reasons and suspicions crisscrossed his mind, but he couldn't narrow it down to anything, though he was sure that explosives would be involved. He was also sure that he would go to jail either way, and that there was no way out. He worked night shifts on Saturdays and, to honour the demands of his blackmailers, he had to officially ask for a swap of shift for that day. He thought of blowing the whistle by going to the authorities, but restrained, knowing that he wouldn't be pardoned by the Riyahd Islamic prosecutors for dealing drugs and alcohol. He was non-Arab and black: if the prosecutors and Islamic judges rendered justice with mercy, life in prison would still be the best deal he could get, and he wasn't ready for that. Life is too short to waste any bit of it behind bars. For Nathan, the most awkward part of the blackmail was that it involved breaking the Sabbath rules. Normally, as an Orthodox Jew, he was supposed to spend Friday evening to Saturday evening in the synagogue. In his case, spend it in his house because he keeps his Judaism a secret in this holiest land of Islam. On the Sabbath day, he was not suppose to operate any machinery or work of any form, cannot drive or be driven – this last option he could circumvent by walking the twenty kilometres stretch from his house to the hotel and work the stairs to his third floor office room to avoid operating the elevator, which is machinery. But what was not avoidable was operating the machinery in the office, which was the core of his task. He had to disconnect the security camera and the bomb detector, both of which were devices. At this point, he was left with only one slim chance of breaking the Sabbath rules without having to atone for it. He had to invoke and exploit the rule of exemption – 'Pikuah Nefesh', a Hebrew clause meaning concern for human life which includes war, health and welfare. Nathan wasn't sure, but disconnecting security cameras and bomb detectors definitely means that there might be robbery, smuggling of bombs and probably an eventual explosion, which is covered by war, health and human lives.

Nathan closed his eyes to pray as the car exited the King Fahd motorway.

"Oh lord, God of Israel. I'm sure you've seen the tight corner I am in, in this land of Islam. Save me oh lord, show me the way out of this trap and if there is no way out, forgive me for breaking the Sabbath rules. Amen," he prayed in silence.

CHAPTER 7
Saturday Morning, Riyahd

Nathan began his day with a prayer:

"Thank you oh lord for making me the way I am" he prayed and set off to work. At 9.30am, Nathan reluctantly disconnected the bomb detecting device and the camera that covered the parking lot area. Five minutes later, Sadiq drove into the parking lot, plugged in the fuse to complete the circuit of the plastic explosive built into the car and boarded the elevator to meet Abdul inside the suite. Abdul checked the receptor for signals, exposing any bomb detecting devices within the vicinity.

'No signal," he said.

"He complied," he said, and both smiled with satisfaction.

Nathan watched the security monitor as two men came out of the penthouse, looked carefully around and took positions before the US Goodwill Ambassador strode out and walked into the presidential elevator. Nathan glanced at the wall clock hanging high and fallow on the office room wall; it was 9.42am. He pushed back in his chair, upped and darted to the elevator control switch box. His eyes searched the numerous knobs inside the box until it rested on the knob inscribed PPE – Penthouse Presidential Elevator, he pulled the knob up and the elevator hung in the mid-air in the well. Alarms started whirling in the security room.

At that moment, Abdul glanced at his wristwatch and picked up his briefcase and made for the exit, Sadiq followed suit.

A loud blasting noise went off in the parking lot. Abdul and Sadiq looked at each other and hurried into the elevator and their descent to the reception and to the open. A car pulled up in front of the hotel and they hurried into the back seat and the car sped away in a disappearing act. Using the cell phone, Abdul put a call through to Afghanistan. Zuba answered the phone at the first ring.

"Our mission is accomplished," Said Abdul gleefully.

"Is it done?" inquired Zuba.

"The blast went off some two minutes ago and soon the rescue department of the Riyahd Police will be picking his bones and flesh," answered Abdul.

Sadiq watched as Abdul spoke into the phone.

"Gora Technology, sometimes I like the Gora so much for his knowledge, but sometimes..." thought Sadiq, as he thought of how western technology had made it possible for Abdul to be speaking to the commanders at their headquarters in Tora Bora.

"Congrats," said Zuba.

"Allahu Akbar!" replied Abdul.

"Allahu Akbar!" rejoined Zuba.

* * *

Nathan was terrified at the bomb blast; he waited few more minutes before pushing the elevator knob up and sending the presidential elevator on its descent to the ground floor.

Minutes later, the Riyahd state owned radio was broadcasting the news of the bomb. The CNN, BBC and other international TV crews and journalists arrived and licked the scene of the bomb blast with their camera flashes. 400 meters inside a cave in Tora Bora, the elite disciples of the Jihadist Movement sat in front of their battery operated TV in their newsroom. They were all animated, gripping hard on the cushion on which they were sitting as the scenes of the bomb blast in Riyahd flashed on the screen.

"Another bomb exploded in Riyahd this morning," began the newscaster. "This time, it was in the Royal Government Guest Hotel, where an American Goodwill Ambassador was lodged. The Goodwill Ambassador was the target of the explosion, but was forty five seconds short of being a victim because he was trapped in the presidential elevator on his descent to the parking lot where the bomb exploded. Officials said the bomb was a medium intensity bomb made from six pounds of explosives and fitted with a timer, and detonated at exactly the second the Goodwill Ambassador was supposed to be boarding his limousine. The entire presidential parking lot and all the cars therein were destroyed, but there were no human casualties. It is known at this moment that the Goodwill Ambassador is safe and sound, and has boarded his white and blue Boeing 757 plane on his way to Cairo, Egypt. A Falash Mura — an Ethiopian Jew — who works in the security department of the hotel has been arrested in connection to the bombing."

"This is sabotage, you bastard," growled the Supreme Disciple in a slow cold voice. He stood up and began to pace back and forth in the newsroom.

Abdul listened in desperation to the Riyahd state owned broadcasting service.

"Allah! I'm finished," he shouted.

"Who did this? That infidel called Nathan. Oh Allah, my Allah, he is a Jew," said Abdul.

"Do you accept trusting an infidel as a sin punishable…?" he remembered the Islamic scholar, the personnel chief of the Movement, saying to him on the indoctrination day.

"I gaffed, Oh Allah I gaffed," he murmured.

The Cell phone beside him vibrated with a call.

"What happened Abdul? What happened?" asked the controlled, icy voice of the military commander.

"I don't really know, everything was fine and in place a minute before the blast. I guess the guy we used to beat the hotel security must've trapped the Goodwill

Ambassador in the elevator to prevent him from reaching the scene before the blast. They said he is a Jew," stammered Abdul.

"A what?"

"Abdul?"

"You trusted him with the secrets of executing the Movement's plot?"

"I swear I never knew he is Jewish. He is a black skinned man, and nothing tells he is Jewish, I was deceived," said Abdul.

A pause.

"But I can still try, they said he was on his way to Cairo. I can catch him in Cairo," Abdul suggested.

"That is nonsense Abdul, his death is not as important as where he died. The more casualties we have inside Arabia, the more likely it is they will leave the holy land. I will get back to you later," said Zuba, and the line went dead.

"What a wasted chance," spat the Supreme Disciple. "You pay me. You pay the Movement. This is the closest we'd get to inflicting a real hurtful injury at infidels and you messed it up."

"He is excluded from the Movement," said the Supreme Disciple.

"Excluded?" echoed Zuba.

"But don't you, highness, think that nobody can exclude anybody from the Movement? Don't you, highness, remember that it is the solemn duty of every Muslim to join the Jihadist Movement officially or in an individual capacity? Besides, doesn't your holiness think that he merits to be given another chance in his quest to make the Islamic renaissance proud?" pleaded Zuba.

"He merits the Movement's moral credit," added Zuba.

"Even after trusting an infidel with the secrets of the Movement?" retorted the Supreme Disciple.

"He never knew he was a Jew. It was a grave mistake. But nobody could've played the part the Jew played. He had no choice but to use that man," said Zuba.

"He should've used the investigative arm of the Movement to find out whom he was trusting that hugely with the secrets of a hit plot. The investigative bureau was there to be used. We have everything. The Movement is no comedy. If he could trust such a man in a task as delicate as that, someday, he could trust the CIA to the secrets of the Movement," said the Supreme Disciple.

"Trusting an infidel knowingly or unknowingly to the secrets of the Movement is an unpardonable sin. Nobody trusts an infidel to the detriment of the Movement and continues in the rank and file of the movement. He is excluded from the Movement, and he must get the minimum sentence," said the Supreme Disciple.

"Death to him," interpreted Zuba.

"That is the minimum sentence for the crime, and he was sworn to that during the indoctrination," said the Supreme Disciple.

"He's done so much for the Movement. He didn't trust that Ethiopian, rather he allotted a part for him to play, and it doesn't infer trust," pleaded Zuba.

"Remember his contribution when the opium poppy cultivation was banned by the Taliban government under the prodding of the USA drug enforcement administration, and the United Nations drug program?" continued Zuba.

"Yes he executed that mission excellently and I'm proud of him for that, but in the Movement, nobody lives on past glory and performances. Even me, the Supreme Disciple, will one day embark on a mission for martyrdom. Nobody is irreplaceable. He's been a good captain, but captains come and go, the Movement remains the same. Besides, he's not been doing anything for the Movement, he's doing whatever for himself as a good Muslim, for his place in heaven, he must rise to defend Islam until the annexed lands of Palestine, Jordan and Syria are recovered and the incursors destroyed, until the infidel forces are driven out of the Arabian Peninsula, no true Muslim ought to rest. He is a true Muslim fighting for his salvation. And as a true Muslim, for his salvation, he is better-off dying while in defence of Islam, and paying for a mistake in carrying out a Jihadist errand is part of it," said the Supreme Disciple.

"He is a collaborator. Tell me at your convenience commander, since when does the Movement condone collaborators?" asked the Supreme Disciple.

"By pardoning him, we would be setting a precedent that will be hard to uphold, anybody could do anything and hide behind the lack of pre-knowledge," added the Supreme Disciple.

In his years in the Movement, Abdul had been invincible even in the most daunting of terror missions, but the target of this very mission had proved totally elusive.

During the opium ban, the Taliban government, in their effort to obtain international help and recognition and avert a looming international isolation, had decreed a ban on opium poppy cultivation, a staple agricultural practice of Afghan farmers. Most opium growers felt the impact of the ban harshly as they replace their plantation with wheat. Wheat doesn't thrive well on the Afghan soil and in the drought prone Afghan country.

Wheat needs more water than opium to grow and earns the farmers less money. Besides, the wheat trade is dominated by veteran wheat growing countries. Afghan farmers are the champs in opium growing, putting out about two-thirds of the world's opium. Afghan was headed to economic ruin and a probable political crisis as the Taliban Islamic Militia threatened to round off and throw into jail the defiant farmers who went back to opium cultivation. And most farmers had sworn to die in jail rather than cultivate money-losing wheat. The Jihadist Movement knew that an economic crisis and an eventual political uprising would destabilize the Taliban government and consequentially the refuge it provided for the movement. The high disciples of the movement met and made a decision to save their sanctuary. Abdul was selected to head the mission code-named "Operation Save the Sanctuary".

Normally, the Afghan farmers earned money in double-digits for an amount of opium that yields a kilogram of heroin, which in turn earned dealers hundreds of thousands when it entered the western market place.

Abdul mobilized farmers, collecting their opium and heroin stockpiles: two tons of heroin in total. He spent months converting the stuff to money: hundreds of millions of dollars. One thousand defiant opium growers, who used to earn an average of $6000 annually from their crops, received $60,000 each: ten years' worth of their income upfront. $60 million was distributed to the farmers with strict advice to each of them never to go back to opium cultivation. The farmers happily obliged. Peace and tranquility returned to Kabul, the UN international drug control program applauded and broadcast the news to the world community.

"Afghanistan has successfully banned and eradicated opium cultivation," the UN lauded.

The American government sent emissaries to verify and confirm. Satisfied, they applauded the Taliban and promised to grant Afghanistan $50 million in emergency aid to tide them over during the draught. The Taliban government was happy and the Jihadist Movement became more entrenched in Afghan soil. Only the Movement's high disciples and the high-ranking Taliban officials knew what had transpired.

CHAPTER 8

Zuba turned to look at the phone as it vibrated with a call on the mat beside him.

"Abdul," he guessed.

"Yes?" he said into the phone. "This is Abdul, commander."

"Can I receive some money to proceed to Egypt?" inquired Abdul.

Silence.

"Abdul, you've been excluded from the Movement," said Zuba.

"It's highly improper to inform a reject that he's been excluded from the Movement, I'm sure you are aware of that."

"You've been excluded for flouting the article four of

the Movement's constitution to which you were sworn as a fadeyin," continued Zuba.

"I wish I could help you," he added, and hung up.

"You are excluded for flouting the fourth article of the constitution," Abdul repeated, mumbling to himself.

"Trusting an infidel with the secrets of the Movement is an unpardonable sin punishable by a minimum sentence of death," Abdul recollected the Islamic Scholar reading out loud to him and he repeated the verse, agreeing to it.

"Soon, Sadiq and company will receive orders to kill me," he thought, and rose to collect his gun and documents from the drawer. He went into the sitting room. He heard the shower running in the bathroom.

"Sadiq?" he called out.

But no one replied. Sadiq was under the shower and couldn't hear as he called.

Abdul went back into the room and packed his briefcase. He stepped into the open and into the car that was parked in the front of the house and drove away with no real destination in mind; his primary concern at the moment was to leave the vicinity before Sadiq received an official order to hit him.

Dismembered from the Movement, no money in hand and with no immediate safe destination in mind, Abdul drove through busy central Riyahd in confusion and very deep in thought. As he drove past the Arab bank of Riyahd, an idea uncoiled in his mind, and he made a u-turn at the end of the street and drove to the bank. He parked the car in the bank's parking lot and tucked his .38 calibre properly inside his waist before entering. He took his place in the line of clients cashing money, his eyes darting from cage to cage as the cashiers in the cages counted and paid out cash to clients. At cage number five, the cashier counted out bundles of cash and stuffed it into a large padded brown envelope and handed it over to an elderly client. The man smiled his courtesy as he received the envelope. Mr Ahmed tucked the envelope into his bag, zipped it shut and turned to leave.

"That's a clean sum," thought Abdul, and eased out from the line and followed Ahmed.

Abdul accosted Ahmed as he opened his 1999 Renault in the parking lot.

"Don't make any move," he said raising his white

brocade jumper to show the short gun at his waist.

"Just open the bag quietly and hand me the envelope," demanded Abdul.

"And your car key also," said Abdul as he collected the envelope from the fear soaked Ahmed.

He opened the car trunk.

"Here," he said to Ahmed, nodding into the car trunk.

Ahmed climbed dutifully into the trunk and Abdul pushed it closed; he dropped the key behind the left rear tire. He made for his car and drove out of the parking lot into the street.

Thirty minutes later, he abandoned the car on a street shoulder north of Riyahd and waved down a taxi. He hastened into the back passenger's seat, and throughout the journey to Damman he looked out the window in deep thought . They arrived uneventfully at Damman, and he hired a car to Manama, Bahrian Island.

Usman noticed the car behind his' shaking, and a faint sound coming from the trunk. He called a bank security officer who opened the car trunk with the key he picked up from beside the rear tire. Mr Ahmed struggled out from the trunk.

"I was robbed! I was robbed!! He took everything I had, he took away my life, my gratuity and my indemnity," shouted Ahmed tearfully.

Ahmed spent the past twenty of his fifty-three years of life working in the Riyahd Royal Amusement Park, where he fed the chimps and orang-utan from 8.00am to 12.00 noon, when he left for an hourly break and resumed work at 1.00pm to feed the sharks and dolphins in the pond. On one fateful Saturday afternoon tourist traffic was quite thick in the park and visitors watched delightfully as Ahmed fed the sharks with fish, and suddenly he slipped on the marble floor around the pond falling into the shark pond. Before he could be rescued, a 10 foot long bull shark named Bob had chopped off his left hand from the elbow, to top off the eclectic array of excitement for the onlookers that bright Tuesday afternoon. Ahmed was sent into a forced retirement at the age of 49 years. After ten years of a drawn out arguments in the Riyahd courtrooms, the amusement park agreed to pay Ahmed $25,000 in indemnity and another $25,000 in gratuity. Ahmed had $50,000 in the envelope that Abdul had stolen from him. Money he'd planned to use starting off a farm, rearing goats and cows.

CHAPTER 9

The phone rang as Sadiq came out from the bathroom.

"Hello!" he said as he picked it up.

His eyes widened as he recognized the person at the other end of the line.

"Salamalek commander," he said and waited.

"Abdul?" asked Sadiq in confusion when the commander had finished counting off his orders.

"Yes, and quickly, before he causes more damage and humiliation to the Movement," said the commander, and hung up.

Sadiq held the phone to his ear as thoughts tumbled down in his mind. He was confused.

"Abdul?" he mumbled.

Sadiq had executed two missions on behalf of the

Movement with Abdul and he trusted him immensely. This was their third mission together and the only mission on which they failed to deliver.

"What must Abdul have done?" he mumbled as he replaced the receiver in its cradle, and walked into the room. He picked up his .45 calibre and walked across the room into the sitting room, expecting to see Abdul.

"Abdul?" he called out.

No answer came.

He walked apprehensively through the doorway into the room, but Abdul was not in sight, and his briefcase was not there either.

"What is happening?" he thought, and darted to the front of the house. The car was not in the driveway, nor was Abdul standing by the corner.

"Does he know that his death warrant has been ordered? Why did he disappear without telling me? Is Abdul guilty of any treachery? Is Abdul a collaborator?" tumbled the thoughts in Sadiq's mind as he walked back into the house.

* * *

Abdul dropped his briefcase on the sofa of the $200

a night hotel suite in Manama Bahrian, and upended the cash-containing envelope on the bed and started to count the money.

"Fifty thousand dollars," he said out loud on counting the last bill. He glanced at the documents in the envelope:

Mr Ahmed
#6 Prophet Mohammed Road
Riyahd, Saudi Arabia
Phone…

He read down the lines into the details of his indemnity.

"Poor Ahmed," he thought.

"Call him or find a way to send him some money, you destroyed him, you took all he had in life," a mind suggested to him.

Abdul glanced again at the name and address on top of the document.

"Keep the money, don't share it with anybody, you will need it. Just mail his documents to him," suggested a mind, and Abdul obliged.

"How can it be," Abdul thought out loud as he lay

bathing in the Jacuzzi, "that I'm now considered a collaborator?"

"By now everybody in the Arab world, and in the Movement especially, wants me dead. To everybody, I'm a filthy man, a traitor, a collaborator. And the sooner I die the better for them. But how can that be oh Allah, you know how much I'm innocent."

"I've liked and worked diligently for the Movement because of the appealing sense it embodies, a hope it offers of a more progressive, happier and more peaceful future for the world under the Islamic renaissance, but I'm excluded from the Movement and branded a collaborator forever and to pay with my life for an error I unknowingly committed. It's so unfair oh Allah. Why me?" Abdul mumbled as a loudspeaker somewhere not very far away from the hotel blasted out the Muezzins call to prayer, reminding all that before Allah, all men are naught.

"Allahu Akbar!
Allahu Akbar!" shouted the Muezzin.

* * *

Sadiq went through an identification parade across

the corridor in the Royal Riyahd district police station.

"It isn't him," said Ahmed to the Riyahd city police.

Sadiq paid the fine for unlawful parking after a long argument that his car was stolen and parked wrongfully on the street shoulder by the thief, and as such he, Sadiq, didn't deserve a fine for being a victim of theft.

"You didn't report your car was stolen before we found the car," replied the traffic officer.

"$50,000! He has my money, he must be somewhere in Manana, Bahrian, no doubt he must be there," Sadiq ruminated as he drove home in his car.

CHAPTER 10
Two Days Later

At the Manama resort hotel, a hotel Abdul had once confessed to Sadiq that he liked a lot, Sadiq paid up-front for five nights.

"In which room is Abdul?" Sadiq asked the receptionist casually as he checked for a vacant suite.

Sadiq knew that Abdul had probably ceased using the name Saif Allah, aware that a middle-east-wide hunt for the bomber of the Royal Guest hotel was going on, and must've resorted to using his original name. Besides, he had no other documents on him except for those issued in his real name. He also knew that Abdul liked checking into hotels with his first name only.

"He is in room...ehm," said the receptionist, hesitating upon recalling that it was against the hotel's ethics to divulge the names and room numbers of guests.

"Which Abdul?" the receptionist asked politely.

"Abdul, he checked in as Abdul, I think three days ago," said Sadiq.

"Let me see," said the receptionist, and punched some keys on the PC keyboard and watched the screen for a moment.

"No Abdul here, I'm sorry sir," he said.

But Sadiq had seen the cautious restraint in his eyes and heard it in his voice. He was sure that Abdul was lodging in the hotel. The elevator stopped at the ground floor and the door slid open. Abdul made a step out of the elevator car, but paused on seeing the two men standing before the reception counter some fifty meters away. One of the men he unmistakably identified as Sadiq. He stepped quietly back into the elevator car and pressed the fifth button, and the elevator began on its ascent to the fifth floor. He got out of the car and made four quick steps across the long, wide corridor to his suite door. He occupied a suite directly across from the elevator. He slotted the key into the keyhole and unlocked the door, pushing it open. He walked hurriedly inside, closed the door and leaned against it, breathing nervously.

"There is no doubt Sadiq and his company have come after me. The hunt has begun and will only end when I drop dead or disappear from the map, and it's very difficult to hide from the powerfully long and worldwide arm of the Movement," thought Abdul, his mind wandering into a deep concentration.

Nothing concentrates the mind more than knowing that one is going to die, and more so after seeing one's killers. Death: a very frightful end but, a natural end whose gradual process begins at the very moment one comes into life.

Abdul waited, his mind whirling in thought. He heard the faint sound of the elevator as it stopped. He turned to observe through the peephole. The elevator door slid open and the bellhop stepped out, followed by Sadiq and his company.

"What's happening?" thought Abdul.

The trio marched down the corridor. Abdul eased the door open and peeped as they continued down the corridor to the last suite in the row of suites on the floor. The last suite was next to the staircase. Suite number thirty, on the even side of the corridor.

Abdul eased the door shut and waited.

"Do they know I'm in this hotel, and on this floor?"

"Could Sadiq have guessed?'

"Good or bad, I mustn't wait for them to come kill me," he mumbled, and made for the gun in the bedroom. He oiled it and reloaded it, took off the safety catch and then fitted it with a silencer. With the muted gun in hand, he moved the curtains and stood before the wide French window that offered a panoramic view of the hotel's Arabic garden, the front entrance and the street beyond. He watched the traffic of people and cars coming in and out of the hotel as his mind went to work.

"They will soon leave the hotel to go look for me in the places Sadiq knows are my favourite joints in Manama city, that's if they don't already know I'm here in the hotel suite," he thought as the breezy evening aged. Nervous and impatient, he walked across the room to the Suite's entrance door and peeped through the peephole, he didn't hear their footsteps as they walked down the thickly carpeted corridor to the elevator. Abdul watched on as Sadiq and his company pressed the button to call the elevator and waited. He was tempted to open the door and spray bullets on them, but he restrained on a second thought.

"Do that and the hunt will intensify, that's if you escape the heavy penalty for murder under the Island's laws. It's a good idea to wipe them both out in one swipe, but it must be done discreetly. The smart criminal is the one who never pays for his or her crimes, the one that never gets caught," exhorted a mind.

The elevator came and Sadiq and company disappeared into the car and descended to the ground floor. Abdul went over to the window and watched as they strode across the hotel entrance into the street beyond. He drew the curtain. With his muted pistol tucked into waist belt and his briefcase at hand, Abdul stepped into the corridor and called the elevator. The receptionist didn't look up at him as he crossed the ample reception area into the open. The money he had in the hotel deposit could still pay his nightly fee for the next ten days. He headed towards the hotel's taxi park, then paused and decided against it.

"No trails," he thought as he turned and started towards the hotel street and quickened up, turning into the adjacent road at the end of the street and moved on, glancing back over his shoulder every few steps. He waved down a taxi and hurried inside. The car dropped him off somewhere in the northern part of the city. He looked nervously around and crossed the road into the next street, waved down another taxi that drove him to the northeast outskirt of Manama, where he checked into a modest hotel for $50 a night.

Chapter 11
Exhibition Avenue
Manama, Bahrian Island

In a pub on Exhibition Avenue, Sadiq skimmed the crowd and weekenders for a glimpse of Abdul. The pub was teeming with droopy faced Arabs. Sadiq spotted a lady somewhere at the centre of the hall, a lady Abdul spent a night with the last time they were in Manama together as comrades. He shouldered his way through the delirious crowd to the girl. Fatima, a tall, spare easy going girl, smiled broadly on recognizing Sadiq.

"How are you?" she said, shaking her body lightly to the music.

"Fine," replied Sadiq.

"Is he here? Where is he?" inquired Fatima.

"I'm looking for him. I don't know where he is," replied Sadiq.

They made their way to the bar counter and Sadiq paid for two glasses of beer.

"Could you call me on this number if you see Abdul? But don't let him know I'm looking for him. I mean don't tell him you saw me, he is always jealous of his women," said Sadiq, handing Fatima a hotel business card with his suite number scribbled behind it.

"Buy a call card or use some coin booth," he added giving her a $50 bill.

"Thank you," said Fatima.

Sadiq gulped down the beer in his glass and turned to leave.

"Tell him I'm here if you see him before me," said Fatima.

Sadiq turned and stared at her.

"I will," he replied.

Isah was holding a dwarf 50 ml bottle of brandy and chatting up one of the local girls in the pub, near the entrance doorway, when Sadiq approached.

"Be on the watch out for him, I'm going to check in the hotel," Sadiq whispered into his ear and turned to leave. Beyond the entrance doorway, he paused.

"Call me if you see him," he said.

"Ok," said Isah and continued his chat with the girl.

From a corner across the road, Abdul watched Sadiq enter a taxi in front of the pub; the car rolled onto the street. Some 50 meters down the street, the car slammed into a concrete electric pole. The driver was dead drunk. Abdul saw Sadiq come down from the vehicle unscratched and say something to the driver who was still inside the car. Sadiq looked up and down the street and started walking down the street.

Isah took a swig on his brandy and raised his hand to the girl's shoulder. The girl moved forward, closer to him. He felt the sweet fragrance of her perfume. She reached for the brandy bottle in his hand and he let go of it and she took a swig and gave it back to him. Abdul waited, calculating what was best to do. Isah paid for another two dwarf bottles of brandy, opened one and handed it to the lady, and opened the other bottle for himself.

Abdul stepped into the open and crossed the street to the taxi stand. At that moment Isah approached from the opposite direction, cuddling the girl at the cradle of her waist. Abdul leaned against the taxi and held h is breath. Tipsy and busy chit-chatting with his new date, Isah passed right in front of Abdul, the man he'd travelled all the way from Riyahd to find and assassinate. Abdul held his breath, his finger tightening on the trigger of the .38 calibre held at a shoot-ready position, pointing toward Isah from under his white Jacade jumper. Isah and his girl entered the first taxi in the row and left. Abdul looked at the other half-drunken revellers, leaving the pub before taking his seat in the front passenger's seat of another taxi. He was driven the hotel in the northeast outskirt of Manama city. By the next morning, Abdul had carved out a clear outline of what he was going to do. As he hurried into the street from his hotel, he contemplated ketchup and real blood: which would serve him better? Real blood won. He went to the blood bank near the city's business district.

"Could I have a 500ml sac of blood please?" he said to the attendant.

"Which blood group?" asked the attendant.

"Which groups do you have?" inquired Abdul, not sure what to say because he didn't know anything about blood grouping.

"We've got all the groups, A, B, O and AB," replied the attendant.

"A is much like it," thought Abdul.

"Let me have group A," he said, in the hope that group A was the best of bloods. The attendant disappeared into the inner room and came back.

"Sorry sir but we have not got the 500ml sacs of the group A blood," said the attendant.

"Have you got the litre sac?' inquired Abdul.

"Yes," replied the attendant.

"Let me have the litre sac," said Abdul.

"But if I may ask, what are you doing with it?" asked the attendant.

"Don't you remember me?" Abdul said.

"I'm afraid not," said the attendant.

"That will be your homework until next time I come around for more litres."

The attendant smiled and went into the inner room and came out to hand Abdul a litre sac of cold blood. Abdul paid and turned into the street on his way back to the hotel room.

Inside the hotel room, he poured some cold blood onto the left side of his chest, some on his face and forehead. He set the Canon automatic camera on its tripod stand and, with the remote controller in hand, he lay sprawled on the floor, in focus to the lens of the camera, and pressed the snap button. He threw the remote controller away before the snap. Wham, came the flash as it snapped. He took several pictures in several positions. Satisfied, he packed the camera and took a quick shower before finding the nearest photographic shop to develop the films. He went to the Manama International Airport – the Al Muharraq airport where he bought an air ticket with Egyptian Air and made reservations on an a DC 10 aircraft for the 12.30am flight to Cairo.

At night, he rehearsed his plot and stepped into the cold breezy night. He flagged down a taxi and headed to Exhibition Avenue. He paid the taxi and trotted across the street to take position behind the kiosk in the corner opposite the pub and waited determinedly. It wasn't long before he sighted Sadiq and Isah as they alighted from a taxi and made for the pub's entrance. He waited, knowing that he had an edge over them for seeing them first.

Two hours later, Sadiq got up from his seat.

"Keep watch here, I will take care of the hotel," he said
to Isah and left.

Abdul watched as he came out from the pub and
walked down the street. He edged out from his corner
and into the street behind him. Sadiq walked at a mod-
erate pace to the end of the street, turned left into an
adjacent street, and continued. Abdul guessed he was
walking back to the hotel. He took a taxi and got to the
hotel minutes before Sadiq. The receptionist sat nodding when Abdul entered the ample reception area.
Abdul quietly crossed the reception hall to the staircase
beside the elevators and took the stairs to the fifth floor,
and sat waiting at the landing. The marbled landing was
cold and the dimly lit stairwell was aired by a cool evening breeze from the nearby river. The hotel was cool
and quiet. Abdul waited.

"Good evening," Sadiq said to the nodding receptionist. He opened his eyes, shook his head, wiped his
hand across his face and squinted at Sadiq.

"Oh you, suite 51," he said, stretching to get the key
to suite 51.

"This is not my key," said Sadiq.

"Abdul? Aint you Abdul?" asked the sleepy receptionist. "Who and what suite are you?"

"He's in suite 51, and he is not yet back," thought Sadiq.

"Mine is suite 58," said Sadiq.

The man grabbed the key and handed it over to Sadiq. Sadiq walked to the far end of the ample reception hall, took a seat and waited. After forty-five minutes of waiting, Sadiq left for his suite. As he slipped out the elevator into the wide quiet corridor, his gaze settled on the door directly opposite the elevator.

"Suite fifty-one," he murmured, and continued down the corridor towards his suite.

Abdul heard the faint halting sound of the elevator and the elevator car door as it slid open and close. He tiptoed to the sixth of the seven steps to the fifth floor and listened to faint footsteps, muffled by the softly carpeted floor. The sound of the steps increased as it came towards him. He drew his gun, put off the safety catch and waited. The person stopped and he heard a key fumbling in the key hole of the door next to the staircase, then a faint squeak as the door opened. He stepped up and rushed to the door in three steps.

Sadiq angled his head to look back, but he was a little

too late: the silenced .38 calibre was already pointing at his temple.

"Both hands on your head," ordered Abdul in a low but icy voice, pushing the door closed behind them as they stepped into the suite.

Abdul reached forward and drew the .45 calibre tucked into Sadiq's waist belt.

"There!" he ordered, waving Sadiq to a sofa in the sitting room.

Sadiq complied hastily.

"Where is your companion?' Abdul quizzed.

"He is in the pub on Exhibition Avenue," replied Sadiq.

"Waiting for me?"

"Yes," replied Sadiq.

"You're here to kill me, ain't you?" asked Abdul.

Sadiq looked Abdul in the face and nodded his yes.

"To kill me," Abdul repeated, and smiled, a smile that didn't soften the hardness and cruel determination in his eyes, but rather strengthened them.

There was a cross current of feelings in the room's atmosphere: hate, resentment and fear as they studied themselves.

"I like you as a person Sadiq," said Abdul, breaking the silence. "But that doesn't mean you would like me in return, because likeness and love ain't respect that is reciprocal, though likeness and love begat themselves in some cases. We have pursued perilous missions together. The last mission was our third mission together and the only mission we failed to deliver on. If I were sent to kill you because our last mission failed, I'd think twice before setting off after you, because neither you nor I ever knew that Nathan, that security guard, was a Jew. And nobody knew he would default on his obligation the way he did, and now here you are on a mission to assassinate me.

If death should be the reward of our effort to execute the organizations plot, I do not merit it any more than yourself.

Why? Because you made the mistake as much as I did. It is true that I coordinated the operation, and I'm proud of it because I believe that any right thinking person who examines our effort will reach the conclusion that we really did our best, though it wasn't enough to hit the target. And for doing our best, they've turned you against me. But thank Allah I take you first. And for now, I want no pardon, no sympathy, because I know how it is in the movement, you're here to get me killed, that's your mission, you are not here to bypass decisions and find excuses and sentiments not to do as directed."

Silence, as both men studied each other cautiously.

Sadiq's killer instincts lurked beneath his fear soaked face. Abdul knew quite well that Sadiq could pounce on him at the slightest opportunity.

"I wasn't told the reason why you must be put to rest. I received order: 'Go kill Abdul, find him wherever he is and kill him.' And you know how it is in the movement, so here I am," said Sadiq.

"Not even the host, I mean the American Goodwill Ambassador, I do not know why his death warrant was issued, I only know he is an American and that what I'm doing is in the interest of Arabian culture and the furtherance of the Islamic renaissance," added Sadiq.

"I know, Sadiq, I know, that to you and the whole of the disciples of the movement, I am a collaborator, and unfortunately that's what I've been branded and it will take planet sized explanation, reason and luck to change it. I'm filthy and deserve to die, that's how everybody feels about me now. So you see I have more necessity to kill you than you have to kill me. Unfortunately, the politicians of the movement don't know or pretend not to know what we went through in the field. Now you're pinned against me and me against you. But gracious Allah, I take you first. Allahu Akbar!" said Abdul.

A pause.

"It is a normal practice that when a disciple turned collaborator is executed away from his base, the elite disciples of the movement, the personnel department of the movement often demand a photo confirmation. Isn't it?" inquired Abdul.

"Yes, it is so," replied Sadiq.

"Have you got a camera with you?" asked Abdul.

"Yes," replied Sadiq.

"To photograph my corpse eh? Well, I've done the job for you," said Abdul, reaching into his jumper pocket to pull out an envelope.

"Here," he said, throwing the envelope to Sadiq, who took it, opened it, and took a moment to study each of the four pictures before putting them back into the envelope.

"You're well prepared," said Sadiq.

"Thank you," Abdul replied.

"So what do we do now?" Sadiq asked, a homing hope in his eyes.

"Address it to the elite disciples," Abdul said throwing him a pen.

Sadiq noticed the cruel and unrepentant determination in Abdul's voice. He caught the pen in mid-air. He knew Abdul would not spare his life.

He decided to tell him a little about himself before he sent him to Allah in paradise.

"Abdul," he began. "I am an Uzbeks militant. Both of us, you and I, and all Islamic militants, are motivated by the same cause – a dislike for the infidels and the Zionists. We all believe they are the cause of the problems and poverty in our various homelands. We both are committed to a violent holy struggle to defeat the infidels and settle the Palestinians and usher wealth and abundance to all Arabs and Muslims with the instatement of the the Islamic renaissance all over the globe. We all belong to the same political religion. I've been longer in the struggle than many of the elite disciples and politicians of the movement. During the years the Supreme Disciple was absent in Afghanistan, I was on the Afghan soil. You started in the militancy movement with your first baptism directly into the Jihadist Movement. I began this journey with a small militancy group; we used to organize our own attacks and contributions to Jihad. My former organization had no intention of usurping power in Saudi Arabia. And I came to recognize the present Movement after the bombing of the American Embassy in Kenya and Tanzania simultaneously," said Sadiq.

"Our organization joined this movement when our funds dwindled following the military coup in Pakistan. I became entirely loyal and swore allegiance to the movement and to the Supreme Disciple in the wake of the American-led Allied bombing of Kabul. I survived the early heavy bombing of the war, and was posted to Saudi Arabia.

I'm really old in the Islamic militancy movement, and as such, I know that the movement is beyond the influence and activities of one man or disciple, or one group or organization. It is rather a multivalent and diverse movement with a broad view on the economic, social, religious and political revival of the Arabic and Islamic culture. Assassinating you based on the reasons you trotted out, which was what came to my mind when I received the orders, is not going to make any positive contribution to the movement, but you know how it works in the movement, receiving and carrying out an order as directed is part of being disciplined, observing the rules and regulations, and from the platform on which we operate, it is part of being a Jihad soldier. It is the reason I came after you, it is nothing personal. And on the other hand, you know that in our religion, if one dies in pursuant of killing and trying to kill a collaborator, an enemy, one has a place in heaven. Before leaving Riyahd, I had to convince myself, with so much effort, that I was going after a collaborator. It was a kind of self brainwashing session. Because of the points I've made so far, I will plead not to address this envelope because it will amount to collaborating with you to deceive the elite disciples of the movement, and it may cost me my place in heaven," said Sadiq.

The phone on the table began to ring, and Sadiq angled his head to look at it. At the third ring, Sadiq pushed forward to grab the receiver.

"Stay where you are," growled Abdul, reaching to get the receiver.

"Hmm," he said into the phone.

"I've not seen him Sadiq," said Isah.

"I will be coming back to the hotel in a few moments," he said, and hung up.

"Don't mind about the envelope then," said Abdul after replacing the receiver to its cradle.

"I will address it myself, and I'd rather you close your eyes so that you don't see me addressing a deceitful envelope to be sent to the elite disciples," said Abdul.

Sadiq obliged. Abdul snatched the pen from his hands and bent to address the envelope with one hand while his other hand held the gun tightly and pointing at Sadiq.

"It will get home fine and safely and they will be very proud of you for a job well executed," he said after addressing the envelope and tucking it back into his jumper pocket.

"Now, over there," he ordered Sadiq, waving his revolver towards the short passage to the bathroom.

Sadiq complied hastily, and Abdul followed him. As Sadiq crossed the doorway into the bathroom, Abdul said a short prayer.

"Take this!" said Abdul pulling the trigger of the

silver silenced .38 calibre. The bullet hit Sadiq at the nape of the neck; he turned to look at Abdul and a second bullet hit him at the temple. He fell head-on to the floor. Abdul bent over him and put the nose of the short gun into his half opened mouth.

"This! In honour of our differences and to our common objective, you die in the service of Allah and I kill you to remain alive and continue in the services of Allah," he said, and pulled the trigger.

He left Sadiq's lifeless body in the bathroom floor and went back into the sitting room and waited. Minutes later, he saw the door-knob turn. He went to hide behind the curtains beside the door. The door opened and Isah stepped into the room and continued to the centre of the sitting room.

"Sadiq?" he called out.

Abdul eased out from behind the curtains.

"Freeze!" he growled.

"To the bathroom and don't look back," added Abdul.

Isah recognized the voice on this second command. He'd never heard the voice as stern and threatening as it sounded then.

"Abdul?" he said.

"Yes, this is Abdul, the man you've come to assassinate in Manama. We made the last escape from the Royal hotel, with you driving us to safety, and now you are here to assassinate me," said Abdul.

"But I'm only…" he started, but stopped on seeing Sadiq's dead body sprawled on the bathroom floor in a pool of blood, his sightless gaze fixed on nothing.

"How did you find us Abdul?" Isah asked, still not turning around, as fear and tension vibrated through him.

Abdul guessed that Isah was trying to engage him in a dialogue while he thought out what to do next to save himself. It is a known tactic to all trained fadeyin.

"I want both your hands on your head," ordered Abdul.

Isah hesitated.

"Now!" shouted Abdul.

Isah was very fast with his hands on guns, and Abdul knew that. Isah obeyed the orders and raised both hands onto his head. Abdul reached forward and disarmed him.

"Let me live, Abdul. Let me live," Isah pleaded.

"I would've loved to, if I wouldn't die myself by leaving you alive. I regret it, but it's nothing personal. It is necessary. Hope you understand," said Abdul as he pulled the trigger three times.

Isah fell forward into the bathtub.

"You fool, you're a traitor, a collaborator, you and your soul will be damned forev..e r..." slurred Isah as he died.

In a briefcase in the bedroom, Abdul found their passports — fake passports. And $15,000 in cash, the mobilization allowance they must have received from headquarters to go after him until he was gunned down. He pocketed the lot. It was obvious they checked into the hotel with fake names other than the names in the passports.

It would be hard to identify and locate their relatives and families, and even harder for the Jihadist Movement to find them.

Abdul glanced at his wrist-watch as he stepped out of the taxi in front of his hotel. He had an hour and a half to prepare and get to the Airport.

Clean-shaven for disguise, in a business suite and carrying a briefcase, Abdul left for the Manama international Airport.

At the Airport, he dropped the addressed envelope in the airport mailbox and boarded the Egypt Air DC 10 to Cairo.

Nathan was arraigned before an Islamic Sharia court Judge and was sentenced to four years in prison for the 15 minute lapse in the security camera recording, the bomb detection device failure and his probable association with terrorists in what the court called "dangerous association and negligence of duty". In addition, he received 100 lashes of the cane on the bare buttocks, in accordance with Islamic corporal punishment.

CHAPTER 12

In an economy class window seat inside the Egypt Air DC 10 plane, Abdul was relaxed, confident and certain of a few things; he was committed to the struggle, to Islam and to the cause of Palestine and the Independence of the Palestine nation, to fighting the infidels wherever they are found, to fighting dominance, hegemony and despotism, and refusing to bow in the face of the most daunting of obstacles. He was going to Egypt to accomplish the assassination of an infidel Goodwill Ambassador on Middle East matters. At the moment, he had no plans of how to accomplish the assassination, and it was his first solo terror mission without a detailed and scripted plot and support from the Jihadist Movement.

"...am I only another desperate and confused Islamic militant staking everything; my life, money, and time, giving them all away merely for the hate of the infidels and hegemon that have caused so much pain to the Arabs, and couldn't generate peace between two neighbours? Peace in search of which my father fled Jerusalem, for which he died fighting for in the 1967 Arab-Israeli war. A hegemony I have no reason to trust?" thought Abdul.

A brief pause.

"Yes, I am," he found himself subconsciously responding. He'd never liked the words desperate and confused to be used in describing his person and actions.

Abdul had often thought that he's been doing it for the Supreme Disciple and the Jihadist Movement, but at this moment, he'd discovered that though the elite disciples and the movement sharpened his mind and senses as to the ills of hegemony and despotism, and the benefits of the fall of the infidels' civilization and dominance, and the benefits of establishing Islamic renaissance so that the children of Islam will celebrate the future, he'd been in it for the dislike of the infidels, for the love of Islam and a free Palestine state.

"I love Islam. Allahu Arkbar," he murmured.

"I will let his blood flow in Cairo like the Nile River," he thought.

"But how?" asked a subconscious voice.

He had no bomb making materials on him, though they were easily available in Cairo, and it could be done with much ease as a suicide mission. But Abdul was not ready to turn into a suicide bomber, because that was not his category as a Jihadist. Besides, he wanted to live and see the infidels crying and the hegemon brought to her knees in his lifetime before going back to Allah as a martyr.

"I can use the Islamic militants in Cairo, they are easily available," he thought.

A pause.

"But they all know the elite disciples, and some are members of the Jihadist Movement. And who knows what they already know about me. A collaborator?"

"Probably, yes."

"The more you disassociate from them the better," suggested a mind.

Ishmail came to mind

Ishmail was a Jenin, a young, robust Palestinian full

of faith and enthusiasm in Islamic rules and renaissance. He'd fought for almost all the Islamic movements
and organizations including the PLO and the Hezbollah. Jenin was a horizontal town with unpaved roads
and potholes situated on the northwest side of the West
Bank, fringed on the north by fig and olive grove dotted
hills, with flat, fertile agricultural land to its west, facing the Mediterranean Sea. To the east was the Jordan
Valley and to its south was Nabulus. Jenin was mostly
inhabited by people who wanted to vent their hostility towards the Zionist state, people drunk on belief in
martyrdom and the Islamic cause.

Jenin bred and harboured many Palestinian hitmen
and henchmen from the Fatah faction of the PLO and
Hezbollah, dating to the 80's riot against the Israelis
and extending into the 90's, when withdrawal from
the West Bank and Gaza by the Isrealis seemed distant
and unattainable so Islamic cells and groups began to
sprout in Jenin.

Abdul met Ishmail in Halhoul, where he'd gone to
celebrate the handing over of the land of Halhoul back
to Palestine control. Halhoul was linked to Hebron by a
bridge, and had been under Israeli control for decades.

That summer day, Halhoul was decorated in all its finery. Its streets were clean and beautiful, replete with red, white, green and black Palestine flags and similarly coloured balloons, as its folks and Palestinians from all neighbouring towns and all walks of life waited for the Palestine Police, guards and horsemen to ride gallantly into town, firing their guns into the high air joyfully in commemoration of the reclaiming of a stolen land. But as the day aged and the evening gloom began to fall, the Israeli soldiers didn't pull out of the town of Halhoul, they stayed put at the Halhoul command post, and no gallant Palestinian Policemen on Jeeps, bikes and horsebacks, waving guns and Palestine flags, galloped into town.

It was a morally drubbing day.

Disappointed, the visibly drooped residents and visitors started to un-decorated the streets and withdrew to their homes and stations.

Abdul was on his way to his hotel room, and pulled by the road shoulder to answer to a young Palestinian who waved him down, asking to hitchhike with him to Hebron.

"Could I come with you to Hebron Comrade?"

pleaded Ishmael.

"Come on in," replied Abdul readily.

Ishmael hopped into the front passenger's seat of the hired Honda car, and they drove in silence for a few minutes. Both were in deep, sad thought.

"It's tragicomedy, eh," said Abdul, breaking the silence.

"Tragicomic, yeah," replied Ishmael sharply, awakening from his thoughts.

"They think we are clowns," said Abdul.

"But time will tell. Time and time alone will say who are the clowns. The rightful owners of the land of Halhoul, Jerusalem and all the occupied territories," said Ishmael.

"They are the clowns," said Abdul.

"As I walked past that regional command post and saw those Zionist soldiers holding their guns in a combat ready pose, I felt an uncontrollable urge to rush into that post and blow up everything and everybody. But alas, I had no munitions on me. I'd come for the celebration and not for war. And look at it, look what they did once again. We've been taken for a ride once again, deceived, lied to and humiliated. And you tell me that peace can be attained by this kind of behaviour. How can they be peaceful neighbours? I feel like dragging all of them to the red sea and...." said Ishmael, sadness in his voice.

"And the infidels that empower and encourage them," said Abdul.

"You know, I've killed lots of our neighbouring enemies for reasons and for fun, but till this date, I've not had an opportunity to hit an infidel or the infidels' interests. How I dislike their mentoring figure to the incursors. How could such an intelligent and clever race and nation be inclining towards evil; incursion is evil, a sin. I wish I could have the opportunity to hit the infidels someday, and if possible, in their homeland," said Ishmael.

"The opportunity to hit the infidels is always there because, in their quest for control and nosing around, they become overly vulnerable. But it is always good and worthwhile to hit them where it hurts the most," said Abdul.

"Sorry, but you ain't from here, I mean you don't reside in Palestine, do you?" inquired Ishmael.

"Your accent, are you a ... ? asked Ishmael.

"Oh, I came from Afghanistan to celebrate liberation of Halhoul. I grew up in Yemen before moving to Afghanistan. But my father is Palestinian, I mean, I'm Palestinian," replied Abdul.

"I was just wondering. You're welcome brother," said Ishmael.

They drove in silence.

"Here," said Ishmael as they drove across a traffic light into a well-lit street in Hebron.

Abdul pulled the car up by the street shoulder, and Ishmael came down and dipped his hand into his breast pocket, pulled out a piece of paper with a handwritten phone number and address, and handed it to Abdul.

"My name is Ishmael. Reach me at this number if need be. Call me anytime and enlist me whenever you need help of any sort against the infidels."

"Whenever and wherever, you can count on me," said Abdul taking the piece of paper.

"And thanks for the ride" said Ishmael.

He crossed the street as Abdul drove off, on his way to the hotel in Jerusalem.

Two days later, Abdul went back to Afghanistan, but he never forgot his new young friend, Ishmael.

* * *

Abdul met Ishmael again in Jerusalem the following year while on a terror mission there. It was a perennial Jihad visit to help the fight during the Tisha B'Av, the day the Jews fast and mourn the destruction of the two Jewish temples in 586BC and 70AD. On this day, hundreds of Jews gather in the western wall of the old city's dung gate in their plastic and canvas sandals and shoes to read the lamentation all day long from the Old Testament. The group, named "Temple Mount Faithfuls", use the day to lay their claims to the "Temple Mount" - what the Muslims calls "The Noble Sanctuary," the Islamic holy sites. The Faithfuls pray and plead to God for more Jewish temples to be built in the area to undermine and eventually replace the Muslim mosques that have been there for centuries. They often come along with a huge stone that they refer to as the cornerstone of the new temple to be built on the holy sanctuary, a stone that provokes and is often seen by the Muslims as an attempt by the Jews to disrespect and destroy the Islamic holy sites. And for years, the Muslims have resisted it by violence. When Abdul came to join the group of Palestinian youths in the elevated compound of Al Aqsa from where they threw stones, tear gas, grenades and bombs at the Jews as they prayed, read lamentations and tore their clothes in mourning, Abdul saw Ishmael behind the wall, standing unblinkingly still and silent as his Islamic Jihad mentor gave him the last instructions. The Islamic Jihad organization had attacked Israeli civilians, with the exception of children. Ishmael and Abdul didn't have time to talk before Ishmael left on his suicide mission. As the Temple Mount Faithfuls ran and cowered away from the onslaught of the stones, grenades and bombs in fear and total confusion, Abdul saw Ishmael tread his way to the truck that was carrying the huge ancient corner stone. Ishmael was armed with a five pound bomb believed by the Islamic Jihad to be capable of smashing the cornerstone to dust, shaming the Temple Mount Faithfuls. Abdul watched as the riot control Policemen approached and Ishmael dropped the bomb at the foot of the truck and hurried away.

The Police chased after him and he ran dodging and ducking to escape into the Al-Aqsa mosque, joining the rest of the Palestinians in the mosque. The Policemen stopped short of entering the mosque because they are not authorized to enter the mosque for the purpose of

enforcing the law – the Israeli law. But for some unknown reason, the bomb failed to explode. However,
the onslaught of stones, grenades and bombs continued
to and from the Al-Aqsa mosque.

Sometimes, when one sits to ruminate on things,
when one thinks of Villa Dolorosa – the road to the
western wall, when one thinks of the western wall, the
Temple Mount, the Holy Sanctuary, an area that is believed to be the area of Jesus' crucifixion, burial and res-
urrection, one wonders why peace eludes. Peace, which
is God's eternal gift and abundant possession, has been
eluding the same land where his only begotten son, the
bastion of peace and truth, the light and the only way
through whom God can be reached, was born, raised
and performed almost all his miracles, and preached
his everlasting gospel. It really leaves so much to be de-
sired, and it is a question one would like to ask God or
Jesus Christ here on earth assuming, he courageously
comes back to earth again after what he underwent on
his first and only visit till date. Jesus is the greatest expression of God's love for humanity. Then why can't
there be peace on the land where he, God and his only
son had a direct contact with humans, a land that's been

trodden by Moses, Abraham, Aeron, Elijah, John the Baptist and all the Angels, Saints and Prophets.

Enigmatic, isn't it?

The next day, Abdul called Ishmael. Ishmael picked up the telephone at the fourth ring.

"Hello," he said, in a dull and depressed voice.

"I'm sad and depressed," he said.

"Why?' asked Abdul.

"The bomb failed to explode. It was a futile attempt. I can't make out any reason for that. And they will say their God is better than Allah, that's why it didn't explode," he lamented.

"I know, I know," responded Abdul.

"But take it easy, you will get there some day," he added.

"It appears targets that are worth a suicide mission and a place in paradise are getting fewer and fewer by each passing day. Don't forget to call and invite me whenever and wherever there is an opportunity to inflict them and be received in paradise," said Ishmael.

"I wont stiff you on that, count on me," Abdul replied.

"Good lad," said Abdul as he replaced the receiver

on its cradle.

Days later, Abdul left Jerusalem for Afghanistan and since then he'd never seen or telephoned Ishmael.

* * *

"It's been a long time" thought Abdul as the plane winged its way to Cairo.

Long time, yes, but once a militant, always a militant.

Abdul knew that Ishmael had been once chosen by the Islamic Jihad for a suicide bombing mission. He must have volunteered for the mission, and he is a clean nationalist and prays in the mosque and is neck deep in Muslim beliefs and doctrines. It was not impulse or vengeance for the death of a relative, but was based purely on Muslim belief, to become a martyr and secure a place in the kingdom of Allah.

CHAPTER 13
Cairo, Egypt

The plane touched the Egyptian soil in the early hours of the morning.

"Welcome to Cairo," said a voice over the public address system as the seat belt signs went off and passengers upped from their seats and made their ways to the exit tube. Cairo is a great city, once the centre of world excellence and ancient civilization, where the first form of writing was invented. A city, replete with historical and archaeological sites, that had been the headquarters of the Arab militancy and hostility towards Israel and America's hegemony before 1978 when United States President Reverend Jimmy Carter lured the Egyptians and the Israeli leaders into a historical peace accord in the highlands of Maryland, the Catoctin mountains, the so called Camp David Accord that many believed led to the assassination of Egyptian president Anwar Sadat in 1981.

"Cairo, give me luck. I count on you Cairo," Abdul intoned silently as he stepped into the arrival hall of the Cairo international airport. After a repast in the airport restaurant, Abdul boarded a taxi to central Cairo. He was calm in the back passenger's seat of the cab, reading the Al-Alkbar – the Egyptian government sponsored newspaper he picked up from the airport newsstand. Occasionally he glanced up from the pages to look sideways into the streets as the taxi glided down the wide road from the airport to the hotel. He read the front page of the paper and smiled indulgently. It read:

"Thanks to Hitler of the blessed memory who, on behalf of the Palestinians, took revenge in advance against the most vile criminals on the face of the earth. Although we do have a compliant against him, for his revenge on them was not enough"

Abdul nodded happily; he was quite familiar with this verse. It kind of formed a part of the creed he read every day. He leafed to yet another page of the newspaper and became thoughtful after reading about the joint presentation in a symposium at the American University of Cairo by the American Goodwill Ambassador and the USA defence secretary. The symposium would be held in the next 72 hours, and would focus on American security policy.

The taxi pulled up in front of the hotel and Abdul stepped out and paid off the driver. He went into the reception hall of the hotel and was checked into a suite on the sixth floor of the hotel. Inside the suite, he unpacked his bag and slumped into the bed and for the next hours he had a sound, dreamless slumber. He bent over his sixth floor window, propping himself with his elbow on the windowsill as he gazed into the redolent city of Cairo. It was a warm afternoon and the Nile was flowing quietly, and Egyptians were going about their normal daily chores.

"I know you give me luck Cairo and Nile. I know, you that is redolent with ancient mystery, Islamic and Arabian tradition and excellence. Don't fail me Cairo, don't fail me Nile," he prayed.

He paused and looked around; he was facing east to Mecca.

"Allahu Akhbar," he added, and turned to walk towards the table in the sitting room. He lifted the receiver from its cradle and put a call through to Ishmael.

"Hello," answered Ishmael at the first ring.

"Hello, this is Abdul."

"Who?"

"Abdul," he repeated.

"Oh! You," replied Ishmael, the expected enthusiasm in his voice.

He went aglow with anticipation, knowing that Abdul wasn't calling just to exchange pleasantries after a long time. He waited for the news and it came.

"Allah is calling you here in Cairo. Your service is most needed here Ishmael. Please do be here in the next 48 hours. Your ticket will be arranged and I will get back to you this evening or tomorrow with the information on your itinerary," said Abdul, and hung up.

A pause.

A smile pulled at the corner of Ishmael's mouth, a smile that would linger long after he replaced the receiver on its cradle. A smile that would linger as he knelt down facing Mecca to say thanks and gratify Allah for the opportunity for martyrdom, because he knew he was in for a terror mission.

Abdul left his hotel suite, called the elevator, descended to the ground floor and walked across the reception into the open and onto the street. Across the street that separates the Nile from the rest of the city, he disappeared into an office building. On the first floor of the building, he spoke with a travel agent.

"An American Airways flight will be leaving Jerusalem tomorrow at 5pm for Cairo, and there are seats in the first class, business class and economy class. Which class do you prefer sir?" inquired the travel agent.

"Ehm," Abdul began saying, as a man appeared from the inner office.

"Good afternoon," said the man as he dropped a note on the table and walked back into the office.

"Afternoon," replied Abdul.

"He's an American?" asked Abdul to the lady.

"Why?" replied the lady.

"His accent," said Abdul.

"Yes, he is the owner of the agency. He is a good man," said the lady, her fingers busy on the computer keyboard.

"I'm sorry, but cancel the booking," Abdul said. He turned and left the office.

"All the good Americans I know are dead."

"He is an imperialist, he is not a good man," murmured Abdul as he left the office, hate and furry boiling inside him.

Strange, eh? But it is the work of hatred. Sometimes one wonders why few Jews use German made cars like the Mercedes, BMW and Volkswagon. It's is part of the ugly tapestry of vengeance and hatred. Down the street, Abdul found an Arab-owned travel agency and bought the ticket. It was a French–made Saudi Arabia Airways plane.

"It's all ours," he thought as he paid for the ticket. He paid cash.

Back in his hotel room, Abdul made a call to Ishmael in Jenin.

"Everything is arranged," he began when Ishmael answered the call.

"Collect your ticket from the Royal Saudi Airways office in downtown Jerusalem. The flight will be leaving tomorrow night. Go to the Hebron branch of the Western Union and collect some money. Here is the money transfer number," he said, and went ahead to quote the numbers for Ishmael.

"Got it," said Ishmael.

"See you soon," said Abdul.

"See you then," replied Ishmael.

CHAPTER 14

The next morning Abdul was in the Airport to welcome Ishmael. They took a taxi to his hotel, and spent the remaining hours of the day going through the minute details of the assassination plot, while the American crew was busy touring historical sites like the Pyramids, the Gizeh monuments and other archaeological sites. Later in the night, they began to assemble the explosives and bombs to be used in the attack.

"Undoubtedly, the Americans are far ahead of the rest members of the global village, but this they achieved through the use of intimidation, propaganda and, admittedly, lots of hard work and little fairness. And in the past two and a half centuries, they've achieved so much, compliments of their leaders who have been leading with great wisdom and foresight," said Abdul.

"Wisdom?" asked Ishmael.

"Yeah, imperialistic wisdom," replied Abdul.

"We helped them against Nazi Germany, but later they discarded us and helped to precipitate the state of Israel and drove us Palestinians away from our home-land. We helped them in Afghanistan to defeat the Soviets, their Cold War enemy, and again when it was over, they turned their backs on us. But thank God to-morrow we will send the message. Tomorrow, we will let them know that being the only superpower and the most powerful and richest nation under the sun doesn't mean doing whatever they want whenever they want it, doesn't mean sitting and watching thousands of Pales-tinians die every day from aerial bombing attacks, nor does it mean bullying treaties and playing truancy on protocol agreements and conferences to address rac-ism. When we send our message tomorrow, the giant will hopefully realise that being so dominant should mean being an exemplary piece, because what the Gi-ant does now, whether inside their own backyard or on a tiny island on the coast of the earth, affects the rest of the world. Tomorrow, we will let the Giant know that, having failed severally in her obligations as the flag bearer, she is accountable to the failures around the global village," Abdul orated.

"I pray it comes to pass," said Ishmael as he tightened a wire on the bomb.

"Allahu Akbar," rejoined Abdul.

They worked into the early hours of the morning before going to bed. They woke up the next morning and, before any other thing, they knelt down and said their morning prayer, closing their prayer with a verse from the creed.

"Oh Allah, let the infidel grow old, let her memories engulf her dreams and let her wither, so that the Islamic kingdom will come and children of Islam will celebrate the future. And we thank oh Allah for having authorized the great attempt."

"Allahu Akhbar," they prayed.

Chapter 15
American University
Cairo, Egypt

Abdul arrived at the university premises in a taxi. The conference hall was besieged by placards bearing students. Some of them read:

"The Protocol Tearing Giant"

"Be an unbiased Judge in the Middle East"

"Environmental Aggressor"

"And more," thought Abdul as he made for the turnstile entrance of the auditorium.

He took his seat and waited. Every few minutes he felt the semi-automatic pistol tucked into the waistband of his pants.

Dressed in an expensive shiny black suit, and bearing an aura befitting the Secretary of Defence of the only surviving economic and military superpower in the global village, the US Secretary took the podium to address the audience. A welcome applause ensued.

"Good day," he said, waving to the audience.

"I'm here today to tell you how glad and prepared the United States is to forge a more peaceful world," he began.

"Peace in the world means peace in the United States of America. That's why the United States must start by defending and protecting America. America has decided to protect herself, a comprehensive protection by employing the latest defence initiative called the strategic defence initiative. But unlike what enemies of freedom are murmuring, it is not just the interest of the United States to put weapons in space to defend only USA assets and attack enemy missiles and satellites, but mainly to forge a more peaceful global village. All the fuss about the strategic defence initiative that will cost the USA about $100 billion is not just an exercise to militarise space as critics keep saying, nor does it mean that the USA wants, thinks and believes that treaties are outdated. No, the USA wants the renegotiation of the Anti-Ballistic Missile and the Comprehensive Test

Ban treaties. We are doing our best to accelerate the implementation of the 1993 START-2 agreement. The agreement that demands the USA and Russia cut back between 3000 and 3500 of deployed strategic nuclear warheads.

Our ABM programme is a defensive system, not an offensive one, and we are doing it because the times demand it. It is very true that the USA won't be spending a $100 billion to build an offensive monster. Ballistic missile technology has spread all over the world, and as such a missile defence system becomes imperative. Besides, the 1972 Anti-Ballistic Missile treaty was all based on Cold War era politics, and now that the Cold War is over, I think the treaty needs amendments, because the politics and circumstances that spurred it are now irrelevant," he orated.

A pause.

"Many of the nations who are clamouring that sidestepping and amending the ABM treaty will weaken the cornerstone of the international arms control are doing so because they are afraid that the USA will become far ahead of the rest of the world and undercut their nuclear deterrent. But Washington hopes to extend this missile protection to Allied countries that want to take part in the program. America respects rules and order. Nobody is more interested in global stability than the USA. There is no doubt who will come out as the biggest beneficiary of an orderly, free world, a world as orderly and freedom-loving as the USA, nor is there any doubt who will come out the greatest loser if world rules and order get destabilized and go awry. Whatever America does is good for America and I bet ya, if it's good for America, then it's good for the rest of the global village," orated the Secretary of Defence.

"Look at it, careless arrogance, always trying to undermine others. Even if it is true in itself that 'good for America, is good for the rest of the world', it is not the kind of public utterance expected of a politically swift and correct nation. But this type of carelessness shows the belief that US sovereignty is superior, and the rest of the world's treaties, protocols and agreements must be treated and amended according to the USA's political whims and caprices. And it is very poor of a modern Giant. The ABM treaty was signed by the US government under the tutelage of Richard Nixon, the Watergate man, and the USSR government under Comrade Leonid Brazher in the cold war, detent era. A treaty that permits each of the superpowers a single missile defence site, but prohibits the development of any national system like the USA government now campaigns.

Now the USA is testing ground, air, sea, and space based systems to intercept ballistic missiles in their ascent, mid-course and at a terminal phase. One wonders why the USA is so afraid and paranoid," thought Abdul, hate burning inside him.

He restrained the urge, a wild urge to draw his gun and spray the podium with hot lead and silver, to pull a grenade and throw it at the podium.

He cast a glance across the stage.

"So many important men of Allah," he thought.

Sitting in the vicinity of the podium were men like the chairman of the Organization of Islamic Countries, OIC, and the secretary general of the Arab League.

"But you, as a professional, shouldn't be afraid of the penalty or casualties when hitting a target," chided the urging evil mind.

"It is certainly chimerical to think that you can wipe out all these Arab leaders only to hit one or two infidels and receive kudos from the Arab world or any militancy organization," came the restraint mind.

Abdul adjusted himself on his seat and listened to the speech, rage coursing through him, his large vivid eyes sizing up the man at the podium, tearing him to bits and pieces

"…the anti-ballistic missile shield, " continued the Secretary of Defence. "…will protect the USA against any nuclear blackmail by rogue nations, and encourage the USA in its intervention missions and wars anywhere in the world against the western interests and the interest of world peace in general," said the defence secretary.

"Rogue nations," echoed Abdul.

"Define Rogue Nation, what characteristics make a Rogue Nation? Nations that abide to the letters of the international treaties, protocols and conferences or nations that disrespect all the treaties, agreements and protocols that they are signatory to, and play truancy on international peace conferences?" thought Abdul.

"In opting out from signing the Germ Warfare draft, the United States is not trying to walk away from the world or to dictate to the rest of the world, because as we all know, the world is increasingly becoming interdependent. We consider that in the face of intense industrial espionage, signing the draft will put US national security, confidential information and businesses at risk. Besides, the draft would not stop the rogue nations from seeking to acquire biological weapons," continued the secretary.

At the mention of germ warfare, 'Vector' came to Abdul's mind and he glanced across the faces in the audience.

"I'm sure that not more than ten percent of this audience know something about Vector," he mused.

Vector, the Soviet era's greatest viral weapons laboratory, is located in the town of Koltsovo. After the fall of the Soviet Union, the USA invested money and effort to dismantle Vector, a Russian military treasure and germ warfare empire, and they succeeded. Backed by the world health organization, the USA turned Vector into a research centre for smallpox vaccines and anti-viral drugs. Some of the vector scientists went to work in the centres for disease control and prevention in Atlanta, USA. America removed Vector from its danger list. Today, Vector is an open library to foreign scientists and researchers, mainly Americans and western Europeans. Some of the Vector scientists went into non-profit research ventures.

"Good for the world and humanity, but why dodge the germ warfare draft accord now?" thought Abdul.

"These treaties, agreements and draft accords only bind and hold the honest nations, and give cover to cheats," continued the Secretary of Defence.

"Good, so if you are an honest nation with an honest leader, then sign the accord and set a good example in all your dealings. Nobody is going to catch you red handed," Abdul thought, almost aloud.

The man beside Abdul turned to look at him.

The Secretary of Defence finished his speech and turned to leave the stage amidst modest ovation as journalists and photographers snapped furiously.

Abdul adjusted himself in his seat and waited for the next speaker – the Goodwill Ambassador – to address the audience on the USA's policies on racism and intolerance. The audience cheered loudly as he took the stage.

"Racism and intolerance is a very sensitive issue and exists everywhere in the global village today," he began.

"But Zionism equated to racism does not pass a product of Soviet era propaganda to pitch the Arabs and Arab sympathisers against Israel and the United States. This notion, that started in 1975 and was approved by the United Nations general assembly then, has been replaced in 1991 by the UN assembly after 16 years of careful study, finding that Zionism is not racism, so much so that it isn't for nothing that Reverend Martin Luther King Jr. in 1967 said thus about Zionism equating to racism:

'It denies the Jewish people the fundamental right that we blacks justly claim for the people of Africa and freely accord to other nations of the globe. It is discrimination against the Jews. My friend because they are Jews, in short it is anti-Semitism'," quoted the Goodwill Ambassador, and looked across the faces in the audience for reactions.

A pause.

"And I don't think any less than this pronouncement of Mr King, a friend of peace," said the Goodwill Ambassador.

"As for reparation for slavery," he continued.

A pause.

"Yes slavery is inhuman and disgraceful. There is no doubt it is a dark side of US history, but it happened centuries back and in the opinion of the US government, the evils of the past are better left to lie. No present or future US government and administration will agree to atone for the irresponsibility of ancient regimes and administrations. The US government is not in the least ready to pay any reparations to the African continent," said the Goodwill Ambassador.

"But the present government and administration of Germany are paying for the evils of the Third Reich. The holocaust happened decades ago. Cash, apologies, compensations, memorials and remembrance foundations have been erected for the holocaust victims. But for slavery, nothing because it happened centuries back. Let's not forget that it only officially stopped in 1867, but unofficially continued till 1900. Time heals wounds, but time doesn't justify evil or warrant evil.

"I would like to hear another quotation of Mr King on this, especially on selective atonements of evils of past regimes and administrations. Mr King, a friend of peace, wouldn't have been in favour of segregation in atonements. In all honesty, the Africans deserve the reparations, 'cause they were so grossly and shamelessly used and underdeveloped. A few hundreds of billion dollars would revive the economy of the African continent, and if the West wouldn't do it in an outright payment, let it be done in form of compulsory investment," thought Abdul in his difference from the quotes of the Goodwill Ambassador.

"It is because of the absurd equating of Zionism to racism and the unreasonable call for reparation for slavery that the United States boycotted the UN-sponsored conferences on racism in 1978, 1983 and again in 2001 in South Africa," continued the Goodwill Ambassador.

"Unreasonable call for reparation?" echoed Abdul.

"Really, times heal wounds, but that's when a wound is not deep enough, when the wound is superficial, but when the wound is marrow deep, no amount of time, whether centuries or millennia, can heal it. Such is the situation of the African continent. Pay the poor Africans reparation, pay them, you owe them so much, pay them Giant, pay them," murmured Abdul, his hateful eyes watching the movement of the Ambassador's lips as he called out his words, his gaze following his hands as he gesticulated occasionally.

"But we will change all this bias and deceit. It must be changed," Abdul murmured on remembering that Ishmael must've been ready at his position, waiting to do his deed. The American government Goodwill Ambassador would soon be leaving Cairo after the symposium, for Alexander, the second largest Egyptian city, situated some 200km north of Cairo. Alexander, an ancient Mediterranean city founded by Alexander the Great. The Ambassador would be visiting the eleven storey disk-shaped Alexander library, one of the oldest libraries in the world. The library dates to the Hellenistic times and contains book collections from the middle ages, with over 700,000 scrolls. The library was built by Ptolemy 1 in 288 BC, with the ambition of acquiring every book in the world, and it'd been visited by big minded scholars as Archimedes, Euclid and, as rumour has it, Jesus Christ himself. It was in the Alexander library that great scientific and mathematical works, including the accurate calculation of the earth's circumference and the mechanics of the solar system, were deciphered. The Goodwill Ambassador would be attacked as he left Cairo for Alexander, that's how Abdul placed the plot. The audience cheered as the Ambassador concluded his discuss and turned to leave the stage, and he smiled placidly and waved a hand to the audience. Abdul was tight-faced and never cheered.

CHAPTER 16

Mounted on an Arabian pony with pounds of explosive hanging down its sides, Ishmael waited on a cross road at the foot of the Nile bridge. The sound of the approaching siren increased with the passing seconds, and he waited, and prayed silently that the target be hit. The siren had grown very loud and Ishmael could see the motorcade approaching. He looked sideways and waited to do his deed. At that moment a children's school bus pulled up by the road shoulder behind him to allow the motorcade a free passage. The Goodwill Ambassador's limousine was some ten meters away from Ishmael now; it was time to pull the fuse and explode the whole goddamn place, but Ishmael's training as a suicide bomber included never to kill children, no matter the circumstances, even Israeli children, and now here were tens of Egyptian children. No way, he couldn't pull the fuse. The Koran says thus:

"Killing an Innocent is like killing the entire humanity and saving an innocent is like saving the entire humanity"

Ishmael watched in frustration as the Ambassador's limousine and entourage glided past. The school bus rolled onto the road and away.

"Allahu Akhbar, Allahu Arkhbar," Ishmael shouted and pulled the detonator as an American Embassy vehicle approached. The bomb exploded tearing him and the pony into tiny bits. The embassy vehicle was damaged and the driver wounded severely.

"Oh Allah, I failed again, Oh Allah, what a shame. I'm denied the glory once again," mourned Abdul as he strode down the tree lined Cairo Avenue that evening, head bent in thought, guilt crisscrossing his mind. Guilt not just because Ishmael died, but because he died alone, with an innocent Egyptian, a father of five severely wounded, who might not be able to walk and work again. His target had claimed many lives without being scratched or even truly frightened. He, Abdul, had been excluded from the Jihadist Movement, a movement he loved with all his heart and blood, and the target remained forever elusive.

"What is happening? Am I too incompetent to carry out this mission? Ain't I worthy enough to take the glory? Is the whole thing wrongly planned?" Abdul ruminated.

"No, not wrongly planned," responded an inner voice.

"Then what and why?" he thought as a prayer call for the evening played up from a public address system of a nearby mosque.

Twenty meters down the street, Abdul walked quietly into the mosque and knelt to pray after the usual washing of the feet, hands, ears, face and mouth.

"Allah, I've always known that glory doesn't often go to the most swift, the best planner, or the strongest, but really stays with perseverance. I won't quit or walk out on the Islamic cause. I will fight hard and fight to the end, as long as I'm alive, because in life, it is persistence that brings about great changes. No misfortune, failure or obstacle can stop me. I will rise and start again whenever the opportunity presents itself. Allahu

Akhbar," he prayed and rose.

Another fortnight crawled by before the crescent moon appeared in the Mediterranean sky and the Ramadan month began. Ramadan is the month when the angel Gabriel presented the word of God, Allah, the holy Koran, to the prophet, Mohammed.

Abdul observed the basic abstinence from food, drinks, tobacco and sex. He spent most of the day inside his hotel room and came out only in the night to walk the streets of the rambunctious Cairo.

After the Ramadan month, Abdul checked out from the hotel and moved into a three bedroom bungalow in the Zamalac neighbourhood of Cairo, at the edge of the neighbourhood where it overlooked the Nile and one could have a beautiful view of the Cairo city spires. The house sat some ten meters from the road and had wide windows with overhanging lintels to shade against the African sun. Days later, aware that he was being sought after by the intelligence agents for his involvement in the bomb explosions in the Royal Saudi government guest hotel, Abdul checked into a cosmetic hospital to have a facial plastic surgery to change his appearance, touching his nose to make it longer and more pointed, widened his eyes, making his lips fuller and pushing his ears back. He replanted some hair on his bald head, and removed the brown patch on the left side of his skin, removing his deep tan with TCA peeling and rejuvenating his appearance, an effect that can last for upwards of five years. When he left the clinic, his skin was lighter and more radiant, he looked far more handsome and responsible, and some ten years younger.

Abdul stood before the mirror in his rest room for the fifth time that day.

"It will really be very difficult for anybody to recognise me properly now, in my shoulder length hair, clean shaven and with all these changes. In Afghanistan, I would be jailed for having long hair and short beard, but Allah knows I'm doing this to stay alive. All I have to watch out for now is the digital scanning security cameras. Just go camera shy," he thought. The security cameras had face recognition software that could turn a facial image into a digital map with some 80-reference points that were as distinguishing as fingerprints or the Iris. The points are matched against a mug-shot database of suspects and criminals with arrest warrants. The software could account for facial hair and aging. Its accuracy depended mostly on the clarity of the mug-shots in the database and the image in focus. Its error rate was less than one percent.

"All one needs to do is avoid public places like the cinema, shopping malls, football stadiums, and casinos."

At the thought of the casinos, he paused. He's been visiting the neighbourhood casino, where he was a registered member and played regularly on slot machines and roulette wheels.

"But in casinos, digital scanning security cameras are used to scan for known cheats that bring loss to the casino, not terrorists," a mind reminded him.

"And the airports have to be avoided too."

"Oh! Allah, when am I going to travel again and to where?" he thought, and looked up at the photo of his old self hung on the wall, and then back at his new reflection in the mirror, his fake self.

America came to mind.

"Oh Allah! They are so proud and loud. America needs to have a look at herself in the mirror, and she may see that she is no longer very young and robust. America has made me mutilate myself and change my god-given appearance. What a bully you are. But thank Allah that I will never quit. I will work hard and one day I will negotiate with you in the only language you use against everybody, the language of terror on all fronts. Economically, politically, culturally and above all militarily, the only language that calls and arrests your attention," he said.

CHAPTER 17
Afghanistan

Mohammed, the personnel secretary of the movement, took the envelope from his personal assistant. He blew air into the envelope and dipped his two fingers in to pull out the pictures inside it. He glanced at the first picture, shovelled it behind, and looked at the second picture for some moments before putting it into the envelope.

"Put Abdul Allan's file among the dead," he said to his secretary.

Three hours later, the Supreme Disciple glanced through the pictures and nodded languidly in satisfaction. He handed the pictures back to the orderly – one of his replicas.

"Dead or alive, that's what Washington wants of me.

Alive because the vindictive America would like to torture and maim me to death. But death is all I want for them, no maiming, no torturing, we do not torture, they do," thought the Supreme Disciple as he reached for the Koran at the foot of the mat on which he was sitting, in a cave some 400 meters below the sea level somewhere near Jalalabad east of Afghanistan. A cave he'd helped the Americans, employing his Civil Engineering skills, refurbish during the 1980's Soviet Invasion of Afghanistan. A cave that had been his last safe sanctuary since the American and coalition bombs rained on the Afghan nation. He opened to chapter two, verse 190 of the Koran and read:

"In the name of Allah, fight those who fight you, but do not trespass limits. Allah doesn't love transgressors"

"I too don't like transgressors and for that I've often said, kill don't talk, don't maim, don't torture nor imprison," thought the Supreme Disciple as he closed and put the Koran down. At that moment, an unmanned CIA predator drone, equipped with high resolution cameras and Hellfire anti-tank missiles, was hunting for the Supreme Disciple and scouting the Afghan airspace in search of him. The sono-thermal sensitive antennas were actively scanning for signs.

"Abdul, that son of a bitch squandered a golden opportunity, and worst still vindicated the American-Jewish ties and favour bank, because the plot was foiled by a Jew. Infidels don't, won't and ought not gain any benefit from the endeavours of the Jihadist Movement's failed or accomplished efforts," soliloquised the Supreme Disciple, stroking his long beard. His mind drifted into memory lane, cruising through the years and details of the Movement's actions and America's reactions in the past. He'd long been at war with America. After studying Engineering in King Abdulaziz University in Jedda, the Supreme Disciple joined and worked in a non-administrative sector of the family construction firm. In the '80's, when the Soviets invaded Afghanistan, he heeded the call of the Muslim clerics to come and defend Islam against the infidel Soviets in a war in which Saudi Arabia and the USA bled over $5 billion through the Pakistani intelligence to the Afghan rebels to defeat the Soviets. The Supreme Disciple worked extensively with the CIA in the Afghan war. He worked so diligently, risking his life on several occasions that the Americans nicknamed him "the good one". He returned to Saudi Arabia after the war, already saddened at the USA for having slipped away back to America immediately after the Soviets were driven away, without any further support to the Afghans to rebuild their nation, leaving them in a land replete with American made landmines, guns, drugs, refugees and victims of war. He met the US troops on the Saudi soil as they warmed up to wage a bloody battle against Iraq, an Islamic nation, in the 1990 "Operation Desert Storm". He outrageously denounced it as an act of treachery by the house of Al Saud against Islam. He led various peaceful demonstrations and bloody riots to show his disapproval. He was subsequently expelled from the kingdom. And he found a home in Sudan.

CHAPTER 18
Sudan

The Supreme Disciple was relatively tranquil in Sudan. He invested in the economy, created jobs and spread his intelligence tentacles to all parts of the globe. In 1994, he noticed a great number of CIA covert and overt agents in Khatoun, Sudan. He'd worked with the CIA and knew how they operated. They often liked to maintain informants within any organization, terrorist or not, and he, the Supreme Disciple wouldn't allow the CIA to use his Movement and his refuge home as their secret service laboratory. The CIA overt agents read local newspapers and magazines, listened to the radio and watched TV programmes, mixed with the locals and collected the facts they needed, while the covert agents stayed in the country as legal attachés to the embassies, or economic and political attachés, but with their eyes wide open and awake. The information collected by both teams would later be assembled in the embassy and sent through diplomatic baggage to the State Department in Washington.

In late 1995, the CIA station in Khatoun was bombed and CIA agents knifed and clubbed in Khatoun. It was a warning attack, nobody died. The 'good one' is not a coward, he never acts without first issuing a warning. But before the attacks, the USA had issued several excruciating remarks to the Khatoun regime for harbouring the Supreme Disciple and condoning international terrorism, and for having a plot underway to assassinate the white house national security adviser who had adduced the Sudanese involvement in terrorism.

Only a life-threatening situation would make a North American leave a tropical nation and head north to the USA in February, one of the coldest months in North America. This was the case with the CIA in Sudan in February 1996, when the attacks on the CIA operatives were getting out of hand, and the CIA station chief in Khatoun advised that all Americans in Sudan withdraw from the Sudanese soil and move back to the

USA. The embassy in Khatoun was closed down and the last American in Sudan, the US Ambassador, made request to the Sudanese government before leaving. "It will please the government of the people of the United States of America that your government expel the Supreme Disciple of the Jihadist Movement from Sudan," said the Ambassador to the Sudanese Foreign Minister.

"We will look into it and we will get back to your government in due course," replied the minister to the Ambassador, as he boarded his plane to the USA.

The Supreme Disciple called a party and celebrated the little victory. He and his followers prayed and feasted in his mansion and thanked Allah for their victory over the CIA.

* * *

Six Months Later

It was summer in America, and the November elections were fast approaching, when the Sudanese Defence Minister disembarked at the Hyatt Arlinghton to meet with the run- away Ambassador and the chief of the State Department of East African Affairs to discuss the Supreme Disciple's case, the accusations of Sudanese involvement in international terrorism and the request of the Ambassador to oust the Supreme Disciple from Sudan. The Sudanese minister's first disappointment and let down came when, instead of meeting with the Ambassador and the East African Affairs chief as scheduled, he was relegated to talk with covert operatives from the CIA's African division that is comprised of the three men who man the CIA's 'Supreme Disciple' Unit. The unit was set up after the Supreme Disciple was alleged to be involved in the 1993 WTC car bomb blast, and Sheik Omar Abdel Rahman was taken prisoner. An American hostage, as the Supreme Disciple would often say. In the Arlinghton government guesthouse, the Sudanese defence minister was handed a document entitled:

"Measures Sudan Can Take To Improve Relations With The United States of America".

The measures enlisted six items, orders rather than suggestions. The defence minister read down the pages in humiliation, knowing that in reality, in the modern free market economic system of the global village, few countries, if any, can survive for a long time being an enemy of the United States of America. He took a sip from the glass of water they offered him, as his eyes moved carefully to number two on the list of orders they would have to follow religiously if they wanted to remain a friend of the USA. The paragraph was devoted to attacks on the CIA station in Khatoun, which Washington believes were commanded by the Sudanese guest, the Supreme Disciple and his terror network. The paragraph demanded that the Sudanese government furnish the CIA with information on the Supreme Disciple and his Jihadist Movement's activities, including names, dates of arrival and departure, destinations and passport details on any of the organization agents that enter and leave Sudan.

"So that they can monitor, track and prevent them from carrying out any terrorist acts and arrest them easily when they carry out attacks," thought the minister.

"The Sudanese government can do this for the USA," said the minister after reading the document. "We can arrest the 'good one' and hand him over to the USA if Washington so demands."

The two operatives exchanged glances.

"Why call him the 'good one'," asked one of the operatives.

"He alleged that was the nickname given to him by the CIA when he was on good terms with US interests," said the Minister.

"And he loves the name," he added.

"We will get back to you in 48 hours," said the lead agent, and the meeting ended on that note.

The agents took the suggestion of the Sudanese minister to their superiors.

"Arrest him and hand him over to the US authorities," echoed the chief of the State Department of East African Affairs.

"That means bringing him into the USA and into the justice system of the USA," began the National Security Adviser.

"And invariably that means an indictment in a US court. And we have no such case against him for now," he said.

"Except if he will be arrested and bundled to Saudi Arabia, where he has a case with the house of Al Saud, the Saudi government. He issued a fatwa – a religious edict denouncing the Saudi government as corrupt hypocrites who must be overthrown. In Saudi Arabia, such offences carry a maximum sentence of beheading and a minimum sentence of life imprisonment."

He looked across the faces around the table in the room.

"It's viable," said the East African Affairs chief.

"Good idea," said the National Security Council Director for Africa.

Emissaries were sent to Riyahd to meet with the Saudi Royals to press the idea. But after hours of negotiations and talks, the Saudi Royals declined to take the part in killing or jailing the 'good one'.

"It is a serious crime he has committed against this government, but we will pass on this, we grant him amnesty on these crimes for now," said the Saudi internal Affairs Minister.

"This government wouldn't want to push things beyond the realms of safety. Expelling and stripping his citizenship is an appropriate punishment within safety limits for the present. His death may cause more uprising than the government will want. One thing about people like that man is that his followers are ready to die for him. If we kill or jail him, Saudi fundamentalists will turn the country upside down. Remember, he is not a plebeian, he is a Saudi noble, from one of the wealthiest families of the land of Arabia. Although his family disowned him long ago, it would not be comfortable for this government to take him to any further war," said the Saudi Minister.

The US emissaries left Riyahd in disappointed.

* * *

Back in the USA

"I'm afraid the Saudi government failed us, they didn't rise to the bait. They don't want anything to do with his death or imprisonment," said the National security adviser to the conference in the well-lit and airy state department situation room on their first meeting after receiving the message from the emissaries.

He paused and his gaze made an arc across their faces and bounced off and rested on the photo frame of George Washington that hung quietly on the brightly painted wall at the far end of the room.

"And now, what next?" he said quietly but thoughtfully, still gazing at the photo frame as if the image might have an immediate answer and solution to the problem.

"Let him go, go out of Sudan," said the chief of East African Affairs.

"But to where?" asked another director.

"We won't let him thin off into the troposphere just like that. I mean let's find a way to hand him over to the prison authority of any government," said the National Security Council director for Africa.

"Where and to who?" asked another.

"To any country with a crude justice system where he has committed the flimsiest of offences, I mean where anything could be scratched up against him," said the National Security Council director for Africa.

"Let him go," said the White House national security adviser.

"But he must not go to Somalia," warned the CIA's African division chief.

He was afraid that the Supreme Disciple, if allowed to stay in Somalia, would fuel and train Somalian rebels who were fighting US intervention and presence on their soil.

"Besides, like what was said some time last year, if we really want him off our back, we can bomb or cause an accident to his jet as it leaves Sudan to cruise the sky to his would-be destination. Like that, we silence him forever," he added.

The heads across the table nodded approvingly, if guardedly, in tandem. They turned and gazed at each other.

"It's a good idea, especially if it is well executed, the investigations into his death if any wouldn't point to the United States. But we all know that the United States have a presidential ban on assassinations," said the White House Security Adviser.

"Can't we find a hand-glove excuse to pull the job?" asked the CIA African division chief, who was also the CIA chief of the special "Supreme Disciple Unit".

"The only viable glove is to link him to the murder of a US citizen, but at this moment, there is none," said the National Security Adviser.

"However, I will talk to the President of the United States about it," he added, and with that the meeting was called off.

CHAPTER 19

The East African Affairs CIA chief ruminated on a gloved hand solution to the Supreme Disciple's case.

"It is very simple," he thought. "A surface to air missile like the sting missile could be fired at his jet from a jungle in Sudan as he flies away to another refuge country. A time bomb could be planted in the jet and it will explode while he's airborne outside of Sudan air space. The pilot might be blackmailed into crashing the aircraft," came the thoughts.

"It could be done, and perfectly too, if the Commander in Chief gives a go ahead."

The American President listened attentively as the National Security Adviser briefed him in minute detail on the Supreme Disciple issue.

"The United States of America is a just nation. To this moment, that terrorist has not been linked to the death of any American citizen, and as such we say let him go out from Sudan, I mean a safe exit. That will uproot him from his business empire in Sudan and his training camps," said the Commander in Chief of the US armed forces.

* * *

The evening sun shun high above the Khatoun sky and its ebbing rays filtered into the large airy sitting room through the wide French window. It was an evening in March 1996, and the Supreme Disciple was in his palace in Khartoun when a Sudanese government car pulled up in the driveway. The Sudanese chief intelligence officer was ushered into the moderately decorated sitting room where the Supreme Disciple was sitting on a low cushion.

"Sudan is no longer safe for you," began the intelligence officer after exchanging pleasantries.

"The government of Sudan can no longer harbour you. The pressure from the USA has become unbearable and the government has decided that you must leave the Sudanese soil, that's the order. We do not want to collaborate with the Americans by leaving you here and informing on you, your troops and your movement. So if you leave, we will be in the clear from being a collaborating party to the defeat of a man of Allah," said the officer.

"In the name of Allah, the government of Sudan is telling you to leave because if you stay here, we will be forced to provide them with information about you, and the activities of your organization. We may choose to give them unimportant information, but information nonetheless. We, the Sudanese government and people of Sudan, are not collaborators, and the only way we can maintain that stance is to tell you to leave and pray that the almighty Allah guide and protect you, your movement and the ideology, the dream of Islamic renaissance," said the intelligence officer.

"I understand," said the Supreme Disciple.

"Any time limit for my departure?" he asked.

"You have one week," replied the Intelligence chief.

At first, it seemed there was no place to go, but on remembering that the Taleban Militia had taken over power in Afghanistan, a ray of homing hope leapt in him. The Talibans were Sunni Muslims who practiced Islam in an ardent manner. Taliban comes from the Islamic word Taleb, which means religious students.

Afghanistan was a country the Supreme Disciple helped to liberate from the Soviet invaders. Afghan owed him a favour. Besides, the Taleban, as Sunni Muslims, hated despotism, hegemony, liberal democracy, western values and the US unilateralism and interventionism around the global village.

"Kabul, here I come," said the Supreme Disciple.

"I wonder why Kabul never came to mind from the onset. It is a country that has provided healthy training grounds for upwards of twenty years for opposition and terrorist groups with the Islamic flag, including the Uzbekistan's neo-Stalinist regime who were exiled to Afghanistan, wrapped in Islamic guerrilla flags, the Uyghur Turkish Muslims in Xinjiang that have been under Chinese oppression are also guests in the Afghan camps, the Chechnya separatist Muslim rebels from Russia, the Tajistan rebels, the Muslim Kashmir who invoke Islam to fight India in Kashmir, and the Jaish-e-Mohammed, a Pakistan based terrorist group run by the Pakistani intelligence service. After training, Pakistani intelligence then deploys them to fight in Kashmir, a bargaining chip for the Pakistani government with India to grant the region a more ample autonomy. Afghan is a fertile land for me and the movement," thought the Supreme Disciple.

Three days after the visit from the Sudanese intelligence chief, the Supreme Disciple packed his belongings and boarded a chartered jet to Afghanistan, where the movement had entrenched camps in Kandahar, Jalalabad, Kabul, Helmund, Nandahar, Namrose, Mazar-al-sharif and Khost. Recruitment for the movement was fast, and the rank and file of the movement fattened by the day with fadeyins, Chechnya Islamic separatists, Arab guerrillas and later the Egyptian Jihad, which merged with the movement.

CHAPTER 20

The Supreme Disciple read with interest the indictment by a US grand jury against him for terrorist conspiracy charges. It was all the US government had been waiting for: to be able to bring him into the US under the justice system. He lowered the newspaper and stroked his beard as thoughts crisscrossed his mind. The evidence for the indictment was extracted from a former Jihadist Movement operative who defected to the USA. Terrorist conspiracy charges carry a minimum of life in prison in the USA.

"I won't, and Allah in his infinite and tender mercy will not allow the infidels to cage me for life. We will kill them in the millions before they lay their bloody, dirty, despotic hands on any officer of the Movement, that's if they ever could," thought the Supreme Disciple.

Two days later, he took the podium in a camp in Kandahar to address some fadeyins, mujahidin and other members of the movement.

"We will take the fight to the infidels, because all they do is sit down in their homes and indict every one of us on trumped up charges, simply because we are men of Allah, pure in heart and very close to our Allah. But we will kill them in millions whenever and wherever they are. The unbelievers, the infidels ought not to live. They are cursed by Allah," he said amidst applause.

The next morning, the National Security chiefs in Washington met in the pentagon situation room to dissect the 'Threat Matrix' — a CIA high-security document containing minute details of new threats on the USA and USA interests around the globe. The Matrix contained details of the Jihadist Movement's threats made and discussions held in Kabul the previous day by the Supreme Disciple. The details were sent by the CIA implant in the Movement, code-named Mr Link by the CIA special Supreme Disciple Unit.

"The USA's interests are at risk everywhere they are around the globe. There is going to be a terrorist attack soon. It is going to be a bloody attack. No knowledge of a specific target at this moment. But the attacks will happen within the next 30 days," read the message from Mr Link to the CIA.

"Ambiguous," murmured the CIA chief of the Supreme Disciple Unit.

"He's never sent clear and specific message. No targets, nothing," he added.

* * *

East Africa, Two Weeks Later

As bomb blasts went off in areas around the horn of Africa and the Somali Peninsula, the 'good one' was sitting with some of the elite disciples of the movement in Jalalabad Afghanistan.

"If the Supreme Disciple and his crew won't stay in East Africa, the yanks won't stay either," seemed to be what the blasting sounds of the explosives were chanting as pieces of the American Embassy buildings and human bodies flew up into the dry hot African air. It was August 6, 1998.

"The attacks were the handwork of the Jihadist Movement," said the CIA chief of the special Terror

Unit.

"Our man sent a message to confirm it," he added as he met with national security chiefs in the state department's situation room, a day after the East African attacks.

"Now, we have enough reasons and evidence to assassinate that son of a bitch. Locate him wherever he is and get him killed," said the National Security Adviser.

"By tomorrow, the President must've signed his death warrant. And don't fail," he said to the CIA chief.

Back in his office, the CIA chief turned to his office manager, a portly Texan.

"Send a telex to Mr Link, let him monitor the Supreme Disciple's movements and gestures. He must find out where he will be for three to four hour stretches over the next few days, weeks and months," he said.

"Yes boss," replied the office manager.

* * *

One Week Later

"Good luck," said the CIA chief of the special terror unit to Mr Cabin as he and his team of seven officers set to board the flight to Pakistan and later proceed to

Afghanistan.

"Thank you," replied Mr Cabin.

"Great luck indeed, one needs it when working in the Islamic camp. The Arabs are very adamant when it comes to religious matters. To them, going against Islam or against whoever clamours for Islamic values is like condemning one to hellfire," thought Mr Cabin as he boarded his plane. The first task they would perform once in Pakistan would be to meet with the security chiefs to plead for authorization to train and send Pakistani intelligence agents to Afghanistan to help in locating and assassinating the Supreme Disciple. If the Pakistani government agreed, Washington would in return lift economic sanctions on Pakistan and give the nation some economic leverage.

"We have a message from Mr Link," said the secretary to the CIA chief of the terror unit as he entered the office.

"Let me see it," he demanded.

The secretary walked around the table, picked up the paper and handed it to him.

"The Supreme Disciple will be attending a meeting in Khost in the next five days. More than 300 members of the Movement will attend the meeting. He will arrive at 4.30pm and the meeting will last until 8.30pm," read the message.

"Good," said the chief, nodding thoughtfully.

"Son of a bitch, you won't escape this," he murmured between his teeth.

"Put me through to the National Security Adviser," he said to his Secretary.

"We've pinned him down to a camp in Khost in the next five days between 4.30 and 8.30pm, where he will be attending a meeting with the Movement's rank and file," he reported.

"Good job," said the NSA.

"No mistakes right? I mean, has the info been proof checked?" probed the NSA.

"Mr Link always comes up with hot info," replied the CIA chief.

"Good!"

Three hours later, the NSA and other security chiefs were meeting with the President. It was decided that Tomahawk cruise missiles would be used to hit the Supreme Disciple as he met and convened with his allies to connive against US interests.

The US navy ship stationed in the Arabian Sea off the coast of Pakistan was put at alert after the meeting with the President at the White House War Room.

* * *

Five Days Later

The day was cool and windy as the Supreme Disciple arrived in his guarded convoy at the camp in Khost. He arrived at 2.30pm, hosted the meeting and left the camp at 4.00pm.

"We thank God for the hell America met in East Africa. Though we regret and plead to Allah to accept the souls of the innocent Africans who died in the attacks. And forever we say death to the infidels, death to the incursors," orated the Supreme Disciple, flanked by the military commander and other dignitaries of the Movement.

"We strictly advise that members stay put in the camp for further information and directives," said the Military Commander.

At 5.30pm, some members were allowed to leave the camp, but fifty members were ordered to stay put in the camp for further instructions. The fifty members had long been under scrutiny for hypocrisy and possible collaboration with the infidels.

An hour later, 66 Tomahawk missile, fired from the American navy ships in the Arabian Sea, rained on the Khost camp. It was at the time the Americans believe the meeting would be at its Peak, probably with the Supreme Disciple at the height of his discussion.

Thirty men were killed in the attack. The Supreme Disciple and his top allies were miles away.

"Fools, you think you can buy me over with your dirty money," murmured Mr Link as he brought out a dirty one-dollar bill from his pocket.

"In God we trust," he read quietly in his heavily accented English.

"You trust in your God. And you want me to go against mine and throw away my salvation. I trust in the Islamic Allah and thank Allah you Infidels are providing me this opportunity to work, to come closer to a place in heaven. The people who died in this attack are as bad and unworthy as all the Infidels," murmured Mr Link, as he watched the strikes of the missiles at the Khost camp from the top of a mountain about three kilometres away. It was the second time Mr Link had misled the Americans in an attempt to assassinate the Supreme Disciple. The first time, he'd allied himself with some CIA-sponsored local Afghans to attack and kill the Supreme Disciple as he drove to Chahar-I-Ansari through Kabul. He'd alerted the military commander and the Supreme Disciple's personal security chief. He led the locals to ambush the convoy that he had convinced them the Supreme Disciple would be travelling in. They blocked the road as the convoy approached, but the Supreme Disciple wasn't in the convoy, which was instead full of militants of the Movement. In the confusion, 10 CIA-sponsored local chiefs were killed. Mr Link and three others escaped.

Chapter 21

"I hope they are alright," thought Mr Cabin of the three CIA operatives he'd sent into Afghanistan some three days back.

Telepathy is a wonderful thing. At the moment, the three CIA operatives were talking with Mr Massoud in northern Afghanistan. Mr Massoud was a Soviet-Afghan war veteran, hero and leader on the Northern Alliance Rebels who were fighting the Taleban regime.

"Search and hunt down the Supreme Disciple and you will have the financial reward, $15 million," said the CIA operatives' lead speaker to Mr Massoud.

Silence, as Mr Massoud weighed the offer.

"It is a good offer and we need the money to continue the struggle against the Taleban regime," said Mr Massoud, tugging his beard.

"But if I could topple the Taleban government and have total control of Afghanistan, then I could capture the Supreme Disciple sound and alive for you. I do not need just the money, but tanks, fighters, military and war intelligence to do the job," replied Massoud.

The three CIA operatives exchanged glances.

"Well, your position is not a bad one, but we've got to speak with our superiors before we can give you any answer," said the lead speaker of the CIA team.

The team left Afghanistan for Pakistan the next day.

Mr Cabin listened attentively as they narrated their report. He later sent a telex to Washington. The national security sages met and analysed Mr Massoud's offer.

"A good and sound offer, but very costly," they decided.

Washington was quite aware that Saudi Arabia and Pakistan had great interest in the Taleban regime. To those two governments and allies of Washington, the Supreme Disciple could go, but not the Taleban government. And Washington wouldn't want to rock the boat.

"He is not worth it," said Washington.

The CIA operatives never went back to Mr Massoud,

but rather got busier with training some 60 Pakistani intelligence officers to invade Afghanistan with the sole mission of capturing and killing the America's arch enemy.

By the second trimester of 1999, the CIA trained Pakistani intelligence officers had slipped into Afghanistan and were acquainting themselves with the Afghan nation and the activities of the Movement and the Supreme Disciple, while waiting for the right time to strike.

Atah, the lead officer of the 60 man mercenary group, had just finished his evening prayers in a rented bungalow in the outskirts of Chahari-i-Ansari when the phone rang.

"Yes!" said Atah into the mouthpiece.

"Evening boss," replied Atah on recognising the voice at the other end.

"Get the job done in the last week of October. Get it done and neatly. Leave no trace. We want no comebacks. Understand?" said the Boss.

"Understood," answered Atah.

It was mid-August of 1999.

Atah sent ten of his men to Kandahar, ten to Jalalabad, to Khost, to Kabul and Masar-al-sharif, and stayed with another nine in Chahar-al-Ansari.

* * *

It was the third week of October, and everything was fine. Mr Cabin tuned his transistor radio on and listened as marshal music petered away on the Kabul radio station. The newscaster continued with the broadcasting of the overthrow of Pakistan's democratically elected government by a group of military generals in a coup d'etat. A military general's airplane was not granted landing rights as he flew home from a meeting abroad, and this triggered the military takeover of power.

Immediately, Mr Cabin knew that the mission was not going to be a success.

He sent for Atah and his men to leave Afghanistan immediately and come back to Pakistan. But before the recall, the Taleban implants in the Pakistani military had warned the Supreme Disciple of the plot and he'd been keeping guard.

The years crawled by and the Taleban got more entrenched on power and tougher on the Afghan subjects. The Supreme Disciple and the movement followed suit and got stronger.

Before October 2000, the Supreme Disciple and the elite disciples of the movement had been planning how to celebrate the failure of the CIA plot to assassinate him. Among the several options they considered, the US destroyer 'Cole' was the chosen target. And as the destroyer refuelled in the Yemeni Aden harbour, a heavy pound bomb struck it. Seventeen US servicemen were killed and thirty-nine sailors were wounded. One year later, when the utmost symbols of the American modernity, capitalism and economic dominance, located at the heart of the world's most cosmopolitan city – New York – were hit and crumbled by two hijacked passenger planes on the eleventh of September 2001, the US government accused the Movement of masterminding the attacks, and demanded that the Taleban government hand the Supreme Disciple over to them. The Taleban government refused, and the USA invoked the NATO charter to defend the homeland, and involved other NATO member nations of the occident into supporting the war against the Taleban government without crossing the grounds by sending their own regular troops into battle. Even Japan was lured into the war against terrorism. Remember Japan and the post second world war legislation? Article 9 of its post-war peace constitution forbids the country from waging war overseas. Washington sent diplomats to nations around the globe to win allies for the battle against the Taleban and against terrorism, a diplomatic game that was led by Washington's traditional ally, Great Britain. In Washington, unprecedented sessions of the American government think tanks ensued. A new world order was in the making.

Chapter 22
Washington DC
November 2001

The US secretary of state was nervously thoughtful as he arrived for the second round of meetings for the day in the White House. In his understanding, the morning session had not been fruitful. He was particularly worried about the allies the USA was beckoning to help in the war against the Taleben and the Jihadist Movement. Most of the countries were complicit in human right abuses, and they had readily agreed to join the war because after the war they would expect Washington to turn blind eyes and deaf ears to their human right abuses and inhuman repression in their respective countries. The problems in the world, human right abuses, torture, and repression in the world, would linger longer than had been envisaged with the present war on terrorism.

The help of the Pakistani government in the present war was of immense importance, but when the war was over, how could the USA condemn the Jaish-e-mohammed terrorist cell that was sponsored by the Pakistani government to help fight India in Kashmir? This war would be better fought and won the same way they fought the cold war, which lasted for 40 years. A war America won because the USA fought it with all sincerity, willpower, foresight and insight, fighting against poverty, corruption and ignorance. Just like the Marshal plan, when the USA extended aid and goodwill to the Europeans in the forties after the Second World War, with all sincerity, and today it is a greater benefit to the USA than ever. It was all these points that the Secretary of State had stressed during the morning session of the US government sages. "When fighting this war, let's fight the conditions that court, fertilize, hatch and breed terrorism and terrorists. Let's not treat it the way we treat the case in Africa, where we refuse to address the real problem in that continent and now every year we keep having refugees and human disaster. Let's address this terror problem with sincerity," he had suggested.

"Let's create a strong and democratic Palestinian state alongside a strong Israel. It will nip all terrorism and terrorists. Let's liberate the Arabs and fight corruption and human rights abuses in the Islamic states".

"Democratic Palestinian state alongside a strong Israel," echoed the NSA.

A pause.

"Don't play with the Jewish American community and its votes. It has a determinant percentage of the American votes. It can deny or earn any aspirant the White House. Advising the president to create a state of Palestine against the wishes of the Jewish-American community will be like telling him to jump off a political cliff, commit a political suicide. And remember, if the President loses his job, obviously, all of us in this room will become unemployed too. It does America no good to increase the unemployment tally, does it?" said the NSA, and paused to look across the faces in the room.

"Let the regime after us do that job," added the NSA.

"We rather start thinking of America, Americans and

the human freedom. Freedom is our guiding principle, the American pride and not regimes and employment," admonished the Secretary of State.

"If we sincerely engage in spreading of democracy in the Arab world, it will harm our oil supplies from the corrupt authoritarian oil rich states. Besides, if we open them up to liberal democracy, the people might bring anti-American leaders to power. Who would want a regime headed by the Supreme Disciple and his likes in Saudi Arabia and Kuwait," said the Secretary of Defence.

"Besides, let nobody think that these fundamentalists, the terrorists, give a damn about Palestine or a secular and democratic government. They are religious fanatics who are absolutely worried with the decadence of the Islamic religion and Islamic societies caused by the intruding rays of the American liberalism into their society, which to them is part of America's sin against Islam. They use the Israel-Palestine case as a mask," said the NSA.

"Mask?" echoed the Secretary of State.

"You mean they kind of say, if you Americans are resolutely sincere in your interventionist policies round the global village, then, resolve the Palestine-Israel issue?"

"Great!"

"You know why?"

"Because it will be great if we start by unmasking them. Remove that favourable opinion joker card they play all the time. That will be the biggest step towards solving the war on terror. Let's deprive them of all the excuses they have," said the Secretary of State

"Arguably right," thought the chairman of the Joint Chiefs of Staff, who'd been listening quietly all along while going through the details of the plan he wanted to present to the house about the looming war against the Taleban regime in Afghanistan.

His plan included using the 'Loya Jirga', the 600 tribal and religious Afghanistan elders that traditionally have the last say in the Afghan affairs. When the Taleban was eventually defeated and uprooted from power, the Loya Jirga would be used to form the supreme council of national unity that would select integrants of an interim government before any new elections in Afghanistan. Like that, America could easily pick the Supreme Disciple from the Afghan soil. Otherwise it would be very hard to lay hands on him. Just as Mr Massoud suggested to the CIA.

CHAPTER 23
Uruzgan, Afghanistan

The Taleban soldiers on the mountain top guarding the entrance to the two hundred meter deep cave in southern Afghanistan in the Hindukush mountain region in Uruzgan, the home of Mullah Omar the spiritual leader of the Taleban Militia, could see, with the aid of binoculars, explosives and fires at the city of Kandahar.

"America's military might is something else. Sometimes I couldn't help thinking that the people think, eat, walk, talk and breathe war, otherwise how could they come up with these monstrous weapons? They advance too fast with their air power, but we must fight to death. We will lose gallantly if we do," said a guard.

"Till the last man, we must fight."

"Problem is, their planes fly so high that we can't hit

them with our air defence system. They fly out of our range," said another guard, referring to 'Sting', the anti-aircraft defence system the Afghans used against the Soviets. It was supplied to them by the USA and had a maximum altitude range of 1500 meters. American planes strike their targets from an altitude of about 3000 meters.

"But we will fight to the end. The truth is with us, Allah is on our side," added yet another guard. As he was talking, an American B-52 aircraft of length 48.5 meters and wing span of 56.4 meters, capable of flying a range of 1400km at a speed of 1000km/h from Diego Garcia – a British controlled Island in the Indian Ocean that had served as an allied base in the 1991 Gulf war – dropped 910kg of joint direct attack munitions, smart bombs and a 227kg MK-82 dumb bomb on the Kandahar airport control tower at the Taleban headquarters, damaging them. At the same moment, tomahawk missiles of 5.5 meters length and 2.7 meters of wing span, each costing about one million dollars, flying at 900km/h, were launched from the USS Enterprise, a nuclear-powered aircraft carrier stationed in the Arabian Sea off the coast of Pakistan. They hit other sites in the heart and the presidential palace of Kabul.

The guards crouched lower to the rocky ground as an F-18 hornet strike fighter launched from the USS Enterprise exploded across the skies at a supersonic speed and continued east to sting targets.

"I bet it is exploding to Jalalabad," said one guard.

"Looks very much like it," replied another.

Meanwhile in Kabul, Kandahar and elsewhere in Afghanistan, leaflets with Images of the Supreme Disciple and Mullah Omar were falling from American planes, heralding the $25 million reward for any person who could give information to the whereabouts of, and aid in the eventual capture of the duo. CIA operatives were going from house to house of the tribal Pashtun elders in their effort to turn them against Mullah Omar and the Supreme Disciple.

"Look at the hardship, the suffering, damage and deaths they've brought to your country and kinsmen. Would you like to continue living your life like this? I guess not, nobody would. Then why not mobilize the people and fish the evil duo out, they are villains. Don't forget the reward, 25 million dollars. It can set your kindred on the free streets of life forever," urged

Mr Cabin. He returned to Afghanistan in charge of the Farah and Kandahar region.

"It is really terribly sad, the war and the pain the pair have brought to this land. I've never seen a war like this, and every Afghan citizen is tired of wars, destruction and the accompanying poverty and hardship. But we owe Islam a duty, fidelity and solidarity. We can hand the pair over to the Americans or any other external authority but not for the money, $25 million. It is a big sum, but I'd rather America add the $25 million to the money to be used in reconstructing my country after the war," said the Pashtun chief, and raised his two hands to clog his ears from the deafening noise outside. He darted towards the door and into the open to have a glimpse of the American B-2 Stealth intercontinental war plane, stretching some 21 meters in length and 54 meters in wingspan, as it tore through the skies of Farah at a supersonic speed after striking targets in Shindnand, on its way to Diego Garcia air base, before returning to Whiteman Air Force base in Missouri, USA.

Mr Cabin upped and followed him to the outside. He raised a shading hand to his brows and angled his head to look at the fighter high above.

"The Afghan people do not deserve this, you know," he said.

"But because of the Supreme Disciple and Mullah Omar of the Taleban, the American government have to do this so as to fish and smoke out the pair wherever they are on the Afghan soil. I'm sure that none of the Pashtun elders ever bargained for this. And I assure you, the moment the pair is captured, the strikes will stop and peace will reign again here in Afghanistan," said Mr Cabin.

"A lasting peace," he added.

"A lasting peace," echoed elder Khan, a distant look in his gaze.

"It's a long time I'd seen or felt peace for the past 20 years. If it isn't the Soviets, it's the civil, or the tribal wars, hunger and deaths from some disease epidemic. And now, it is the mighty America. I wish peace comes to this land in my lifetime," he thought.

"I hope it reigns," he turned to say to Mr Cabin, who beamed politely.

"But sincerely, I can't help you. I wish you luck in your manhunt for the duo," said the Pashtun chief, a tinge of native pride in his voice and bearing.

CHAPTER 24
Uruzgan Cave

"America won't go unpunished by the almighty Allah," thought the Supreme Disciple as he knelt, facing east to Mecca with other high ranking disciples of the movement for the fifteenth session of the year. After praying, he rose to speak.

"At this moment, the American F-14 Tomahawk aircrafts and F-18 hornet strike fighters launched from the American USS Carl Vinson nuclear-powered aircraft carrier stationed in the Arabian Sea are busy striking what is left of our camps and positions in Mazar-I-sharif, Kabul, Jalalabad, Kundus, Shiberghan and other towns and villages. The Americans and their stooges have pushed us to the mountains and caves. The Taleban government has fallen. The Infidels have reactivated their embassy in Kabul and their diplomatic ties and services with Kabul. But in the next few months, the Infidel's Goodwill Ambassador will be touring the Arab states to influence the OIC – Organization of Islamic Countries summit in Taba, Egypt. I want capable emissaries and fadeyins to be sent to the holy land, Saudi Arabia, the first port of call of the Goodwill Ambassador."

A pause.

"Allah will never allow the infidels to have peace before peace reigns in Palestine and the entire Arab land," said the Supreme Disciple, with a languid wave of the hand.

A pause.

"We will work it out fine," said the military commander.

"They can drive the Taleban out of power and us into hiding, but they can't stop the time and they will never stay here in Afghanistan. We will get them where we want them. It may take long but America will crumble. The Movement will bring the Infidel hegemon to her knees," thought the Supreme Disciple as he rose and walked into the inner chamber of the cave. The military commander, the military planer and other think tanks remained in the outer room to work out the details of the assassination plot to be executed in Riyahd.

Three hours later an orderly, one of the three doubles of the Supreme Disciple, crossed the heavy stone doorway of the inner private quarters of the cave.

"May Allah bless your holiness," he bowed.

"It's time to leave," he added.

The Supreme Disciple was sitting on a mat on the floor, with a prayer chaplet in hand. He looked up at him and nodded languidly. He was a bit irritated, but on a thought of an ugly horde of American rangers or any of the groups of the American marshal services and British special forces that were marauding the streets, caves and mountains of Afghan nation in search of him, putting a handcuff on his wrist and ankles, and probably slapping and kicking him, he rose dutifully and got ready to move. It had been decided by his personal security department that he should stay not more than 4 hours in any particular place. He glanced at his right wrist, at the Timeless wristwatch, a piece of America strapped tightly to his wrist. Timeless is an American product. The time was 6.35pm. The sun was moving slowly over the other side of the mountain in its brilliant and colourful evening glow. He'd been in the cave for upwards of 3 hours and fifty-eight minutes. His eyes remained fixed on the inscription, 'Timeless', behind the glass screen of the watch.

"A piece of America on my wrist," he thought.

He thought of how indispensable America is to the modern world and civilization.

"But no nation, no civilization is indispensable, and this hegemon must be substituted with the Islamic renaissance," he thought as he crossed into the outer chambers of the cave and made haste to leave for another hideout.

* * *

At the foot of the mountain, the Supreme Disciple and his retinue mounted their horses and galloped off. And some 10 km away, the lead guard, a tall, lanky, rumpled Afghan named Shamak, pulled up and went back along the line of the 25 man retinue of guards. He stopped at the centre, looked at the three replicate figures on their horses, approached the man in the centre and began to talk.

"Here," said the Supreme Disciple from behind the replica.

"I'm sorry your holiness," said Shamak and moved over to him.

The Supreme Disciple climbed down from his horse to listen to him

"We are not moving west to Herat as in the itinerary. We are moving east to Khost instead. The general security chief changed it at the last minute as we were about leaving," he whispered in his ear.

"Good," replied the Supreme Disciple, and mounted his horse.

They moved through unmotorable treed and rutted mountain footpaths for the first quarter of the night before joining a wider dusty road that led to the tarred road which then connected to Khost. Some ten kilometres down the road, moving uphill, they branched into a green wooded mountain valley, a cautious retreat in fear that their convoy might have been picked up and identified by the American satellite. They improvised a temporary camp in the valley and waited as the night slowly crawled to day, and continued until a little before dark when the Supreme Disciple, the replicas, three other guards and Shamak climbed to the mountain top and, with the aid of infra-red binoculars, could see towns and villages separated by lonely, dusty and dirty roads and paths: towns and villages they had to move through before getting to Khost. On the other side was a convoy of trucks crawling uphill towards them.

"Military convoy," said one guard.

"Northern Alliance military convoy probably going to Khost," said Shamak.

"I'm not sure, but we will see as they come closer," said one of the doubles.

They all clenched tightly to their binoculars as the trucks crawled and groaned forward uphill. One of the guards kept watch around them to alert them of any approaching unidentified person.

"Relief trucks probably coming from Herat," said the Supreme Disciple as the convoy of the Russian-biult Kamaz trucks came into clearer view.

"With supplies to refugees in Khost," said Shamak.

"Certainly," replied the Supreme Disciple, and at the same time, an idea came into him.

"Send ten men to interrupt the convoy," he ordered.

Shamak, one guard and a replica hurried down hill to prepare ten men to simulate a roadblock on the road beyond. Ten men changed into camouflage uniforms acquired from stripping some dead northern Alliance and coalition soldiers, marched up to the road and mounted a road block. They waved down the trucks as they inched up the hilly road, unleashing a plume of powdery dust mixed with black exhaust smoke.

"Good Morning officer," said the driver of the lead truck.

"Morning," replied Shamak.

"Where are you coming from?" he asked, climbing up into the truck from the passenger's side as the other ten of his men went to interrogate and keep the remaining six trucks under control.

"We are coming from Herat to Khost," replied the driver.

"To deliver goods to the refugees," he added.

"What kind of goods?' asked Shamak.

"The whole seven trucks have powdered milk, sugar, biscuits and medicinal drugs."

The Supreme Disciple and some guards watched from the mountain top.

"Come down from the truck," ordered Shamak.

The lead driver climbed down from the truck to see the other drivers clustered beside the second truck with their hands tied tightly behind them.

"Over there!" ordered one guard, nodding him towards the other drivers.

At that moment, the Supreme Disciple and the rest of the retinue came down from the mountain on their horses.

"Keep your heads down and don't look up or sideways," one guard ordered the drivers.

Shamak hurried up to the Supreme Disciple.

"Your holiness," he said.

"What do they have in the trucks?" asked the Supreme Disciple.

"Biscuits, powdered milk, medicinal drugs and sugar," replied Shamak.

"Send four of the trucks to Uruzgan cave to stock up the caves."

"And the drivers?" asked Shamak.

"How many are they?" asked the Supreme Disciple.

"Ten men," replied Shamak.

"Take seven of them aside and send them to New

York. We will need the other three," replied the Supreme Disciple.

Shamak turned to execute the order.

"Silently," said the Supreme Disciple.

Shamak nodded in concordance, delighted at the opportunity to pull the trigger again. It had been more than two weeks that he'd not pulled the trigger and sent someone to Manhattan, as execution of unbelievers was referred to in the parlance of the movement. He selected three men from the cluster of drivers, including the driver of the lead truck, and led the rest seven into the shrub. With his riffle slung and fallow over his shoulder, he drew his .45 calibre from its holster.

"On your knees," he growled quietly to the handcuffed men. And one after the other he shot them twice each in the nape of the neck. He came out of the shrub smiling coldly.

Let ten of our men drive the trucks and horses back to the Uruzgan caves. And the rest come with us. As the four trucks turned to return to the Uruzgan caves, the Supreme Disciple and the replicas entered the truck in the middle while Shamak took the seat in the front truck, and they set off to Khost.

"The other trucks going back?" asked the driver.

"To our camps, yes. The charity will make it up for the refugees in Khost," replied Shamak.

The trucks groaned and lumbered uphill and hot, dry, dusty wind blew down the hill, lifting pieces of pamphlets high into the air. The pamphlets had the image of the Supreme Disciple and Mullah Omar, and announced the $25 million reward for the information that might lead to their capture and assassination.

"For how long will you be staying in Khost?" asked the driver, more to alleviate the tension than for curiosity.

"Till the Supreme Disciple and Mullah Omar is captured or assassinated," replied Shamak.

"In all honesty, I wouldn't want him to be captured. Because, his actions lead to the ousting of the Taleban regime by the American led coalition forces."

"At least for that, I say Allah bless him. And forgive me America for blessing your arch enemy," he added quickly.

"So you're anti-Taleban?" inquired Shamak.

The driver noticed the timbre of anger and caution in his voice. To the best of his knowledge, the man beside him was a northern alliance soldier, but his voice, his question, seemed to be pro-Taleban.

"Careful," admonished a mind.

"I mean their regime could have been better if they had allowed our children to be educated, allowed us to listen to radio, TV and music. Music is good for the mind. It sooths a sorrowful mind and you know how sorrowful it is here."

"I'm a liberal Sunni Muslim," said the driver cautiously and turned to glance at Shamak.

"Eh?" said Shamak.

"It doesn't pay to let him know who we are at this moment," thought Shamak.

He was burning with anger that he was sitting next to an anti-Taleban and couldn't put him to death instantly.

The Supreme Disciple increased the volume of his pocket transistor radio a notch higher as the newscaster announced:

"Good evening, this is radio Shariat, the official Afghan radio."

The Supreme Disciple gazed into the distance, an idea taking shape in his mind with the thoughtfulness of a numerate terrorist. His eyes narrowed, trying to chase down and dovetail something into place. Mullah Lahir came to mind. Mullah Lahir was a traditional head of Shamshaad.

"Mullah Lahir could do it. At least with this the Infidels will know that the Islamic community is no mafia they often disintegrate with monetary rewards for treachery and betrayals," he thought.

They arrived in Khost in the morning and drove into a boarding school at the outskirts of Khost. The school was on holidays and there were no students. The principal of the school, a tall hirsute man in his mid fifties, was in bed with his wife in the principal's residence when he heard a knock on the door.

"Strange," murmured his wife.

"Very strange, at this time, but we are at war," said the man.

"Hope it's not the soldiers," the wife said.

"God's great," he replied, and climbed out of the bed to answer the door.

Ten minutes later, the wife turned in the bed to climb out, to know why her husband had not returned from answering the door. She swung her legs onto the floor and looked up; there by the doorway were three soldiers, one with a gun pointed at her husband's head. The other two moved quickly towards her, seized her, gagged and handcuffed her. Husband and wife were gagged, handcuffed and put on their matrimonial bed. Two of the disciples took comfortable positions in the room and started to snooze. Three other disciples went into the kitchen and with a carton of milk, sugar and biscuits taken from the trucks, and prepared breakfast for all.

As the retinue was busy in the house, the Supreme Disciple and two replicas found a mosque some 100 meters away from the house, a small school mosque. He went into the mosque and knelt to pray.

"I'm in your temple Oh Allah to pray to thee. Oh Allah, don't allow the infidels to lay their bloody hands on your servant. Shame the infidels Oh Allah. Because you know how much they need to be shamed. How much the Islamic renaissance needs to reign. Protect me and my retinue and the entire Jihadist Movement Oh Allah. You know I do not begin my wave of terror and retaliation against the infidels with any sense of arrogance, entitlement or demagogery, but rather with a huge dose of humility, reason and truth. I'm a son, grandson and great grandson of Muslims and I was born into Islam and in Islam I will brood my family and raise my children to have a great sense of pride and purpose of serving the cause of Islamic causes greater than themselves. For Islam I shall live and die. It is because I ardently believe in Islam and owe Islam more than ever, that I decided to bear the cross of Islamic Jihad against the Infidels. And if you, Allah, permit, I will be alive to see the future. It's no personal ambition, but rather a selfless pursuit. Then my Allah, don't let America defeat your son. Why defeat the Taleban, why humiliate the Jihadist Movement. I wait on thee Oh merciful Allah to tumble the infidels, to bring the hegemon to her knees, to cut short her dreams and her memories, to overturn her dreams. In thee I do trust Oh Allah.

Allahu Arkhbar!" he prayed.

They stayed at the mosque praying and fasting till night.

"I thought you would let us go as soon as we got to Khost," said the driver.

"I'd hoped so too," replied Shamak.

"How?"

"The person in control has not ordered your release. And you better be quiet, you go when you go," warned Shamal.

At this moment, the driver had not seen the Supreme Disciple.

* * *

The journey to Shamashaad was made through rutted, dirty motor paths. The Supreme Disciple, the replicas, Shamak and five guards went to Mullah Lahir's house while the three drivers under the control of the rest of the guards stayed in a nearby mosque. Mullah Lahir had been a fan of the Supreme Disciple. He received them warmly and heartedly and ushered them to a comfortable bunker in his compound.

"We are very happy and proud of you. And we all thanked Allah immensely for you. We prayed hugely for Allah to guide and protect you and the movement. You can stay here as long as you desire," said Mullah Lahir, as he showed him around the bunker. The bunker was 50 meters deep and had one living room, a conference room, three bedrooms, a kitchen and a scullery.

"It is safe here, nobody can find you here," said Mullah Lahir.

We are really happy for you. We pray for you and the movement, and we thank Allah for having you," said Mullah Lahir.

The Supreme Disciple stooped to brush a kiss on both his cheeks.

"You know, human beings change for two things: either for love or hate and hurt. For years, we tried to get the hegemon to listen through love, peace and dialogue. We tried that in Jerusalem, through demonstrations in the streets of Saudi Arabia. At other times, we used ill-coordinated attacks, but nobody heeded our calls. But on the 11th of September, their attention was drawn and arrested by our gallant disciples," said the Supreme Disciple gleefully.

A pause.

"That day, the eleventh of September, reminds me of the Hiroshima on the 6th of August 1945, and the repeat in Nagasaki on the 9th of August 1945, and the daily bloodshed in the Palestinian occupied territories," said Mullah Lahir.

"The infidels, in their most over orchestrated intelligence and foresight, forgot that when they embroil themselves in cruel and brutal treatment of other nations and races outside their country, that the cruelty and brutality will one day rebound on their own community," said the Supreme Disciple.

"We thank Allah for you," said Mullah Lahir.

"You will do me and Allah a favour," said the Supreme Disciple as he lowered into a cushion.

"Anything you ask, that is within my limits," replied Mullah Lahir.

He listened as the Supreme Disciple narrated his request.

"I will be doing that for myself, for fun and for Islam," he replied when the Supreme Disciple finished his request.

"I'm elated at this opportunity to scratch the infidels in my own style," he added

He recalled what one American Colonel and a CIA operative had told him some weeks before in his sitting room, one dry sunny afternoon.

"Help us to locate him, any time you hear anything, any clue to his where-about, call us, here is our number," they'd told him.

"Tell them you will need the money in cash,

in $1000 bills," said the Supreme Disciple. "$50 million in cash," said Mullah Omar thoughtfully.

"$50 million," echoed the Supreme Disciple and a smile of delight creased his face at the thought of it all, not just for the money, but for the sadness and desperation the plot woule cause the CIA, Homeland Security and the FBI terrorist task force and most especially the chief of the special Terror and Supreme Disciple Units and all the sages of the American government and the American society at large.

One of the replicas standing by the doorway looked over his shoulder and saw the Supreme Disciple smiling.

"I'm blessed, oh Allah, I'm blessed to see the Supreme Disciple smile," he soliloquized. A feeling of excitement and pleasure ran through him. It had been along time since he had seen him smile or look delighted. Sometimes he'd believed that his system had stopped secreting the pleasure hormone into his brain, though there is nothing to smile and feel pleasure about when Palestine lives in awe and is under occupation, and the American military bases are still rooted in the Islamic holiest land and the house of al-Saud has done nothing about it. But a little deception, a $50 million trick on the infidels, could bring him a meagre joy but joy nonetheless.

CHAPTER 25
Shamshaad, Afghanistan

"Get ready we are leaving for Kabul. We need to be there by tomorrow morning," said the Supreme Disciple to Shamak after they had the fifth and last prayer of the day in the mosque, in the company of the three drivers and the rest of the guards.

"Kabul?' inquired Shamak.

"Yes Kabul," replied the Supreme Disciple with a knowing wink of the eye.

Shamak now understood. "He wanted to mislead the fools," he thought.

The three drivers, who were now allowed to look up at the Supreme Disciple, stood agape on standing face to face with the Supreme Disciple.

"Why? Your holiness, why?" asked Shamak, entirely

confused about why he had ordered that the drivers see him.

"Get them released in the next two hours," ordered the Supreme Disciple, and started towards the exit of the mosque.

Shamak passed down the order and followed the Supreme Disciple.

"They will tell the allied and American forces that you are here in Shamshaad," argued Shamak.

"That will be good for us. It is part of our game plan," replied the Supreme Disciple.

Mullah Lahir dialled a number from his house phone, and waited as the phone rang at the other end of the line.

The phone got answered at the third ring.

"I've got news for you. Good news," said Mullah Lahir into the mouthpiece, dispensing all pleasantries and preambles.

"Interesting news. This is Mullah Lahir," he said.

"Oh, you. Good Morning," replied the cool, cautious voice from the other end of the line.

It was the voice of Colonel Damsel, an American army colonel attached to the CIA.

"Good news?"

"Good news, yes," replied Mullah Lahir.

Three hours later Colonel Damsel's jeep pulled up in front of Mullah Lahir's house in Shamshaad.

"What is up?" asked Damsel as he stepped onto the mezzanine of Mullah Lahir's house. Mulah Lahir stood smiling proudly.

"It is the best news you will have heard since the surrender of the Taleban and the war against terror," said Mullah Lahir, extending a hand for a shake.

They shook hands and matched into the house.

"I know where the Supreme Disciple is hiding. He came into town last night and probably will be leaving tonight," he said.

"You ain't joking, are you?" said Colonel Damsel.

"I'm serious," assured Lahir.

"So it is all true," said Colonel Damsel, a distant thought in his gaze.

"What?"

"The rumour I heard this morning," replied Damsel.

"What rumour?"

"That the Supreme Disciple is in town," replied

Damsel.

"Yes he is in town and only I know where he is hiding," said Mullah Lahir.

"What are we waiting for, tell me. Where is that son of a bitch?"

"No, he is not a son of a bitch, he is an Arab prince, the prince f Islam," said Mullah Lahir.

Damsel glared at him.

"I will tell you where he is Colonel, but I need the reward upfront and in cash," said Mulla Lahir.

Damsel glanced up at him and held the gaze for a few seconds.

"Sure, you get your reward, but let me see him. Let's arrest him. Call some troops," he said and reached for his cellular phone and began to place a call.

Mullah reached forward and snatched the phone from him.

"Look Colonel, I want the money upfront, the cash, the $50 million. I'm doing this for the money, not for fun, the risk, the betrayal, for you, for America, not even for justice, ok?" said Mullah Lahir.

A pause as both men studied each other.

"Let's get talking about my reward first before anything else. If you want to confirm, I will get you dressed up as a Taleban fighter and take you to his hideout, and you will see him in bone and flesh," said Mullah Lahir.

"Yes, I want to see for myself," replied colonel Damsel hastily.

"Excuse me," said Mullah Lahir as he disappeared into the inner room. He came out with a long artificial beard, headgear and a Russian made Kalakaskov rifle.

"Dress up in this," said Lahir, handing the Colonel the ensemble.

Colonel Damsel dressed up and was ready to go.

"Sorry colonel, but I will have to blindfold you before we set off," said Lahir.

"Why?"

"Because you're not supposed to know the route to get to the hideout before I get my reward, $50 million."

"How will I see him then if I'm blindfolded?" asked Colonel Damsel.

"If we get there, I will unblind you," replied Mullah Lahir.

"Alright," obliged the Colonel.

Mullah Lahir drove around the town and, after thirty minutes, drove into a stud farm where one of the replicas and some ten guards were waiting.

At the second gate inside the stud farm, they were stopped and searched by guards and their rifles were taken from them. They walked past the wood gate into a lawn and were searched again by another set of three guards before being ushered into a room in the farmhouse where the Supreme Disciple was sitting on a prayer mat with a prayer chaplet in hand. He was dressed in elaborate white headgear and camouflage army wear, and flanked by two guards while another guard stood behind with his rifle at a shoot ready position. Lahir crouched to plant a kiss on his checks in greeting, and Colonel Damsel did the same, his eyes as large as tennis ball as surprise and hate burned in them.

"Son of a bitch," he thought as he kissed the air near his cheeks.

"You're damned. Soon you will be groaning and moaning to answer my questions," he thought.

Colonel Damsel was quiet as Mullah Lahir and the Supreme Disciple discussed things in Arabic. He couldn't understand anything, but pretended to be following the discussion by nodding approvingly when Lahir nodded, smiling when he smiled.

Minutes later, they rose to leave. It was the only time during his stay on Afghan soil he'd soulfully regretted not being able to speak and understand the Arabic language. But he was sure of one thing: he was sitting right across from America's supreme enemy. Inside the jeep, Lahir wanted to blindfold the Colonel, but he objected.

"Put the fold on now or else ..." threatened Lahir.

"I get killed here and blow up the plot of catching the supreme enemy of America," thought Colonel Damsel as he reached to put on the blindfold.

They made the 35 minute journey to Lahir's home in silence.

"Are you convinced now?" quizzed Mullah Lahir as they settled onto low cushions in his sitting room.

"That will be the best present anyone gives the American populace this Christmas," said Colonel Damsel.

"Christmas is the celebration of the death of Jesus Christ, right?' asked Lahir.

"His birth," replied Damsel.

"To the Americans, Jesus is their saviour, founder of their Christian faith. To the Muslims, Mohammed is the saviour and the prophet. The Koran recognizes Jesus Christ. We Muslims believe that Jesus Christ was a great prophet but not the son of God. We believe he may come back to earth like many other great prophets, but not the son of God," said Mullah Lahir.

"And the $50 million will be the best present to be received from America," added Lahir.

"Speaking of money, let me make a call to Islamabad, Pakistan," said Colonel Damsel, and reached for the satellite phone in his pocket.

Lahir listened as he spoke with somebody in Islamabad.

"Couldn't be trying to get smart? I hope not," he thought.

"We will get him arrested as soon as the money is here," said Colonel Damsel, and waited.

"Yes, the whole $50 million," he replied.

A pause.

"That's how he wants it?"

A pause.

"I saw the devil himself."

"I shook his hand."

A pause.

"Of course I was disguised as a Taleban warrior."

Silence.

"I will try to talk to Washington after speaking with you. Please do send the money down here today, the devil might be leaving town today. You never know."

A pause.

"Alright bye," said Damsel, and lowered his hand from his ear and immediately began dialling another number while Lahir looked on.

* * *

"If we sail through with this plot, they will be put out of leads as to my whereabouts. I mean put them off my back for a very long time, if not forever. By that time we will have time to regroup and reorganize," said the Supreme Disciple to the Movement's financial secretary, who had just came into town from Jalalabad where he'd been hiding since Kabul was captured.

"It will really help the organization a lot. Besides, the cash will do wonders to the Movement's battered economy. It is quite typical of you. I mean the idea, it is ingenious," said the financial secretary, his face lit with a delightful smile.

"The harder they come, the more ingenious we become," said the Supreme Disciple.

"But that country has weapons. Their air power is devastating," said the secretary.

"I'd never expected any niceties and civility from America. What do you expect from a nation that spends more than one-third of her annual budget on her military and military technology? What do you expect from a hegemon, an imperialist? America is even more terrifying than terror itself," said the Supreme Disciple.

"I wonder if the attacks on the WTC and the pentagon could be repeated, assuming time and opportunity is rewound," said the secretary.

"Oh!...don't talk."

A pause.

"That marvellous moment will be difficult to come upon again. But the almighty Allah never goes back on his word, never regrets his actions. He's promised to bring the hegemon to her knees, and he won't go back on his word. And that's why I will never say never on seeing the infidel despot crumble. I miss Zawahiri and Mohammed. If the opportunity crops up again, and the Palestinian brothers are still under attack and occupation, and infidel forces are still stationed on the Arabian

Peninsula, I will be most delighted to live that euphoria again," said the Supreme Disciple.

* * *

Five Hours Later

Mr Cabin and two of the Colonel Damsel's men pulled up in front of Mullah Lahir's home. One of the men wheeled a metal suitcase into Mullah Lahir's living room.

"Must be trying to do something smart. I don't believe this metal box contains a whole lot of $50 million," thought Mullah Lahir.

"Here is your reward. $50 million in $1000 bills," said Colonel Damsel.

"Now let's go get the asshole. The boys are thirsty, thirsty for his blood, for his life. I mean the whole of America is thirsty for his blood," said Colonel Damsel.

"I've told you he is an Arab prince, not an asshole. I'm doing what I'm doing not because I believe America and the accusations, but because of money, $50 million," said Mullah Lahir.

"I will need to confirm if the money is real and complete," added Mullah Lahir.

Damsel gazed at him for a moment.

"Confirm? That's real cash," he said nodding towards the metal suitcase.

"Well said, but the only way I can be sure is by confirming," said Mullah Lahir.

"Ok, go ahead and confirm it," said Damsel.

He pushed up to reach and open the metal suitcase.

"Here, raw cash"

"Ibrahim!" Mullah Lahir called out.

The financial secretary of the movement came out from the adjacent room and went straight to the metal box without looking at the men in the room. He pulled the box to a corner and bent over to count the bundle manually. Each bundle had $50,000. After two hours he looked up.

"$50 million," he said as he counted the last of the 50000 bills. There was an arrogant mischief in his gaze as he gazed down on the heap of cash.

He closed the suitcase and pulled it along as he disappeared into the adjacent room.

Mullah Lahir, Colonel Damsel, Mr Cabin and two Rangers left in the two jeeps for the stud farm, all disguised as Taleban soldiers.

At the second gate on the farm, the guard asked Mullah Lahir about the new faces he'd brought along this time around.

"The Supreme Disciple knows they are coming," said another guard.

The five guests were patted down in turn.

"You can go," said one of the guards.

At this moment, the two rangers and Mr Cabin drew their .45 calibers from nowhere and subdued the guards. They were too fast; the guards had no time to wink a reaction. They were handcuffed and gagged up and huddled into a corner and advanced into the stud farm. At the next security post, they repeated their act and put the security under their control successfully.

As Damsel and his men advanced into the stud farm, Radio Shariat was broadcasting the news of the capture of the Supreme Disciple of the Jihadist Movement by the American Forces.

"American Marines, Rangers and CIA agents have surrounded a stud farm West of Shamshaad where the Supreme Disciple is believed to be hiding," announced the newscaster, whose voice sounded more desperate than enthusiastic.

"Minutes later, men, women and children began to cluster in the dusty bill and dirt strewn field in front of the farm. In the farmhouse, the Rangers dominated the guards and shackled the Supreme Disciple."

"The time has come."

"Allahu Akhbar," he shouted .

Colonel Damsel rushed forward, held him by his long beard and pulled, kicking him on the knee cap. He bristled in defiance, ignoring the pain. Damsel was annoyed at his defiance and stoicism.

"No! No! Not here, not yet!"

"Take him to your station, to America, wherever you choose, and do what suits you. Just don't do it here," pleaded Mullah Lahir.

The Americans removed their artificial long beards, headgear and the flowing robes they had over their camouflage uniforms. Now in their full American Military attire, they dragged the man, the Supreme Disciple, into the open to the field besieged by a crowd of locals. One of the Rangers darted forward to open the Jeep door. Colonel Damsel held his captive tightly by his shirt collar and dragged him forward. He pushed him into the back seat of the military Jeep and climbed in after him. One Ranger climbed in from the other side, so that their captive was sandwiched between them. The other Ranger took his seat in the front passenger's seat, and Mr Cabin took the driver's wheel.

There was a pregnant quietude among the crowd in the field. It was perceivable that they were waiting for the first person to act. The roads were blocked and nobody was making way for the Jeep to pass. The Afghans didn't hate the Supreme Disciple any more than they liked the Americans, despite the effort of the USA forces to paint him as a terrorist using the media and the news-papers. They were rather grateful to him for his selfless service to the Afghan nation during the Soviet invasion. He was an Afghan hero, and heroes are respected and protected from humiliation in Afghanistan. The crowd inched forward towards the centre of the field, towards the Jeep, at each passing second. Colonel Damsel was befuddled by the attitude of the crowd.

"They applauded the advent of the Americans and the coalition forces and the ousting of the Taleban regime, and now the Devil has been captured, and they won't make way to whisk him off," thought Colonel Damsel as he dialled a number from his satellite phone.

"Send us an helicopter down here, and reinforcements. The crowd won't make way for us to leave. Fast please, I'm afraid we might be mobbed. I don't know what is happening here. It is all very strange," he said into the phone and hung up.

Shamak, one replica and the Supreme Disciple, disguised as Afghan women in their veils, watched the scene silently from among the crowd and attracted no second glances.

"You won't take him away cheaply," shouted one man in the crowd.

"He is no devil. You won't leave here with him," said another.

"You mustn't take him away from here. He is a good one," said yet another.

"The good one," the Supreme Disciple echoed in thought.

"You're a good one," he could recall one American Commander saying to him when he presented his plan for the expansion, reconstruction and refurbishing of the Tora Bora caves.

"It is a good one," the American colonel had said as he examined the construction plan.

"With this, we can hide the entire army here, conduct the war safely and defeat the Soviets," he had added.

"The good one, that's what they used to call me when I allied with them against the Soviets. But today I'm the devil, the villain, or so they think. But Allah knows and the American god knows that I'm still a good one, though now I have no superpower to work with, no good support to fight this holy cause, and they think they can paint me a devil overnight. No way! The people know their heroes. We unleashed terror for a good cause, and the people know," thought the Supreme Disciple.

Through the checkered holes on the veil his eyes were fixed on the Jeep in the centre of the crowd, occasionally glancing up at the helicopter hovering overhead.

A ladder descended slowly from the helicopter to the Jeep. Colonel Damsel and the Ranger fastened their captive between them and began to ascend the ladder, and the ladder in turn ascended slowly into the air towards the chopper. The crowd inched forward and forward towards the upping trio on the rope. A stone projected towards the helicopter, then another and another. The helicopter flew up high and higher as the trio inched upwards towards it. The Supreme Disciple stood still in the crowd, his eyes darting around, taking note of everything that was happening around him. Damsel, two Rangers, their captive and Cabin climbed into the military helicopter. The Supreme Disciple was very unhappy that the crowd stood there and let the Americans ascend into the chopper. He reached a button on his Timeless watch, which had been turned into a remote detonator of the microchip bomb implanted into the inner thorax of the replica, and which could be detonated with a particular combination from any part of the global village, using satellite waves. He held his hand on the button and began his countdown:

"….3, 2, 1, Allahu Arkhbar!" he counted and pressed the button. The explosion that followed was deafening There was chaos as the crowd scattered in search of shelter from the falling debris of the helicopter.

In the confusion, the Supreme Disciple and his retinue made their way on a disappearing mission to Tora Bora mountains and caves. When the crowd recovered from the shock of the explosion, they whooped and sang an honorific song in commemoration and honour of the Supreme Disciple. They sang not for joy that he was dead, but for the fact that it was now over, the struggle, the search, the apprehension that he would be captured, that he would forever be remembered as a hero, an Islamic hero, a hero of the Arabian people. Whooped and sang because they know he would have a dignified place prepared for him by Mohamed and Allah in paradise. That it all ended with gallant flourish, three American Rangers, two American Colonels, an American Pilot and a senior CIA official blown up in the Afghan stratosphere. He wasn't caught like an idiot in some sleazy spider hole. Spider hole sucks. At least he was not captured and taken to America to be snuffed out like nothing. When they looked at the bones, flesh, clothes and metal they saw great resistance and a mound of hope for the struggle to exalt Islam.

Chapter 26
Washington DC.

The Secretary of Defence sat back in his seat and folded his arms across his chest. In his face was a sullen disappointment. There was an icy, ominous quietude in the Pentagon situation room, amongst the ten men in the room are the most powerful voices in the US government. The national security Adviser uncrossed his legs, lit a cigarette, took a drag and stubbed it out. He tugged at his tie and adjusted himself on his seat. The Chairman of the Joint Chiefs of Staff removed his spectacles and crouched, leaning forward with his mouth agape. The combined team of four CIA and FBI scientists from the crime laboratory were expressionless; they'd had their shocks in the lab, when the result of the DNA tests showed a positive identification for all the US service-men, but showed negative identification for the man believed to be the Supreme Disciple of the Jihadist Movement. His DNA didn't match that of his mother and brothers, collected by the CIA operatives.

"What is the margin of error for a DNA test?" asked the defence secretary.

"99.99%," replied the CIA Crime Lab Scientist.

"Zero, that's if the blood samples collected from Saudi Arabia were from his real mother and real broth-ers," added one of the FBI scientists, a man who had put in 25 years of service in the FBI crime laboratory in Washington.

"The blood collections were all on video and attested to," said the CIA chief of the special terror unit.

"Three Rangers dead, two American colonels, an American combat helicopter, an American Marine, a CIA operative, an unidentified man supposedly the Supreme Disciple, probably an Arab, all dead, and $50 million in cash, American tax payers' dollars, gone," said the Secretary of State.

"Four Rangers," corrected the NSA.

"Damsel knew the Supreme Disciple very well, I

mean every American soldier and civilian knows that devil and can identify him on sight," said the Chairman of the Joint Chiefs of Staff.

"Then the Supreme Disciple has a real double," said the head of the CIA terror unit.

"What a heartless, conscienceless son of a bitch," hissed the FBI chief.

"Heartless? Conscienceless? He is a terrorist, a bandit, he has no obligation, no compromise and responsibility to nothing and nobody, not even his loyal servants. He is only engaged to his ambition, his selfish aims and objectives. He gives no damn about who gets sacrificed," said the CIA chief.

"I wonder how many of these replicas are still there to be sacrificed to deceive our operatives," said the defence secretary.

"Who mediated the capture?" asked the secretary of state.

"Mullah Lahir, an Islamic teacher who runs a mosque in the city of Shamshaad, his birth place. He is a Sunni Muslim and has two wives and seven children. His eldest son was killed by US air strikes at the onset of the war. He owns the stud farm where the replica was arrested. The farm has once been mistakenly bombed by a US war plane, but the bomb didn't explode for some unknown reason. He is a Pashtun and the traditional leader of Shamshaad. He is a member of the 'Loya Jirga'. In the mosque where he presides over daily prayers, fifteen Taleban tanks and 50 AK-47 assault rifles were found. Information gathered from locals and the faithful who pray in the mosque suggests that Taleban parked their weapons in the mosque against Mullah Lahir's consent. He was afraid it would attract the US and the allied strikes to the mosque. Like most typical Arabs, Mullah Khalid Lahir hates the Zionist state and the sufferings of the Palestinian people, but he's never made any deplorable statement in the public against the USA. He was educated in Saudi Arabia in the '60's. That is all we know about him for now," said the CIA chief of special terror unit.

Silence.

"Could he have been deceived also, or does anything suggest that he is complicit in the swindle, that he knew more or something we don't know?" asked the Secretary of State.

"Nobody can say for sure at this moment what he

knew. But from record, we think the Supreme Disciple, under present circumstances, wouldn't trust anybody outside the inner circle of the Movement. Mullah Lahir is not a member of the Jihadist Movement or a Taleban. He is just a Muslim Cleric," replied the CIA chief.

"A Muslim cleric," echoed the secretary of state thoughtfully.

CHAPTER 27
Tora Bora

"What a deception, what a swindle. It sounds like a Hollywood movie," thought the Supreme Disciple with a satisfying smile after listening to the radio announcements of the capture and death of America's arch enemy.

He was happily ensconced by the fireplace, a Koran and an idle Russian Kalashnikov submachine gun beside him, a radio tuned in to the BBC, and two replicas standing by the doorway of the War chest some 500 meters below the ground in a Pakistani border village. The War chest had its entrance through the Tora Bora Mountains of Afghanistan and extended through a 500 km tortuous tunnel connecting with other, smaller caves as it extended to the neighbouring Pakistani village. The War chest was a 100 meter square underground expanse divided into ten rooms including three sitting rooms, a conference room and two laboratories equipped with the latest equipment and machines, where a team of Arabic scientists were putting finishing touches to nuclear and ballistic missiles intelligent enough to deceive the ABM systems that the USA was developing unilaterally, against the agreement signed with USSR in 1972. The Walls and the roof of the cave were reinforced with two-meter thick stainless sheets. The entrance to the underground sanctuary had electric sensors and the whole complex had a closed circuit system, and an emergency alarms connected wirelessly to the vigilante headquarters of the Jihadist Movement – a residential house in the Tora Bora area. The elite squad was a reserve squad of 200 men scattered in Tora Bora, Jalalabad, Kunar, Shamshaad and Kabul, and the elites lived among the civilian population, waiting for action, and could be regrouped in less than an hour in the case of an invasion and capture attempt by the American and coalition forces. The order was 'nobody leaves with the Supreme Disciple alive'. The Supreme Disciple felt totally safe in the sanctuary, stuffed with enough food and medicine to last 200 people for over five years. The Americans, in their hurry to slip home after defeating the Soviets, had forgotten to take a copy of the building plans for the Tora Bora caves. And what was left of the Tora Bora caves in the Afghan government archives was totally destroyed in the air campaign to oust the Taleban regime. Only the Supreme Disciple had an authentic copy of the Tora Bora cave construction plan.

Chapter 28
Cairo, Egypt

In the waiting room of a clinic in central Cairo, Abdul sat in wait for the surgeon. He looked up from the magazine he was reading and, through the transparent wide glass window, he saw a young girl sitting on the grass under a shrub in the twenty meter square lawn that separated the cosmetic ward from the hospital ward. Her sandals were neatly arranged beside her, and her legs stretched out at full length in front of her. Her veil dropped gently over her shoulder and the edge of the black cotton veil outlined her face, highlighting her rich textured, tanned and beautiful face. Abdul walked closer to the window and watched the young woman as she basked in the open evening air. It was the first-sight sort of arresting hit. Abdul was touched by the drug, the magic that changes everything and enriches all experiences, the thing called love. Love is very necessary to every human heart, as is air to our lungs. There is no living being under the sun that doesn't desire love, even when they don't show and dispense love. And one very marvellous thing about the overpowering force of love is that when it hits you, no matter how hard it hits, one feels no pain, even with a red eyed Islamic fundamentalist terrorist as Abdul. Abdul didn't know the age of the young woman, but he was sure she was old enough to take care of her womanly circles. He made for the exit door.

At age 17, Amina, a girl from a poor Muslim family of 9, was doing what a girl her age should be doing. She liked exotic places, went to the marriage ceremonies of friends, studied in a secondary school without the full support and blessing of her father. She watched the television, socialized with boys and worked as a babysitter in the home of Canadian residents some three kilometres from her neighbourhood, where she worked from 8.30 am to 2.00pm, three times a week. Her father had warned her several times against receiving male visitors, watching TV and working, but she insisted, and continued working to pay for her schooling.

One day, Amina was coming back from school in the gloom of the late evening. As she descended the steps to her neighbourhood, a guy who looked to be in his mid twenties appeared from behind the concrete rail and pointed a gun at her head, lead her down the steps and walked her under the staircase.

"Please don't hurt me!" pleaded Amina.

"Shshh!" he shushed.

"Any word from you again, you feel the steel from this," he warned, nodding to the gun in his hand.

"Remove everything," he commanded.

Trembling, Amina obliged and removed her clothes.

The boy pushed her onto the grass and deflowered her. She screamed and groaned in pain and agony. Ahmil, a municipal guard who was going to his home from work, heard a faint agonizing moan coming from under the staircase, as he walked up the stairs. He paused and listened up and the moaning continued. He tiptoed down the steps and towards the groaning sound. It was hard to see anything clearly in the gloom underneath, but the rapist saw the faint outline of Ahmil and sprang to his feet and a chase ensued.

Amina dressed up and crawled out from under the staircase. Ahmil caught the rapist some 120 meters from the staircase. Amina cowered beside the concrete staircase banister and sobbed. The police came to the scene minutes later. The rapist was taken into custody and was arraigned before a judge in an Islamic court. His lawyer urged the court for a reduced sentence of two years; he argued that the girl was not a virgin and high-lighted that losing one's virginity before marriage is a crime in itself in Arab culture. The court succumbed to the defence lawyer's argument and sentenced Rashid, the rapist, to two years in prison. Rashid was hauled to jail to start his sentence. Amina's family was enraged. Two weeks later, Amina resumed work and schooling. One afternoon while Amina was in school, her seven brothers and her father gathered in their sitting room to discuss and vote on her fate, so as to save the fam-ily honour. They call it honour killing in the parlance of Arabian cultures. The youngest son of the family, who was 15 years old, was chosen by the family to slay Ami-na. He was chosen to do the killing because he was less than 18 years, and as a minor he would receive a lenient treatment by the state court and the law. If his conduct was satisfactory during the trial and detention in jail, he could stay for 2 years or even less in prison for a first-degree murder because it was an honour killing. It was all agreed on, and the slaying date was arranged.

Amina, a rape victim, was voted to die to preserve her family's honour. It is an old part of Arabian culture that has little to do with the Islamic religion. The Arabian culture has it that women are devils that the society has a duty to protect, and the male is the only protector for the women, and ought to have total control over her. And when this duty is violated, the male loses his honour, and to reinstate this honour, the woman has to be sacrificed.

* * *

One month Later

Dr. Walabi descended the first front steps of the Islamic courthouse in central Cairo and hurried to his car. He'd made a submission on behalf of his client, Ahmed Rashid the rapist. In his submission, he asked for the release of Ahmed Rashid because Rashid had decided to marry his victim, Amina – the most exonerating claim for rapists in any Islamic court, and most absolving for any family honour restoration victim. Dr. Walabi and Ahmed Rashid's family were at Amina's family compound to inform her family that Rashid had decided to take their daughter's hand in marriage. The family embraced the proposal gratefully and the scheduled slaying was discarded. Seven days later, Rashid was released from the prison and the traditional marriage rights were observed and Rashid took Amina home to become his second wife. The marriage lasted only eight months before Amina left her matrimonial home. She was molested, harassed and humiliated in the eight months of marriage. Amina didn't go back to her family home, but rather to the female sorority complex owned and managed by the Association for the Enhancement and Development of Women – AEDW. Her family was furious and re-invoked the death sentence passed on her, to redeem the family honour.

The evening's gathering gloom was evident. As Amina walked from school to the dormitory, Suleman her younger brother appeared from the corner and fired two gunshots at her. Though it was gloaming, Amina had no doubt that the bullets that hit her shoulder were from Suleman. She was rushed to the hospital, and while recovering from the bullet wounds, she had her first epileptic seizure. She was treated by Dr Saddat.

Dr Saddat had been recruiting patients and research subjects for an American drug company for experimental drug tests. When Amina recovered from her bullet wounds, Dr Saddat offered her a form written in English, a language she didn't yet speak or understand properly. The form was full of legalese. It was the famous consent form: a form that will be saying that she volunteered to undergo the tests. But most of the time, the forms are prepared to protect the researchers from any lawsuits and never, as they are often presented, to protect the patients. Though Dr. Saddat knew that this practice was against the Nuremberg code of 1947 and the World Medical Association's declaration of Helsinki, which made it clear that:

"Companies, People, Countries seeking to conduct medical tests on humans must explain the purpose, risks and methods of study and obtain each subject's voluntary consent."

Dr. Saddat made all the patients he recruited believe that they were being provided with free and volunteer treatment, as opposed to volunteering for an experimental drug that had not been tested on humans.

However, Amina signed the form and was tagged with a number. She was patient number 11345 and was taken to ward two of the hospital complex, which was the experimental ward of the complex. This experimental complex was next to the cosmetic ward. Amina met other young Egyptian and Arabian girls of her age in the experimental drug ward, some of them suffering from meningitis, others from breast cancer. All were under the care of foreign doctors. Since Amina got to the ward, she'd never seen any patient leave for home alive. They all left wrapped in the hospital white, on a stretcher and rigor mortised.

Amina had been staying under the shrub for about thirty minutes, bathing in the fresh evening air, and having a deep thought about some friends she met in the hospital that had died. Latifa was her friend, and she died of meningitis. Before she died, doctors had sucked up fluid from her spine and evaluated her symptoms and administered drugs and injections. Though her condition got worse with each passing day, she kept receiving the same ineffective treatment for her illness.

Latifa became lame, deaf and almost blind, and died. Another friend had breast cancer and was under gene therapy – an experimental medicine that aims to cure diseases by changing people's genetic make-up, and has side effects which includes high fever, clotting irregularities and low blood pressure. In other cases, where genes were injected into tumours like cancer tumours, side effects range from partial paralysis to speech impairment. She died of high fever; she was almost dumb when she died.

"In my next life, I will be a man. If I'm born in the Muslim world, if not I will remain a woman in the West," thought Amina.

The only thing about life that sometimes irks is that life has no duplicate that can be used for replacement and correction when one is damaged or ill-lived. Well, it is life's uniqueness that makes it exciting and worth living. Though people talk about reincarnation, which arguably could be possible, but the thing about reincarnation is that one knows not about the details of the previous life's mistakes, successes and accolades, so as to administer corrective measures.

"Hello," said a voice from behind.

Amina angled her head to look over her shoulder to the complementing voice.

Abdul wore a broad grin.

"Hello," replied Amina.

"You're alright?" said Abdul.

Amina looked up at him and nodded her yes.

"Are you happy?"

"No, I'm sad, very sad," replied Amina.

Abdul paused. He regretted having asked the question, especially now she had said she was very sad. It was off-putting to have a lady say she was sad when he had no immediate, positive response to her sadness.

"Sad?' said Abdul.

"No, not just sad, I'm very sad," she replied.

"Very, very sad," she added.

"But you don't look that very sad," said Abdul.

"How do you mean?" inquired Amina.

"Your way of expression, your posture, your facial appearance," said Abdul.

"Well, I'm very sad, not angry or bitter. Besides, when people are sad, they look sorrowful. It shows and everybody notices it on a glance. But when people are very sad, the sorrow crosses the natural threshold, and we look normal and probably relaxed on the surface. But deep inside, at the southernmost lobe of the soul, lodges the hanging weight of the block of sadness," she said, and angled her head to gaze into the distance.

"Are you taking care of a relative here?" asked Abdul.

"No."

"I'm ill, or so they told me," she replied.

"So what's your illness? You don't look ill," said Abdul.

"I don't know, for now, what my exact illness is," she said.

"I was brought here in the hospital into the emergency ward, and while I was being treated for the bullet wounds I sustained, I had an epileptic seizure, or so they told me…"

"Why do you say that?" asked Abdul.

"Because I have never had it in my life, and since the day they told me I had it, I've not had it again. I was given a form to fill and transferred to ward two, where I was told I'm patient number 11345, and since then I have been here with a whole lot of other Egyptian girls in the experimental ward. A whole lot of people I met in the ward have died," said Amina, gloom in her gaze.

"And your family? Are they here with you?" asked Abdul.

"No, I'm alone."

"How do you pay the hospital bills?"

"They ain't charging us any money," replied Amina.

"They ain't charging you any…?"

"It is the experimental nonsense," thought Abdul.

"And they gave you forms to fill and sign right?" quizzed Abdul.

"Yes" replied Amina.

"Oh the evil consent form. Did you read it?" asked Abdul.

"I tried but it was written in English."

Abdul drifted into deep thought.

He bit his lips as a single tear ran down his check, hate chipping away at his heart, that Arabian youths have been seriously deceived and used as guinea pigs for an experimental drug by an American drug company and doctors. Drugs that would later become unaffordable to them.

"Oh! America, what a cheat you are, even in medical and health issues, casting your medical lines, surfing in the blood of Arabs and the poor for your medical experiments and discoveries that will most benefit your citizens. And what rankles is the mask of politeness and charity behind which you hide your prejudice," murmured Abdul.

Amina uncrossed her legs and sat up, eyeing Abdul curiously in his reverie.

Abdul thought of children dying of diseases and starvation in Afghanistan, India, Pakistan, Sudan, the Philippines and Haiti, children that would've been in intensive care were they in America and the West, but who beg for food in the streets of their respective countries.

"Oh capitalism!"

"And here on Arabian soil, see what is being done to the beautiful children of Islam," thought Abdul as he looked east towards Mecca and offered a silent, short prayer for the fall of America.

Amina was quiet, dissecting all Abdul's questions by mind. Abdul had a mixed accent she found a bit difficult to place.

"Where are you from?" asked Amina.

"I'm a Palestinian," replied Abdul.

"But how come, I mean why the bullet wounds? Victim of armed robbery?" asked Abdul.

"No," replied Amina.

A pause.

"Then what?" continued Abdul.

Amina reluctantly dabbled into details of the events that finally landed her in the emergency ward of the hospital. Abdul nodded understandingly as Amina narrated her life saga.

What makes love such a wonderful thing is that it encompasses everything, including understanding and tolerance, and it discriminates against nothing. It is very generous.

Abdul had never thought of marriage until that moment. He'd never been worried of meeting a wife with her hymen intact and bleeding on the nuptial night, though he'd never thought of marrying a leftover, a rape victim, a social and family outcast. Even as an Islamic fundamentalist, moving from one nation to the other and knowing international politics, customs and cultures had made Abdul more liberal with regards to certain foibles of life. Besides, in his present condition, Abdul knew he needed a friend, male or female, who would be extra loyal and glad for having a friend, for being accepted into his world. Abdul thought quite a little about family honour as it regarded women, chastity and rape, but his real and immediate concern was seeing the infidels grow old and crumble to their knees and seeing the incursors pushed back and all the Palestinian refugees go home to the land of Judah. The rest of the ills of the Arabian society could be arranged and fixed. Amina made him remember Nadia, whom he met in west Beirut, but who was later killed by the phalanges in the Palestinian refugee camp massacre of the early '80s. Abdul took Amina with him to his house and later met with her family, and all traditional marriage obligations were observed and they lived together as husband and wife.

A month later, the team of American and western doctors who were working in the experimental drug ward of the hospital boarded a chartered Boeing corporate Jet 757 and hopped into the skies on their return home. Mission accomplished.

CHAPTER 29

Abdul and Amina lived happily, and in the autumn of their love, they had a baby boy whom Abdul named Omar.

Omar was registered in a nursery school for children whose parents wouldn't have problems paying 400 Egyptian pounds monthly. At the age of four, Omar came home one afternoon with a lottery coupon, an education lottery that gave a child a scholarship till University level if he won the draw.

"Dad, the teacher said I must give this to you," Omar said to his father, Abdul.

Abdul read and filled the coupon and paid the £30 lottery fee. A year later when the lottery was drawn, Omar won the 7th of the twenty available positions, granting him a scholarship until University education to study any course of his choice.

"Nuclear physics," Abdul thought.

On the appropriate date, Amina took her son to the new primary school for enrolment. Amina waited with the other 19 mothers who had brought their children to be enrolled. She filled out all the forms and documents given to her, and returned them and waited while the school director called them alphabetically into the office.

Amina went into the director's office at her turn, and the director looked up at the door as she entered.

"Mrs Amina?"

"Yes sir," replied Amina.

"Have you seat please," said the director, waving her to a seat.

"I'm sorry madam, but we cannot enrol your child," said the director.

"Why?" Amina questioned.

"If we enrol him, then he must pay tuition," said the director.

"But why? He won the lottery, the education lottery, didn't he? Why must he pay tuition?" asked Amina.

"Madam, the lottery is strictly for Egyptians, Egyptian citizens," said the director.

"Good, he is an Egyptian citizen," replied Amina.

"You are an Egyptian, correct, but he is not Egyptian."

"What do you mean?" retorted Amina.

"You filled this form didn't you?" asked the director pushing the form towards Amina.

"Your husband, the father of your child is Palestinian, correct?" quizzed the director.

"Here in Egypt, children of foreign fathers cannot go to public schools or state Universities for free, and they are not allowed to read courses like medicine and engineering, even when paying. They are not allowed to compete in strictly Egyptian competitions or play lotteries meant for Egyptians like your son mistakenly did and unfortunately won," said the director. Unfortunately, because the £30 lottery fee you paid is non-refundable, and the emotional inconvenience of uncovering this hard fact was huge and disturbing. And it's cost another child a chance," said the director.

Amina watched and listened in disbelief as the director trotted out the absurdities about the Egyptian citizenship. Amina recalled the section of the Egyptian constitution that proclaimed all Egyptian citizens equal. The director watched Amina's desperation and anger.

"I'm sorry but that's how it is here. To be enrolled here, he must pay tuition. I wish I could help you," said the director, a hint of dismissal in his voice.

Amina and Abdul employed a lawyer and sued the school. The court sat and ruled in favour of the school, citing the section of the state law that grants such discrimination, arguing that the child of an Israeli father and Egyptian mother would be a natural spy, and since children in such cases are more attached to their fathers, the child would become a spy for Israel against Egypt.

Amina and Abdul appealed to a higher court, and tried to enrol Omar in another public school, but received the same reception: Omar had to pay tuition. Amina went to the office of the Association for the Enhancement and Development of Women and Women's Rights - a group that leads the fight to rewrite Egypt's immigration and citizenship laws.

"Yours is one of the one million or so children affected by the Egyptian citizenship law that discriminates and prevents children of foreign fathers from attending public schools and state universities free, and bars them from some professional courses. And some wouldn't get jobs without the residency and work permits required of all foreigners," said the AEDW director.

Amina gazed thoughtfully into the distance, unable to comprehend this injustice.

"It is incredible that the state supports such discrimination, such violation of the country's constitution that guarantees equal rights for all Egyptians – men, women and children. The children of foreign mothers and Egyptian fathers are granted automatic citizenship. It's all very incredible, but we are working on it and with each passing day, the number of children affected increases and so does the pressure, we will surely get to dismantle this institutional discrimination some day," said the AEDW director.

"Thank you," Amina said to the director, and rose to leave.

"It's all part of the Arab male chauvinism. It is so tribal," she thought.

Amina recalled that Arab culture had it that families

be linked to the man. A man gives the children their social status in the society. In the Arab world, women belong to the tribe and, if they marry into another tribe, they are no longer members of the original tribe and neither are thier children. But it is all very confusing and very ridiculous, because if one goes on religious track one sees that the prophet Mohamed, the founder of the Islamic religion – the most viable uniting force amongst Arabs and the faith for 98% of the Arab enclave, never had a male child. All his children were women, his descendants all came through women. And the Islamic tradition has it that the righteous will be summoned according to their mother's name on the judgement day.

"If that is all about it, then why can't I give status to my child in my community?" thought Amina as she rode home.

Amina was found dead in the restroom in her home the next morning. She'd cut the arteries on her wrists and bled to death. The suicide note found beside her read:

"Killed by the society

By the institutional male chauvinism

The stupid foolish customs"

CHAPTER 30

Abdul was now father and nanny, without a homeland or citizenship for his son.

"Problem is that nobody can survive this Anglo-American lead capitalist century without adequate education," thought Abdul as he relaxed on the carpeted floor of his sitting room. Omar lay stretched on the floor, pillowing his head on his father's thighs.

"What can I do for you son?" Abdul thought, stroking Omar's head.

Canada came to mind. Abdul was aware of the Canadian lenient Immigration laws, especially towards stateless people and Palestinians in particular. In Canada, Omar and he could acquire Canadian citizenship after due immigration process, and Omar could go to school in any of the Canadian Universities and study any course of his choice.

"Nuclear Physics," he thought.

In Canada, he would get on with life and if any viable opportunity to inflict harm on the infidels arose, he would grab it.

On the fifteenth of May, the Catastrophe day anniversary, Abdul, in the company of Omar, arrived at the Cairo international airport to board an Egyptian Air plane to Toronto with a stopover in Washington DC. After hours of cruising through the quiet Mediterranean skies, the Boeing airplane touched ground at Ronald Reagan international airport Washington. As passengers filed through security check points and into the transit hall and arrivals hall respectively, Abdul noticed airport security men at strategic posts, skimming the passengers, their searching eyes very alert, not missing anything, trying to catch any tell-tale clue of tension and restlessness in any of the passengers. The skimming gaze of one of the security men caught Abdul and lingered on him for some moments.

"An Arab," thought the security officer.

"Let him go, he's with a child, must be clean," suggested a mind.

"With these people, you never know, the child might even be the terrorist himself," another mind said.

"You!" said the security officer, pointing to Abdul "Come here."

"Me?" inquired Abdul.

"Yes, you," replied the security officer.

Abdul approached the officer.

"Wait here for a moment sir," said the security officer.

"The assholes, of all the 400 passengers in the airplane, I'm the only one to be singled off the line for special searching, just because I'm Arab," thought Abdul.

Abdul became very worried, not just because of having been stopped, but because he knew what he had in the false bottom of his briefcase.

"Did you pack your bags yourself sir?" asked the security man.

"Yes I did," replied Abdul.

"Did any person give you any parcel to deliver to someone?"

"No sir," replied Abdul.

"Did you at any time leave your baggage unattended

since you packed it?"

"Pardon?" said Abdul, not because he didn't hear or understand him, but because he was trying to buy time to think out an adequate response to his question.

"I mean has this bag been in your possession since you packed it?" repeated the security man, rephrasing the question.

"At the Cairo airport, I left it with Omar in the departure hall while I used the gents," replied Abdul.

"Omar is your son?" asked the security man.

"Yes."

"Come with me," said the man.

They walked to the security check post.

"Put it here," he ordered, nodding to the security x-ray conveyor belt.

Abdul obliged, and he pressed the button beside the table and the belt hummed alive and conveyed the bag across the x-ray chamber and pushed the bag to the other end, and red light began flashing on the table.

The security man spoke some codes into his radio.

Within minutes, five security men came hurrying towards them. Abdul knew immediately that something was wrong. The machine must've detected the stuff in his bag. The security men took Abdul and Omar to an inner room where they ripped the bag open. The radioactive detector one of the security men was holding beeped out loud, and he looked at it and kept his gaze on it for some time.

"This is 90% grade enriched Uranium 235," he murmured.

"Weigh it," he ordered.

One of the security agents put the substance onto a scale.

"One kilogram sir," he said.

"What were you planning to do with this?" shouted one of them.

Abdul gazed at him but said nothing.

"I'm asking you," he shouted.

"Take it easy, my son is here, do not shout at me," said Abdul.

"But if you have respect for your son, you shouldn't be travelling with him and a substance as dangerous as this," replied the security agent.

Another agent approached with handcuffs, and Abdul was handcuffed.

"Do you smoke?" he asked after handcuffing him

"I'm handcuffed, how can I smoke, even if I'm a smoker? Stupid thing," cursed Abdul.

"Bring him along and take the child to the guest centre," ordered the senior security agent.

"Where are you taking Dad to?" Omar asked as one of the agents held Abdul by the elbow and dragged him on.

"Your Dad is alright. He is going to the hospital for a check-up, he will come to see you later ok," one of the agents consoled Omar.

"Do you handcuff people when you take them to the hospital?" Omar asked.

"Please let me talk to my son," pleaded Abdul to the security man who was leading him away.

The man looked at him for some moments; his gaze then dropped and fixed on Omar.

"Poor boy," he thought.

"Ok, talk to him," he said to Abdul.

"I'm sick too, I will go to the hospital with my Dad," Omar protested.

"Please remove the handcuffs for a few minutes while I speak with him," pleaded Abdul.

The security agent obliged.

Abdul removed the ring on his small finger and, crouching before Omar, he put the ring onto Omar's left thumb. It was a ring he inherited from his own father Allan.

"Son, this is all I have for you now, but I believe it will protect and guide you wherever they take you to, till when next we see each other. I'm not very well, I'm going to the hospital, but always remember daddy loves you and never wished to abandon you. Daddy was only working hard to make you proud, but it came out all wrong. But it's going to be alright. You will be a nuclear physicist just as Daddy had planned," said Abdul to Omar.

Abdul noticed the fear and confusion in Omar's eyes, but it was the fear inside him, which was certainly showing in his own eyes, that worried him more, because it wasn't good for his son to ever see him afraid.

The security man came forward and tapped Abdul on the shoulder. Abdul looked up at him.

"It's enough, let's go," he said.

Abdul kissed Omar on both his cheeks and his forehead and rose. The security agent handcuffed him and pulled him away, holding him at the elbow.

Father and son gazed at each other for a brief moment before the security man took the child away and through the doorway.

Separating from Omar was the most terrible time Abdul had witnessed since the death of Amina his wife. Guilt filled his heart, not guilt for having a controlled dangerous substance, but guilt for the unknown that would befall his only child.

"No need to feel guilty now, just pray he is taken to a good Orphanage," a mind said to him.

CHAPTER 31
Washington DC

Abdul pleaded not guilty before a federal judge in a Washington federal court.

His defence lawyer argued that Abdul's finger prints were not found on any of the items inside the brief-case containing the controlled dangerous substance: enriched Uranuim 235. He pointed out that the album inside the briefcase bore no photos of his client or his child. The addresses in the address book found inside the briefcase matched no known address of the accused. The two rings found inside the briefcase didn't fit any of Abdul's fingers. A small comb inside the briefcase was not adequate for Abdul's long hair. And the eyeglasses found inside the briefcase, which had been confirmed to be for a myopic patient, didn't befit Abdul, as tests confirmed he was not suffering from myopia. An identical briefcase containing Abdul's real belongings, album, identification and underpants that matched his waistline was found on an Egypt Air Boeing plane in Toronto and recorded as a forgotten luggage.

."Abdul must've picked up some other person's briefcase mistakenly. Justice, quite unlike history, ought not to leave room for doubts. There is so much doubt in the prosecutor's case. But our justice is popular because of the high standard of evidence and proof it requires before dishing out its judgement and its accompanying irreversible consequences. My client is innocent," orated the defence lawyer.

Abdul had bought two identical briefcases and, using hand gloves, he'd packed one of them with one kg of enriched uranium hidden in the false bottom. He put albums with photos of innocent pedestrians, Arab gardens, the Nile, and the Pyramids. Photos he took randomly in the city of Cairo. He'd ordered an oculist to make myopic eyeglasses for him. He'd plotted it so beautifully well, hoping to deny ownership of the briefcase if arrested. His fingerprints were only detected on the bag handle.

It was really a tough case for the judge to decide, but the court finally put two and two together, found Abdul guilty and sentenced him to ten years in Jail.

The reason?

Anti-Arab sentiment.

A briefcase containing nuclear material, and an Arab standing within the vicinity, and the briefcase had not been linked to any other passenger on the Egypt Air Boeing flight. And there was no way the briefcase could've got into the flight without an owner. After all, the anti-terrorism regulations prohibit any baggage on board an airplane unless it belongs to a passenger aboard that flight. Abdul was found in possession of the briefcase. It was his briefcase.

"My lord," Abdul said as the Judge finished reading the sentence.

"Speak," said the Judge.

"Your honour. I plead that you grant me the opportunity to see my child regularly," pleaded Abdul.

"Once a month my lord," said Abdul.

"You got it," replied the Judge.

CHAPTER 32

Thoughts tumbled down Abdul's mind as he sat crouched inside the police prison vehicle that drove him to a federal prison facility east of Washington to start serving his sentence.

"All my life, I've enjoyed nothing till this day. I am a reject of the Jihadist Movement.

A collaborator. And now, I'm an American prisoner.

I'm in a real mess.

Where have I gone wrong?

Is the whole goal wrong?

Is it a wrong life to lead, being a terrorist? What a life?"

The thoughts tumbled down in his mind.

"You shouldn't be asking yourself what the meaning of life is, because the definition of life is found in each and every one of us. And life encompasses both wrongs and rights, failures and successes. And its enigmatic singularity makes it exciting and worth living. There is no right or wrong way to live life, so one mustn't complain about mistakes and all that is done well or ill-done because both success and failure, good and wrong are opportune impostors. I had only wanted to give my child a good future and at least a citizenship, a country to call a home. And the right to carry out the duty I owe to Islam. There are the things I've believed will make me happy, and I'm entitled to seek happiness, which in itself is not directly brought by material wealth. But in a capitalist world like ours, it is impossible to be happy when the essential amenities and necessities of life are lacking in one's life. It's impossible for a man in the 21st century, an American century, to be happy being unable to give his child even an elementary education. How can a child cope in this digital world without basic education? It is not greed or ambition and not just fundamentalism. I was only trying to carry out a duty I owe a child I deliberately put into this world. A duty that means more to me than anything because it is the duty I owe this child that makes me worthy to be called a father, in all sense of it , and not only the biological link, the mere sperm contribution to his genetic makeup. What really creates the love for a child is not just that biological link but also the duty to rear, care and educate and watch your child grow into an adult, and with luck into a responsible adult.

Abdul listened up as his train of thought was interrupted by the squeaking sound of an opening gate, the prison gate. The prison compound was triple fenced with electronic sensors, bright lights, thick steel doors and gates, closed circuit TV monitors, emergency alarms and red–eyed, weird armed guards. Abdul was handed over to the prison authority and was escorted by a prison warder to the prison inclusion office.

The warder sitting behind the desk in the registration office looked Abdul over and waved him to a seat opposite him, and without further preamble he began.

"Name?"

"Abdul," he replied.

"Complete name."

"Abdul Allan."

"Civil Status?"

"Widower."

"Have children?"

"Yes, a boy."

"Country of origin?"

"Palestine."

"Religion?"

"Islam."

"Place of birth?"

"Yemen."

"Age?"

"36."

"Do you smoke?"

"No."

"Crime?"

"Possession of a controlled substance."

"Name of substance?"

"Enriched Uranium 235."

The warder looked up from the computer screen at Abdul, his fingers busy on the keyboard.

"A terrorist," he thought.

"Sentence?"

"Ten years," replied Abdul.

"Over there," he said to Abdul nodding towards a door to the left. Abdul crossed the doorway into the room and his fingerprints were taken and stored. Abdul was supplied with a prison garb. He was federal prisoner number 200,002.

CHAPTER 33
Federal Prison, Washington

Abdul stepped into the prison cell, and the warder pushed the door closed and turned the key in the lock. He paused apprehensively and looked around the cell. There were three-bunk beds, with a ladder to the top-most bed. The first level bed was dressed in a white bedspread, the floor was uncarpeted and a fairly large reading table stood to his right. At the far end of the cell was a white curtain separating the washroom.

"And this will be my home till they transfer me to a one-person cell," thought Abdul as a man came out from behind the curtain separating the washroom.

"Good evening," he said warmly in an Italian accented voice.

"I'm Mendes," he said.

"Mendes Cachiola," he added.

"I am Abdul."

"Just arrived?" quizzed Mendes.

"Yes," replied Abdul.

"From another prison, on transfer, or a fresh from the streets?" probed Mendes.

"From the court, from the streets," replied Abdul.

"You're Arab, right?"

"Yes, Palestinian. And you?"

"Italian American," said Mendes and walked to the table, drew a stool and sat down.

"Sit down," he invited Abdul, waving him to a stool.

"So how is the outside world?" Mendes quizzed.

"The same old thing, same old world," replied Abdul.

"For how long did they decide to have you as their guest?" asked Mendes.

"Ten years," replied Abdul.

"Oh, that's a short time. Soon you will be outta here and back to the streets," said Mendes.

Abdul looked askance at him in surprise.

"A short time?" he asked.

"In the next six years, you will be due for parole, and

I mean it is a short time, and time passes rapidly."

"Even at that, it isn't anything short," thought Abdul.

"How long have you been here?" inquired Abdul.

"Fifteen years," he replied.

"I was sentenced to 35 years," he added.

"I will be due for parole in the next five years, so we will be leaving here in about the same time," he added.

Abdul was tempted to ask his crime, but restrained.

"Thirty five years behind bars is a tough one," he thought.

A pause.

Mendes was gazing at the vent high above the cell wall opposite him, his gaze distant, as he surfed through his past.

Abdul looked on.

"My cell mate, now our cellmate, Rodrigue, is here to complete a 9 years sentence for having been caught in possession of a controlled substance," resumed Mendes.

"What substance is that?" asked Abdul.

"Cocaine," replied Mendes.

At that moment, the curtain covering the second

bunk-bed drew open and Rodrigue jumped down and joined them at the table.

"Rodrigue," he said, stretching out his hand for a shake, a barely-there smile on his face.

Abdul took his hand in a warm shake.

"Abdul."

"You look Indian," said Abdul.

"Sim, sou Indigina Columbiano," replied Rodrigue.

"Eh?" inquired Abdul.

"I'm from Columbia, an American-Indian," repeated Rodrigue.

"They lashed you nine years eh?" said Abdul.

"Yes, nine years, and I've stayed six years in this hell for possessing a produce of my land. A product so mystified that it seems to be the worst crime under the sun. But it is such a common compound, a salt of cocaine — Cocaine chloride. America and the rest of the West said it causes violence, death, destroys lives and families. Arguably, it does, primarily because of the mysticism that surrounds it due to the prohibition. Besides, there are so many substances and things that cause death and violence, that damage families and the human society at large, things that destroys tenfold more than the salt of Cocaine. Things like cigarettes, arms, landmines, bombs, explosives, weapons of mass destruction and imperialism. But I think that the human race has advanced so much that we are now even capable of making the duplicates of ourselves through the advent of the cloning technology, amongst other achievements including visiting the moon, internet and so on. Then, why can't we find a solution to cocaine chloride. And to me, the solution is simple and handy — legalize it," said Rodrigue.

"Why do you think that legalizing it will stop the abuse and the problems associated with it?" quizzed Abdul.

"Because when it is legalized, firstly, there would be no more illegal drug dealers. Dealers would pay taxes to the crown as it is with other products and businesses. When this is done, the price of the substance will crash, since the price hike of the drug is only caused by the clandestine nature of the trade. And when the clandestine veil that clouds the trade is lifted, the violence it generates will also disappear. I've never heard anybody say that cigarettes and alcohol of the present day cause urban violence. The health authority would establish a legal concentration, so as not to get people addicted or cause dependency. It could be sold alongside other substances that remove its addiction and dependency qualities, without removing its hallucinatory and euphoric effects. I mean you can use it and get all the kick you desire from it without getting addicted to it. Alkaloids sharpen the mind, you know, alkaloids are what you have in cocaine chloride. I mean something positive get to be done to resolve the problem of drugs, it can not be resolved by throwing people into jail. The same mistake was made during prohibition era, when so many people died, went to jail and so much money wasted fighting alcohol until the government braved up and legalized it. And today, one can drink the best of whiskies, brandies and alcohol in general in the corridors and cocktail parties in Downing Street, London, England, and Pennsylvania Avenue, Washington, USA. And alcohol related deaths and violence have been reduced ever since the ban was lifted. I believe the same could be done and achieved with the white powder of South American origin," orated Rodrigue.

A pause.

"And opium of the Asian origin," said Abdul.

"Look, cocaine is to my people what arms are to the people of the United States. Just like the USA knows how best and more than anybody else to build, market and use weapons and arms of all sorts, my country Columbia knows more than anybody else how to make cocaine. And I love my country and our produce. Remember, drugs have come to stay and the only thing left for the global authority to do is to learn to live with it. Besides, it is not just meant for its raw usage and abuse, we use cocaine and heroine to make other useful things like anaesthetics. And it has a legal medicinal usage, it will always be with us, and will make sense if we start learning to live with it as a legal substance.

Recently the US government sent $1.8 billion in military aid and social aid in what they call 'Plan Columbia', the anti-drug strategy to the Columbian government to fight drugs and FARC —'Forcas Armardas Revolutionario Columbiano'.

FARC is a 30 year old, 18000 member leftist guerrilla insurgency that have their stronghold in Southern Columbia including Putumayo and Caquetta, which the Columbian and US governments accuse of condoning drug dealers and sympathizing with the drug trade by selling protection to Coca farmers who grew coca without fear of government intervention. The $1.8 billion sent to Columbia was not in cash but in arms and pesticides," said Rodrigue.

"All were American products," chirped Abdul.

"Pesticides to be spread on coca plantation in Putumayo, in Caquetta and Amazonas where you have three-quarters of all coca cultivation in Columbia. They don't, I mean the Yanks don't give a damn about the ecological problems this would cause to the South American Ecosystem."

"Terrorism, isn't it?" said Abdul, his gaze fixed on the table.

"Pure terrorism, eco-terrorism and deprivation of natural resources," replied Rodrigue.

"Just imagine where $1.8 billion dollars worth of chemicals and biological agents are expended in a region. Thought of that?" said Rodrigue.

A pause.

Abdul nodded indulgently.

Mendes looked on.

"Drugs in their illegal trade status take billions of dollars out from the US economy annually, and if and when it is legalized, I believe it would take less money out from the economy because the multinational drug companies that would spring up at every corner of South America, and the USA would pay taxes, and on the other hand make their heavy profits. The tax payers' money that is being used to fight the un-winnable war against drugs would be channelled to some other useful things in the society. Besides, if one looks at the human behavioural pattern and comportment, one sees that somehow, human beings are very inclined to the use of stimulants to jar up the brain. The human brain seems to have a permanent depressive tendency. Depending on the race, time and epoch, if it isn't cigarettes, with their nicotine and other noxious substances, it is coffee, alcohol and other sorts of drug known and unknown to keep the brain from depression," exhorted Abdul.

Really the human predilection for leisure and pleasure will never go out of style especially as long as the Amygdala still forms part of the brain.

Amygdala is the slightly oval brain structure that recollects the details of pleasure and leisure and to some extent may be responsible for the human susceptibility to substance abuse. Some humans are replete in a type of dopamine receptor. This receptor brings about feelings of pleasure when stimulated with dopamine or other stimulants. The people who are deficient in this receptor came into life with a defect in the gene responsible for forming the receptors and consequently experience life with less joy and happiness and always need something, a stimulant to psyche them up. That's why sometimes we have some friends who, while in a social gathering, say disco, party, night clubs, never switch on to enjoy the razzle of the moment unless they have a glass of drink, a cigarette, a joint or any other drug, legal or illegal. It is all genetic and one mustn't punish the lands of Asia and South America for giving the genetically less fortunate people what they need to keep up with in this short life of ours, after all, what's better than pleasure?

Money?

You may say so, but remember the words of the richest and wisest man of all times. Said King Solomon:

"There is nothing better for a man than that he should eat, and drink and make his soul enjoy the good of all his days."

Dreams?

Well, dreams are good because they give us the reason to continue with life, without dreams, life becomes boring, so tedious it wouldn't worth living. But still better than dreams is the realisation of dreams.

"And besides..." resumed Rodrigue.

"...Coca plant is a cultural heritage, we use Coca leaves as a vegetable, a staple food. It is the West that came and showed us how to transform it into a white powder that can yield more money than selling it as vegetables. And today, I'm here as a criminal and later will be marked as an ex-convict for the rest of my life," said Rodrigue.

"No, don't say that, because that's what they want you to think of yourself. They want to use the moral conscience against you and your produce. Don't fall for their game. You are a businessman. It is all buying and selling even at its illegal status. Like you rightly said, so many things cause death and violence in the human community today. Things like arms and imperialistic forces that impoverish poor nations like yours and mine and force people to resort to crime. What you did is no crime as they portray it to be. And if you choose to take back some wealth in drops through the sale of your produce so that your land doesn't get depleted, go on and do it," said Abdul.

Mendes, who had been quiet till then, looked up at Rodrigue.

"But if you want to stay out from prisons, if you value your freedom, all you have to do when you get outa here is don't trade drugs again, because it is still a prohibited trade. All we think against drug prohibition doesn't warrant drug trafficking and all the stress associated with it. Yes, it is a legitimate produce of a country and its people, but it is still illegal and a crime to sell and possess cocaine," said Mendes.

Rodrigue looked askance at him but said no word.

"Having been here with you all these years, I'd noticed that crime is not your beach. You don't fit the profile of a drug dealer," said Mendes.

"A drug dealer? Yes I am, but a criminal? No I'm not. Drug dealing is not a crime in itself. It is only a question of buying and selling. It is the folly of the West not to legalize it and thus mystifying it that creates the criminality around it.

All my life, I harvested Coca leaves. I acted out of necessity, my credit card interest rate was high, Cars are expensive, auto and engine parts, computer chips are expensive. The cost of communication is high. It is cheaper to call the USA from my country than it is to make an intercity call inside Columbia. The chemicals I use in producing my stuff, the Putumayo product, ether, acetone, sulphuric acid, ammonia are very expensive so you can see that for one to survive the economic constraints caused by the occidental imperialism, one has to sell ones product to the West.

My family had a big farm in Maguare area of Caquetta. Daddy had waited for years for the government crop substitution subsidy as promised by Bogota, but none came. We had never processed our produce into Coca paste, Base and then Cocaine. We'd often sold the Coca leaves in the market. One day, while I, my father and some farm workers were in the farm pruning the shrubs, four agricultural helicopters flew overhead spraying pesticides. It is very sad to see planes spraying poison on your farm, killing the plants. You see foreigners inside a helicopter spraying your farm in your own land, your backyard in your country. Dad and I opened fire on the invaders and they returned fire. We shot down two of the helicopters and they crashed onto the farm, exploded and killed the occupants. The other two helicopters continued firing at us and unfortunately Dad was killed in the confrontation and two farm workers were also killed. I escaped and flew to San Vincente del Caguan and later to Putumayo. In Putumayo, a city in the Apurimac valley of Peru, where I started a little farm, and with the help of an agronomist, I grafted a Palma-pampa Peruvian coca stem into the Columbian native coca species, creating a great and high yielding hybrid that can be harvested up to ten times a year with a high alkaloid content. In my effort to maximize the value of my stock like any other businessman, I processed the first harvest from my farm and planned this trip to the USA. A trip that I believe was well planned and scripted, though it failed and landed me in jail. While processing the base into cocaine, as I poured the last absolute acetone into the base to cake out the Cocaine crystal, I was sure it was a good stuff," said Rodrigue.

"You produced it yourself?" asked Abdul

Rodrigue shot him a glance.

"Careful, he might be a jail house snitch," a mind warned.

Jailhouse snitches squeal on other inmates, taking

confessions they make during casual discussion to the authorities, and when there is none, they make one up just to earn reduced sentences.

"But I've been sentenced and already served half my sentence," thought Rodrigue.

"But it could affect your parole," argued another mind.

"Not Arabs, they are never friends of the USA," insisted Rodrigue, and continued his story.

"Yes," he resumed.

"I produced it myself. Firstly I put the leaves in a large and wide thick plastic bowl and poured in some kerosene and mashed the lot into a paste, then I added petrol to turn it to base and decanted it, then I added ether followed by absolute acetone to cake out stuff. I sun-dried it and it was ready. When I weighed it, I had ten Kilograms of stuff. I parked it into a false bottom of my trunk bag and had wanted to sell it in the streets of America to raise some money to expand my family farm, the farm destroyed by the American anti-narcotics forces," said Rodrigue.

Silence.

"Daddy was a successful and satisfied country farmer, you know," he continued in a tearful voice.

"I'd planned my trip very well because I'd wanted to avoid American Jails. I was told it's terrible and having been here I think it is horrible, miserable and violent. I started by not flying the American Airlines, because it flies directly to Washington, and the American Customs and exercise department treats everybody on such a direct flight from Columbia and Peru as narcotics suspects. I flew British Airways and transited in the London Heathrow airport. In London, we changed flights and continued to Washington, USA. As we alighted from the aircraft and proceeded to the baggage conveyor belt to claim our baggage, I saw some DEA agents patrolling the arrival area in the company of sniffer dogs, but I cared less, knowing that some of the sniffer dogs in the airport terminals are not always looking for drugs but also for bombs, fruits that might carry imported flies, pathogens and other potential scourges. Besides, the compartment in the bag where the stuff was hidden was airtight so dogs can't perceive no smell because, just like sound, air is the vector of smell. Not even the detectors that detect rays from substances could accuse anything in the bag. Everything was taken care of. So I was confident. But alas, I waited for our baggage but it didn't roll out. I went to the British airways counter and complained.

'We are sorry sir, but your bag was left behind in London. The baggage handlers in the London Heathrow airport were on strike yesterday. If you furnish me with your address and phone number, we will forward the luggage to you as soon as it arrives. Here is our number, you can call to inquire about the status of your luggage,' said the blond lady as she handed me the card.

I left the airport really worried. I never bordered to put a call through to Riche, my contact. I knew his emissaries were in the airport monitoring me, and activities around me. I checked into a three star hotel north of Washington and waited in trepidation. The next evening, I called the British airways counter at the Ronald Reagan national airport to inquire after my bag, but was informed that it hadn't arrived.

Thoughts came tumbling into my mind.

Had they detected the drugs inside the bag?

Were they waiting to see my contacts so that they could round off everybody and put us in jail?

Nothing, I assured myself. They can't find it.

The only way they could find it was to destroy the bag. Whatever the case was, they wouldn't lay their stupid bloody hands on any of my contacts. Riche didn't live in Washington, and the plan was that nobody would see me or talk to me in Washington. Even when I get to Dallas, Texas, I still had to stay upwards of two weeks in the hotel before handing over the bag, to make sure that any agent on my trail must've been shaken off.

The next day I had a casual tour of the city of Washington, I was quite pleased with the numerous fine places in the American Capital. I was relaxing on the divan in the hotel suite when the room phone buzzed. I reached and answered it. The receptionist informed me that a British Airways official was at the reception area and would like to see me.

I hurried to the reception area.

"Mr Rodrigue?" asked the short, stout airways official

"Yes," I replied.

"I'm from the British airways, your luggage sir," he said looking at the bag before him.

"Do you still have your passenger's piece of the boarding pass and luggage tag sir?" he inquired.

"Yes," I said and opened my wallet to pull out my boarding pass and luggage check-in tag.

"Here," I said.

"And your ticket?" he demanded.

"Sorry, it's just to make sure I'm handing the bag over to the right person," he added.

I pulled out the folded return coupon and ticket jacket from my wallet and showed him.

"Your bag sir," he said.

I bent forward and picked up the bag.

"Could you open it to confirm the content before me sir?" he suggested.

"Open, confirm, why?" I thought.

"Probably routine, just act normal, you're into it, open and confirm," suggested a mind.

I arranged the combination number of the lock and opened it. I touched and turned two, three items inside the bag and nodded my satisfaction.

"It's okay," I said and pulled upright to look at the man. At that moment, a man approached from behind him and two other men flanked me, men I'd seen reading newspapers at the other end of the reception area. The trio pulled their identity cards and guns simultaneously.

"DEA, freeze!"

"Mr Rodrigue, you are under arrest!"

I was handcuffed and my hotel room searched. I was later hauled to the Police detention centre and, after due legal process, I was sentenced and brought to this dungeon to complete my jail term," said Rodrigue.

A pause.

"How did you plead before the Judge?" asked Abdul.

"I pleaded not guilty," said Rodrigue.

"Not guilty," thought Mendes.

The ills of drugs in the society and miserable addicts came to mind. The Brooklyn heroin, cocaine and crack addicts, their rituals when they take their doses, their highs and lows, They are everywhere in America and the world over, dying in their millions and ruined in their millions. They are everywhere in the sidewalks, in the parks, under the bridges, behind trucks, against banisters of street steps and beneath girders of sidewalks leading a deplorable existence.

"And you ain't guilty? Murderer," thought Mendes.

Silence.

"But what about the victims of imperialistic forces, the miserable of Iraq, Vietnam, Guatamela, Haiti, Afghanistan, India, South America, Bangladesh and Africa? What comes around goes around in different ways," said a mind to Mendes.

"Have you ever been addicted to drugs?" he asked.

"Occasionally I use cocaine, but I eat a lot of coca leaf. It is a staple vegetable of the indigenous people of Columbia, my country," replied Rodrigue.

"And you?" said Mendes to Abdul.

"No, I don't use drugs," replied Abdul.

"And nobody has the right to take it away from us, even America, the righteous," added Rodrigue.

"America the righteous," echoed Abdul.

At six O'clock, Abdul knelt facing east to Mecca to pray, his fifth and last prayer for the day.

"Oh Allah, you have seen where the infidel has put me for virtually nothing, for being in possession of what they called a controlled substance, Uranium 235. A substance they know more than any other race how to manipulate. An element found in the bombs and explosives rained on the people of Iraq in the gulf war and the war on terrorism. And they say here will be my home for the next ten years, as though they own me. You and nobody owns me Oh Allah. Look at Rodrigue, an innocent South American Indian farmer who was only trying to globalize the sale of his produce. He's been caged here for years, because the infidel is despotic. Oh Allah, remember what you said in the holy Koran: 'victimising an innocent is victimising humanity at large'. Allah, I've been victimized, Rodrigue has been victimized. How long will you stand aside while the infidels perpetuate evil against your children. Oh Allah, strike the infidel, strike the hegemon.

Bring the hegemon to her knees.

Let her grow old.

For the Islamic kingdom to reign!

Allahu Akbarr!

Allahu Akbar!" he prayed and rose.

Rodrigue and Mendes watched on as Abdul prayed silently in deep concentration, dipped his head to the floor, stood up, bent and dipped his head to the floor again.

"Since he was a toddler," thought Mendes as he imagined how long Abdul has indulged in this act of meditation, high concentration and prayer. The act is

known to produce hallucinogenic effects and, indirect-
ly, the religious sensation of being in the presence of
God and a graceful state of the mind. Mendes was born
and baptized in the Christian faith, Catholic to be precise, but he was not a practising Catholic. Mendes was
practically an atheist, but he never defined or intro-
duced himself as one.

"His neurotransmitters are at work now, producing
a lot of brain chemicals and chemistry, giving the mys-
tical sensation and experience that there is a supernatural controller, who sits somewhere overlooking and
listening to his supplications. It's all a product of the
brain. Nobody is out there in the clouds above in all his
righteousness and omnipotence, listening, analysing,
answering to supplications," thought Mendes.

"You are a Muslim eh?" asked Mendes when Abdul
rose.

"Yes, and you?' said Abdul.

Ehmm... Christian, Catholic," said Mendes.

"And you?" asked Abdul looking at Rodrigue.

"I have no religion, though I believe in the supernatural force. The origin and sole controller of the universe and the solar system, but I pray more to my ances-

tors," replied Rodrigue.

CHAPTER 34

"What a life I am offering you, son," thought Abdul as he walked into the prison infirmary waiting room where Omar, his son, was sitting on a sofa waiting to see him.

Omar was brought to the prison by the Orphanage authority to see his father as authorized by the court. Abdul knew he was looking pale and exhausted and, as such, fit the profile of an ill person in a hospital as he would say to Omar.

"Daddy! Daddy!" shouted Omar as he jumped onto Abdul and held him in a tight embrace.

Abdul took him in his arms, kissed him on the cheeks and on the forehead.

"Daddy loves you Omar," he whispered into Omar's left ear. The left ear, we've been told by researchers, is more sensitive to love titbits.

"And I love you too Daddy," replied Omar.

"I want to stay with you here," Omar pleaded.

"You can't son."

"Yes I can," said Omar.

"I can only stay here alone, it's not for children," said Abdul.

"When will we go home Daddy?" asked Omar.

"I don't know yet, but it wouldn't be long. One day we will go home," replied Abdul.

"How are you fairing in the home? Is it good there?" quizzed Abdul.

"Yes," answered Omar.

"But I want to stay with you," he added.

"I know."

"Do you have friends?" probed Abdul.

"Hope, Nerry, Benneth and John."

"Hope is my good friend. Reverend father Robert said Jesus loves Hope, and sister Agnes said the heavenly father loves and will protect Hope. She is my friend," said Omar.

Since Hope arrived at the Orphanage, Rev. Father Robert had visited the home twelve times. The city orphanage was run by Mrs Poem and catered to thirty children. On the day Hope arrived in the Home, Mrs Poem had woken early as usual, collected letters and packages from the mail box at the gate, and went inside to the mail room to read the correspondences. The first package she opened contained two-dozen children's stockings from an anonymous donor.

"Bless you dear," she said softly and reached for the third package. It was somewhat heavy. Though she had received heavier packages, something about this very package quickened her heart beat, something that hadn't really got anything to do with the careful and beautiful way that the perforated bright yellow, blue and white expensive wrapping paper was assembled, but something not tangible or visible to the naked eyes. She looked the package over again and gently began to unwrap it. The smell of the newly born wafted to her nostrils as she opened the perforated flap of the padded carton. Lying supine in a peaceful slumber inside the carton was Hope. She was some hours old. Mrs Poem's heart skipped and she was showered with goose pimples. She gazed at the little peaceful and innocent baby for some seconds before lifting her up cuddling her gently in her arms.

"You are welcome dear baby, you are welcome to this home, to the world, to life," she said.

"Only God could mail such a beautiful little angel, such a gift to me," she said, a tear running down her cheek as she glanced back at the carton and at the piece of note inside it.

She stretched to pick up the note and read:

"Please call her Hope, Hope Tidings is her name. See the notes under the baby mat. God bless you."

Mrs Poem took the baby into the maternity room of the Orphanage and left her in the care of a nurse.

"Her name is Hope Tidings," she said to the nurse.

"She is a beautiful angel, isn't she?" she added.

Back in the mailroom, Mrs Poem found ten crispy $1000 bills under the baby mat in the carton.

* * *

One Month Later

Mrs Poem received a correspondence from the orphanage bankers, the Chase Manhattan Bank. The Bank was writing to inform the Orphanage that $3 million dollars had been deposited into the Orphanage's account by an anonymous donor.

Mrs Poem received another letter three days later, and the letter advised thus:

"The cash deposited in the Orphanage account is for the education of all the children who are in the Orphanage at the time of the deposit. Education to the University level."

Since then, Hope Tidings had been in the Orphanage, a happy and intelligent girl. She developed healthily, her brilliant green eyes and honey blond hair getting even more beautiful, as was her effervescent nature, with the passing days.

Reverend Robert visited the Orphanage for the first time two years after Hope Tidings arrived at the Orphanage, and continued visiting the Home twice a year thereafter. At his first visit, he prayed collectively for the children in the Orphanage, and afterwards he took each of the thirty children in his arms. At Hope's turn, he held her longer than he did any other child.

"Jesus loves you Hope," he said kissing her on the cheek.

Nobody in the home ever suspected that the glassy

green eyes of the infant Hope Tidings had any biological link to Rev. Robert's bright green eyes, let alone knowing that father Robert was the person that cut Hope's umbilical cord, bathed and put her in a carton well padded with very soft and delicate medicated cotton materials and packaged it to let in enough oxygen and warmth to keep the baby alive. Father Robert had disguised as a mailman, parked his car some two kilometres away and walked to the orphanage and gently dropped the package inside the mailbox at the Orphanage gate. It was 5.35am when he crossed the street that early Monday morning and turned into the next street on his two-kilometre trek to his car. He wriggled into his doctor's coat and drove off to work at the Washington Catholic Hospital, thoughts tumbling down his mind about the child's future. He knew that the child would be taken care of, but would irremediably miss her maternal breast milk. She would be formula-fed, and of all the numerous health benefits of breastfeeding, including obesity prevention, and intelligence at adulthood. She would find it hard as an obsessed woman in today's ever-aesthetic world. But cosmetic medicine makes it easier for everyone nowadays. The only person who remains obsessed and ugly is the person who wants to stay the same, otherwise the aesthetic medical surgery theatres were everywhere to be used.

Sister Agnes was lying on her bed in the exclusive private ward of the Catholic hospital. She opened her eyes as the door to her room opened and Rev Dr. Robert came in and went to her bedside, bent and kissed her on her lips.

"It's alright now, She is in safe hands," he said.

CHAPTER 35

Sister Agnes visited the Orphanage three and half years after Hope arrived at the Orphanage. She acted much like Rev. Robert, praying collectively for the children and having each in turn in her arms. She kissed Hope on her lips.

"The heavenly father will guide and protect you my daughter," she said to her.

Hope was as honey blonde as Sister Agnes, and had her sensual lips.

Sister Agnes was a nun with an unshakable faith in God and the Catholic church of the Benedictan order at the Washington city convent. She met Rev. father Robert at the city catholic cathedral on a day the nuns attended a mass outside the convent. Ever since then, they'd exchanged letters and verses in the bible. Some months later, Sister Agnes fell ill. Special prayers and fasting were made on her behalf, but to no avail. She was later admitted into the exclusive private ward of the catholic hospital where Rev Dr. Robert works. Agnes stayed ten months in the hospital. On the second month into her stay in the hospital, Dr. Robert knew her nakedness.

Agnes should've been discharged from the hospital on the fifth month after being admitted, but Rev. Robert had known that Agnes has fallen pregnant, so he ordered that she remain in the hospital ward so that he could observe her to complete recovery and arrest any possible re-emergence of the disease, an autoimmune disease. He assured that patients of autoimmune disease are at increased risk of developing another within short time of escaping one, because autoimmune disease is a situation where the body immune system turns against itself and launches assaults on its own organs. His assertions were good as medical science had it. Sister Agnes suffered from the disorder of the tear ducts. She wept, or rather tears streamed down her eyes every minute of the day, morning, afternoon and night, even in her sleep. At the onset of the disorder, everybody in the convent believed she was weeping for the sins of the world and humanity, but when the tears couldn't stop, prayers and fasting were conducted on her behalf before turning her over to the catholic hospital. At the seventh month of gestation, Rev. Roberts injected her with Bromocriptine to suppress prolactin – a pituitary hormone that ingress into pregnant women's blood stream late into pregnancy to stimulate milk production. Nobody in the hospital noticed Sister Agnes was pregnant because she wore her robe always. It was agreed between Rev. Robert and Sister Agnes that the baby would be given away as soon as she is born, as such the baby wouldn't need the maternal milk. By cutting the milk production, Rev. Roberts saved Sister Agnes the pains caused by a breast replete with milk without being sucked by an infant.

When Sister Agnes received the Bromocriptine injection, the nurses at the hospital didn't suspect any fowl play because they thought it was injected to prevent 'Lupus', another autoimmune disease prevalent in women of child-bearing age.

Three days after giving birth to Hope Tidings at exactly 4.30am, Agnes rose from her bed and tiptoed out

of the room into the corridor and made it to the staircase avoiding the elevators. She glanced back over her
shoulders to make sure nobody was watching her. She
took the steps one at a time in the dimly lit stairwell to
the underground parking lot where Rev. Robert was
waiting for her in the car. He saw her sidling towards
the car, and stretched to open the front passenger's
door.

Did anybody see you?" asked Rev. Robert as she adjusted herself in the seat.

"No, I hope not, they were all asleep," she replied,
referring to the nurses at the ward.

Twenty minutes later, they were at Rev. Robert
guesthouse. The next morning, Rev Robert sent a mail
to the convent.

"Your holiness:

Sister Agnes is in our custody, we kidnapped her
from the hospital bed in her sleep early this morning,
and if you want her back, we will need $3 million in
$100 bills, it has to be used notes, all loose, no bundles.
Remember, if we find any kind of tracing chip in the
money or the bag containing it, the sister will be killed
and her decapitated head will be sent to the convent for

identification. We have a tracing chip detector, so you are warned. No need informing the police or any other security body. They all must be kept out this negotiation if you want your nun back to the convent. We will return the sister safe and sound to the convent if our requests are met. Pack the money in a large black Sensolite trunk bag and let a sister of your Benedictan order wait in line with the bag at the central bus terminal, at the ticket counter of the Grey Hound sector at exactly 10.30pm Friday night. We will recognize your emissary not just by her brown wimple, but by a medium size black cross pendant over her neck, a brown shoe, and let her wear a black lipstick.

Signed,

Collaborators."

The convent authorities were shocked at receiving the letter, they first contacted the Vatican and later the catholic hospital arguing that the hospital has to pay the ransom because Sister Agnes was in the hospital's custody when she was kidnapped. The hospital bluffed. Later the Vatican paid the ransom when they couldn't argue anymore. Through Banco Ambrosioli, they advanced the cash to resolve the impasse and save Sister Agnes' life.

Chapter 36
Washington DC Bus Terminal

Rev. Robert arrived at the bus terminal in a Harley Davidson 2001 model motorbike, wearing a buffalo skin jacket, a black leather hat, an immaculate clean jeans and a dusty winter boots. His wrists were belted with numerous bangles and a dark sun glasses completed his ensemble. Chewing on a gum, he tootled towards the nun who was last on line to the ticket counter.

"Hi Sister," he said brandishing a ticket as if he wanted to obtain information from her. The Sister turned to glance at him. He lowered his voice and said solemnly:

"Just drop the bag gently and as I leave, pick mine up and remain quiet on the line as if nothing has happened, and Agnes will be very grateful you did."

"Bless you," said the nun, her heart racing.

"Forgive him Lord for he knows not what he is doing," prayed the nun silently as he walked casually away, trailing the bag on its wheeled carrier.

The next morning Sister Agnes was found behind the convent. She was blindfolded and shackled at the wrist and ankles. A special prayer was offered for having saved her life from the devils. The nuns also prayed and asked God to forgive and bless the perpetrators because they knew not what they had done. They prayed that the perpetrators know Jesus Christ, the lord and saviour. A thanks-giving service was observed in the city's cathedral the next Sunday after Sister Agnes' release from the devils. Rev. Robert was in the cathedral.

"Jesus loves you," he said as he bent to brush a kiss on both of Sister Agnes' cheeks.

"He loves you too, father" replied Sister Agnes.

Three days after the thanksgiving, Rev. Robert went to New York. He spent about three hours to complete the task he's come to perform. As his taxi belted across the Huston bridge to the airport where he would join a flight to Washington, he drew a pen and a paper to knit the words of his four-line letter to the Orphanage. Chase Manhattan Bank also prepared a correspondence to notify the Orphanage that its account has been topped up with a whooping $3 million by an anonymous philanthropist.

CHAPTER 37
Prison Infirmary

"Are you happy with your friends?" asked Abdul stroking Omar's head.

"Yes, I like Nerry, she makes me laugh a lot. She is good and intelligent. Benett likes her too. He likes her a lot. The other day, Jackie pushed Nerry down violently, Benett was quick to pick her up and dust her down. He eyed Jackie furiously.

'Next time you push her down this hard, you will have a dust-up with me, make no mistakes about it,' he'd say to Jackie, and turned to Nerry.

'Are you ok Nei?' he crooned.

Then I knew he loves her," said Omar.

Nerry is a Jewish girl who was brought to the Orphanage at the age of one. Her parents were killed by shots in the head by a Jewish killer. Nerry's parents were liberal Jews, and were ambushed by Moshe the killer as they came back from a concert one summer night. They were in their newly bought Mercedes Sedan, the fourth in their fleet of cars that's made up of a Volvo, a Chrysler and a Chevy Sedan. As they turned into the close where they reside, a car belted past them and screeched to a stop some meters ahead of them blocking their way forward. A huge tall man came down the Ford Escort convertible, his right hand inside his pocket as he went to the driver's side of the Mercedes.

"How may I help you?' asked Nerry's father, a soft spoken man in his late thirties. The bullet hit him in the upper mouth palate and burrowed into his inner skull before he could finish. The second bullet went into his right eye and came out the back of his head. Nerry's mother was paralysed by fear and shock. She sat agape as Moshe turned the nose of his gun to her and pulled the trigger three times, and the bullets burrowed into her head.

"This is a Mercedes, it is a German product. Have you forgotten your roots? Have you forgotten the Nazi era and wickedness? The holocaust? How dare you patronise the murderers? How dare you carry the German flag? You fools," he snorted

At that moment, Nerry turned in her crib and woke up from her sleep. She began to cry. The babysitter came hurrying to her crib. She lifted Nerry out from the cradle and crooned her back to sleep. Husband and wife died at the spot and Nerry became an Orphan. A month later, she was taken to the Orphanage and since then Benett had been her close friend and protector.

On another occasion Moshe had shot and killed another Jewish man because he was playing and listening to music by Richard Wagner. Richard Wagner was alleged to be Hitler's favorite composer. The man was playing 'Die Walkuere' from the Wagner's work "Ring Circle". Wagner was a 19th century German Opera composer whose music was played often at Nazi gatherings and propaganda sessions. Many Jews believed that Wagner's music inspired and had a strong influence on Adolf Hitler. Even before the Second World War broke out, an informal ban had been placed on performing and playing Wagne's music in Jewish gatherings, a ban conceived in the Jewish community of the British ruled Palestine after the Kristallnacht in Germany. Kristall-

natch was anti Jewish rioting in Germany in which riot-
ers shouted anti-Semitic verses from Wagner's compo-
sitions. The ban became even more vehement after the
holocaust.

"Nazi fascist, Jews don't play concentration camp
music," snorted Moshe as he pulled the trigger several
times. Moshe himself was a son of a holocaust victim
whose mother, a holocaust survivor, was in her first trimester of his gestation when she escaped the concentration camp. Moshe's friend, a staunch supporter of
the Jewish cause and a grandchild of a holocaust victim
had once told Moshe.

"Playing and listening to Wagner doesn't in itself
mean enjoying it or necessarily mean being anti-Semitic. One might play Wagner out of curiosity to exam-
ine and dissect his lyrics, weighing their deep mean-
ings and figuring out all their undertones. It could serve
as a reminder to keep Jews at alert and on guard against
anti-Semitism."

"We don't need to kill fellow Jews for such indul-
gence."

But Moshe had not listened to him. He was still at
large and yet to pay for hate crimes committed against

his own folks.

"I like John because he is very quiet," said Omar.

Abdul nodded indulgently.

They had the afternoon prayer session together before Omar was taken back to the Orphanage, and Abdul was dragged back to his cell.

CHAPTER 38

Mendes turned to glance towards the doorway as the cell door squeaked open.

"Are you ok?" he asked as Abdul stepped into the cell.

"No I'm not ok," replied Abdul.

"Why not?"

"Because I'm lying to my son," replied Abdul.

"How?"

"By telling him that I'm in the hospital," said Abdul.

"You are not lying to him. Jail is a form of hospital. You are morally sick, judging from the reasons for which you are being incarcerated, and the penitentiary system was invented as a corrective measure, a corrective social engineering. You are being re-educated and rehabilitated. What you told your son is not a lie in itself. Besides, lies are sometimes necessary in life," consoled Mendes.

Back in the Orphanage, Omar was among his peers. "My father is big and handsome. He has beautiful teddy bear and he loves me," said Omar to Hope.

"Did you see you r father?" asked Hope.

"Yes I did" replied Omar.

"Why didn't your father take you to his house to live with you?" asked Hope.

"Because my father is sick and he is in the hospital. He cannot stay in the hospital with me," said Omar.

"But you can stay in the hospital with him," said Hope.

"No, I can't," replied Omar.

"Yes you can," insisted Hope.

"But Daddy said that I can't. It is true. I can't. Daddy doesn't lie," said Omar.

"Did you see my father in the Hospital?" asked Hope.

"No I didn't. But I don't know your father," replied

Omar.

"If I see him, I will know, he will look like you, but he will be tall, big and bearded but not a beard like my father's. Daddy's beard is very beautiful," said Omar.

"My father will be handsome too," said Hope.

"Next time you see your father, tell him to ask my father to come and see me," said Hope.

"Yes, I will tell him," promised Omar.

"Do you know why my parents left me here?" asked Hope.

"Yes, I know," replied Omar.

"Why?" asked Hope.

"Because Jesus loves you and the heavenly father will protect you," said Omar.

Hope gazed at him, then gazed up into the skies as though she would see the heavenly father watching over them.

Silence.

"Yes, Sister Agnes said so," said Hope.

"And father Robert said it too," added Omar.

CHAPTER 39

It had been two years since Abdul was caught and thrown into a US jail. He still had five years before being eligible for parole.

"The Helicopter will land in the patio in the night," said a voice.

"And the noise of the engine and rotor?" asked another voice.

"It will rouse the whole prison and wake everybody up. Don't you think so?"

"It is a MH.60 Pave Hawk military Helicopter. It could fly in the night without light and noiseless too, it is equipped with a hush kit."

Abdul knew the voices to belong to Joe and Edward.

Joe was an ex-UNO worker who was in Jail for embezzlement.

"We could saw the steel door to a convenient point and immediately the helicopter lands on the patio, we push the door down and off we go," said Joe.

"At 10.30pm on Tuesday," he added.

As Abdul came out from the bakery area that abutted the Kitchen, Joe saw him and opened the boiling stainless steel pot on the cooker unleashing a waft of meat and onion scented steam into the kitchen. It was a mouth-watering smell.

Abdul breathed in deeply, relishing the delicious smell in the kitchen as he passed on, pretending not to have heard anything of the discussion the pair was having.

"How could I ask him now?" Abdul thought.

"Could they agree to bring him aboard the escape plot?" The problem was not asking to get aboard and probably get rejected, but if he happened to be rejected and the plot for any other reason failed to go through successfully, then he would be in a difficult situation. It would be assumed that he foiled the plot by squealing on them. In the prison, the price of such betrayal was death.

"The moment you get into the cell at 5.30pm on Tuesday evening, start sawing your door. From what I found out, a five-hour sawing would open a large enough hole on the steel door," said Joe as soon as he felt Abdul was gone.

"It is obvious that the whole plan had been set and I would be intruding by asking to get aboard. They may even decide to kill me before the escape day to make sure that the plot succeeds. When one is in jail for a very long sentence, one of the things that give merit to taking another person's life is escape from the prison. You could tell the director, squeal on them at least you will receive some kudos from the authorities and some privileges too," thought Abdul.

"Squealing on a fellow prisoner? An informant of the American prison authority? Is that what you have become? Abdul?" a mind quizzed.

"For a prison privilege, yes," answered another mind.

"It is putting America against Americans. Joe and Edward, and probably another four inmates, including their roommates, are all Americans. Besides, Joe is an ex-UNO worker. The UNO is a tool of all past and present Washington regimes. It has always been Washington puppet organization. It substituted the defunct League of Nations, another puppet organization, all are brainchildren of American thinker tanks. America entered the World War One, holding at the back of the mind to create a global system to buffer World security. After the WWI, the USA created the League of Nations which unfortunately failed but not before its mandate was used to create new states in the former Ottoman enclaves and territories thus introducing the taste of secularism and liberalism in the heart of the Islamic enclave. Later came Hitler and the Second World War, opening yet another chance for the USA to join the war and foster another ambitious secret agenda of replacing the League of Nations with the UNO, and the global financial institutions. After the Second World War, the UNO was born with its financial arms – the World Bank and the International Monetary Fund, all are the strangulating functional arms of imperialism. And they've been under the merciful whims and caprices of the Mighty infidels," thought Abdul.

There will be no regrets for betraying Joe.

"And Edward?" asked a mind.

"He's fished out," thought Abdul gleefully.

Abdul had his turn of betrayal and backbiting at the hands of Edward. Abdul worked in a fireworks factory in the prison premises. Benco Fireworks Ltd. was a factory with about $300,000 in annual revenue and employed inmates to make firework explosives. It was owned by Mr Benedict, a balding man in his late forties. Mr Benedict had often tried running his factory as much like a factory in the street as he could, believing that it would be good for the mental state of the prisoners. He knew that it was a kind of therapeutic relief period for the prisoners from the crushing prison time. In the factory, uniformed guards armed with automatic pistols and whistles inspected the prisoners closely, but they were not prison warder. Abdul's workday in the factory started and ended by lining up in the front of the factory door for inspection and a path-down, it was a precautionary measure to make sure the prisoners didn't take anything dangerous into and out of the factory premises. Two weeks into his job in the factory, Abdul was withdrawn from the factory by the prison authority.

"You don't allow an Islamic fundamentalist, a terrorist, to work in a fireworks factory in the prison. It is artificial though, but fireworks nonetheless," the director general of the prison said to the prison disciplinary chief on discovering that Abdul worked in the Benco Fireworks Factory.

Two days later, Abdul was sent to work in the prison Kitchen, where he worked alongside other prisoners, including Edward and Joe the embezzler.

Abdul's responsibility in the kitchen involved general cleaning and washing. He washed the kitchen floor, the washrooms, plates, ladles, tables, and giant kitchen pots. In the evenings, he had to wait for the cooks to cook and dish out before he washed the tables, floors, ladles and pots. He was often the last prisoner to leave the kitchen. In the kitchen, armed prison wardens inspected the prisoners. On his first day, Abdul began with washing the washrooms, kitchen butchery and tables. Intermittently, he washed and mopped the floor. In the evening, before leaving the kitchen for the cells, the prisoners were patted down carefully to make sure that nobody was taking a knife or any other weapon to the cells. One day, Abdul went to the kitchen with an Arabic language edition of the Sun Magazine to which he subscribed and which he read to know and keep abreast of the happenings in the Arab world and the world at large.

Edward approached Abdul as he read the magazine.

"Could I have a look?" inquired Edward, taking the magazine from Abdul even before he could respond to his request.

"Oh…"

"Arabic," said Edward, handed the magazine back to Abdul and let out a loud sigh as he turned to leave.

Subsequently, Whenever Edward saw Abdul reading the Magazine, he would snort:

"Asshole, only he could read and understand that magazine."

On one occasion, Edward went to complain to the Kitchen inspector, Mr Bone, a short and stout Texan.

"See boss, that Islamist doesn't do anything, he sits there all day and read his Arabic language magazine while other people do the job. I've told him severally but he wouldn't listen to me. Please tell him the whole kitchen floor is dirty and slippery and needs washing and mopping. The butchery is dirty," Edward complained.

At other times, Edward would deliberately pour oil, soap, solutions and dirty water on clean marbled kitchen floor just to get Abdul to work, or to report him to Mr Bone. But despite every ploy by Edward to dissuade him from reading his magazine, Abdul never failed to utilise any ten minutes of spare time he might have to sit himself in a corner of the kitchen to read his magazine. He preferred it to gossiping with fellow prisoners.

"Look at him at his repose while the whole place, the pots and the ladles, are dirty," Edward would say to Mr Bone, pointing towards Abdul as he read his magazine in concentration.

Mr Bone made a short, low whistle to call Abdul's attention.

Abdul looked his way and Mr Bone beckoned him with his index finger.

"Fuck you, I am no dog," Abdul thought, then bent and continued reading.

Mr Bone whistled again and again Abdul looked up. He beckoned with his index finger again, and again Abdul looked back at the pages and continued reading.

"Abdul!" Mr Bone called out loud, a tinge of anger and frustration in his voice.

Abdul looked up.

"That's my name," he thought and started towards Mr Bone.

"Isn't there anything to do at this moment?" asked Mr Bone.

"I just finished cleaning the whole place some ten minutes ago. I'm waiting for some time before I do the next round of cleaning," replied Abdul.

"Go boil some water in one of the 150 litre pots and pour the boiling water on the floor to mop it," said Mr Bone.

"I will use the hot water hose sir," replied Abdul.

"It is not hot enough. Boil water to 100 degrees celcius to be hot enough to sterilize the floor," rejoined Mr Bone.

Abdul lifted a 150 litre pot onto the cooker and filled it with water. While the water was heating, Abdul stood beside it and read a column in the magazine.

Mr Bone approached him.

"I don't want to see you reading magazines in the kitchen," said Mr Bone.

"But sir, while the water is being brought to boil, I see no other way to spend this spare time than by reading a few verses in the magazine. Please do allow me this privilege of reading because it is the only way I can find to keep me sane while serving my sentence. It is my only way of knowing what is happening in the free world, besides, what is a better way of re-educating a prisoner than reading and writing?" pleaded Abdul.

"But you read it all the time," objected Mr Bone.

"No sir, it's not all the time. It happens that the times you choose to notice me are the times I'm reading. But you fail to observe that I've never failed to carry out all the tasks I'm assigned to perform. You see, there is always ten, five or fifteen minutes of free time for every worker in this kitchen. It is the way I spend my own free time. It's just simple variation, because some prisoners spend their own time discussing and chatting, others walk around and other hypocrites pretend to be doing one thing or the other whenever you come into view. But I'm no hypocrite, I can't pretend, I don't know how to pretend. My work is defined, I'm a cleaner and it is as easy as that. When everything is clean, I'm free to read. Isn't it?" Abdul said with confidence.

"I do not like it, I've told you," said Mr Bone as he turned to leave.

Chapter 40
Five Days Later

At 13.45pm, the kitchen alarm bell rang. It was a signal for all kitchen workers to identify themselves and go out to the open patio for observation. At this time, the trash truck came to collect the kitchen trash. Abdul identified himself and went to the patio. He chose a comfortable part in the patio and began leafing through the pages of the magazine.

"In great Britain, the old ban on Jews to taking up residences in the city of Leicester has been officially renounced. It is 800 years old ban. The Earl of Leicester, better known as the father of the British parliament, ordered the ban. The ban was placed in the year 1221 when Earl Simon de Montfort chaired the British parliament," read a verse in Abdul's magazine.

"Ever before the holocaust and Hitler, people have been at issues with them, so much as to ban them from living and taking residency in their cities and towns. What a holy city, Leicester," thought Abdul.

"Why lift the ban now, why?"

"One of the few places they have not inhabited and have been kept holy for such a long time. I wish I'd been to this holy city before now to take a handful of its soil as a souvenir," thought Abdul.

"Don't be naive, Jews have been living in Leicester for centuries, only that the ban was never officially lifted, so for documentation, it was officially lifted this week," admonished a mind.

"He is reading again," Edward whispered to Mr Bone.

Mr Bone looked around and saw Abdul bent in concentration over the pages of the magazine. He walked up to him.

"You must stop reading now!" Abdul heard a familiar voice growl near him. It was Mr Bone's voice he recollected, and looked up towards the voice.

"The disciplinary director will soon be here, he mustn't see you reading the magazine in here," said Mr

Bone.

"Oh, he wouldn't mind, he wouldn't be angry to meet a prisoner reading, after all we are being re-educated," replied Abdul.

"You must stop reading now," insisted Mr Bone.

"The director will think you ain't doing nothing, aren't working," said Mr Bone.

"Then tell him that I've done my own part of the duties for the hour. He will understand. He is no fool," insisted Abdul, unable to stop reading the article about the city of Leicester.

Mr Bone darted across the corridor behind the door that separated the kitchen from the washroom area and came back with a broomstick and a dustpan.

"You must get busy now," said Mr Bone, handing Abdul the pair.

Abdul accepted the two and pretended to be dusting the floor.

Minutes later the director came into the kitchen, he walked round and left. The trash truck had left too.

Abdul went back to the patio, arranged the trash drums and anchored in a corner and began to read again. Edward peeped into the patio and saw Abdul. He went to call Mr Bone.

"We need some help on the table to make the pancake, would you please tell Abdul to give us a hand. I've tried talking to him but he is busy reading in the patio," said Edward.

Mr Bone got visibly angry and darted towards the patio.

"Abdul!" he called out across the door that links the patio.

"Come and help in the kitchen, to prepare the pancakes," said Edward.

"I can't sir," replied Abdul.

"I'm a cleaner, not a cook, besides, I've just finished washing the washroom, arranging the trash drums," said Abdul.

"Use the kitchen hand gloves," said Mr Bone.

"I feel filthy, I don't want to touch any edible now," replied Abdul.

"I give you till the end of the day, if you don't improve on your conduct here, you will be dismissed from working in the kitchen," said Mr Bone, and went back to his table.

"Ok sir," replied Abdul.

Minutes later

"Go and speak with Abdul, strike a conversation on any topic," said Edward to Joe.

Edward waited until Joe and Abdul were deep into their conversation before he went to Mr Bone.

"You know what sir? That Islamist is boasting that he doesn't obey you or panic when you raise your voice and give ultimatums. He said he is not afraid of being dismissed from the kitchen. He is still there in the patio with Joe and some other prisoners telling them how tough he is," lied Edward.

Mr Bone nodded thoughtfully.

"I will get him," he said.

"Mr Bone is planning to dismiss you from working here in the kitchen," Edward said to Abdul on joining him and Joe on the patio.

"I'm not bordered," replied Abdul.

"I guess someone must have been talking bad about you to him," said Edward.

"Who might it be?" asked Abdul.

"I will find out for you," replied Edward.

The next day Edward approached Abdul.

"I've spoken to Mr Bone. I explained to him that you are a good guy and he has to exercise patience with you. He understood and promised to go it easy with you. Ok?" said Edward.

"OK," said Abdul.

"And the guy?" asked Abdul.

"Who?" inquired Edward.

"The person who's been talking bad about me to Mr Bone," said Abdul.

"Oh! I'm yet to find out," replied Edward.

"Though that is not very important, but we will fish him out with time," said Edward and turned to leave.

"Fish him out with time," echoed Abdul thoughtfully.

Two hours later, Edward went to Abdul.

"Could you please come help me prepare some soufflés?" Edward said to Abdul

"I'm sorry but I don't like to touch edibles. I hate cooking," replied Abdul.

The next minute, Edward was at Mr Bone's table.

"That Islamist is really very lazy. He wouldn't even help us make soufflés. He is not fit to work here in the kitchen. I don't know why you still retain him," complained Edward.

"What will you be doing after this?" asked Mr Pattern.

Mr Pattern was the assistant to Mr Bone.

"I will have five minutes rest, by which time they must have finished making preparations for the soufflés and I will get busy again cleaning up," replied Abdul as he mopped the floor.

"Do join them in preparing the soufflés," said Mr Pattern.

"I'm not a cook, I'm a cleaner," replied Abdul.

"Yes I know that, I'm only asking you for a favour," said Mr Pattern.

"I'm afraid I wouldn't want to do you this favour. I've got enough work to do as a cleaner," replied Abdul.

"Well, we won't force you to do it," murmured Pattern and turned to leave.

He went straight to Mr Bone, to discuss his observation.

"He's an asshole, saucy and arrogant. Let him get out of this kitchen," said Mr Pattern.

"He won't get past tomorrow," replied Mr Bone.

Chapter 41
The Next Morning

Abdul felt a little uncomfortable with the way he was looked at by the folks in the kitchen. There was this knowing and gleeful glint in their eyes. He went to work, mopped the floor, washed the pots, ladles and tables and cleaned the washroom. He took position in a corner and, while on the wait for the next round of cleaning, he opened a page on his magazine and began to read. He'd just read the second line of the first paragraph of the first article when Mr Bone touched him on the shoulder from behind.

"Go help the butchers cut the meat please," said Mr Bone.

"But it's not my sector sir," protested Abdul.

"I insist you go and help them now," said Mr Bone.

"Fact is that the infidels want to switch me on like a motor and switch me off when they want. And if I get switched once, I will remain switched forever," thought Abdul.

"I prefer to resign from working in this kitchen instead of suffering this discrimination. There are so many inmates to be sent to the butchery, but I'm the person you have chosen. See them in the patio chatting. You can transfer me from the sanitary department to the butchery sector," said Abdul.

"I won't transfer you, I insist you go help in the butchery," said Mr Bone.

"I resign from working here," Abdul said and turned to leave.

Abdul knew that Mr Bone couldn't send him to the punishment cell as the disciplinary director won't allow that. After all he, Abdul, was right. He was not working in the butchery sector and as such has no business giving them any helping hand except on voluntary basis. He had obligations as a cleaner. Besides, though working was compulsory in federal prisons, no one had the right to force anybody to work or render punishment for refusal to work in any particular sector. One must be given a free hand to work in the sector he deems fit.

"Are you going?" inquired Mr Pattern.

"No, you are sending me away," replied Abdul.

"Now you will have enough time to read your Arabic literature," said Mr Bone.

"Allahu Akbar!" said Abdul.

Abdul crossed the doorway and waited by the corner for a warder to come walk him to the cell.

"He is a fuckin guy," said Mr Bone.

"Very Boring guy," said Mr Pattern.

"I lost my job today," Abdul said to cell mates.

"Why?" asked Mendes as he turned the tap to fill his plastic cup.

"That arrogant kitchen twit. I can't stand him and his humiliating attitudes any longer," replied Abdul.

"The warder in the kitchen?"

"Yes," said Abdul.

"It's good for you. I've always considered working in the kitchen to be a very serious job," said Rodrigue.

"Why?" asked Mendes.

"It isn't safe working with those junkies and freaks with knives at their disposal," said Rodrigue.

"Most of them in the kitchen and butchery don't

have any nostril hairs," added Rodrigue.

"That means?" asked Mendes.

"Their nostril hairs have been eaten up by drugs — cocaine they use," said Rodrigue.

"Your produce, a good produce," joked Mendes.

"Well, I'm proud of that produce. If you don't know how to use it, it fucks you up, just like most things in life," said Rodrigue.

Abdul laughed.

Mendes took a gulp from his cup. The water smelled of minerals.

"Prison, it's tough. Look at me drinking tap water," said Mendes.

"It's good," said Abdul.

"How?"

"Positive psychology, eh?"

"Since there is no alternative, we'd better find what's available good and tasty, eh?" said Mendes.

"Not just that," said Abdul.

"First of all, I believe the tap water here is good enough for consumption, but also it's good to drink tap water, as a friend of the environment. It is sort of contributing to environmental cleaning and preservation.

You know, tons of plastic is used in the yearly packaging of bottled water. The chemicals and heat released into the atmosphere during the making and disposal of the water containers also contribute to climatic changes. And remember that any tiny contribution towards keeping the environment and climate clean and lowering green house gases and temperature helps immensely since the USA, the world super power, moral custodian and global police, have adamantly refused to sign the Kyoto accord to reduce climatic heating," said Abdul.

"You would make a good environmentalist," said Rodrigue.

"Will always find one way or another to criticize the USA, eh terrorist?" said Mendes laughing.

"Not really, It is the ozone nonsense, if a hole had not been opened in the ozone layer, who would be bordered about global warming. But now we have to. One cannot turn deaf ears and blind eyes to the alarming 5% annual increase of melanoma – skin cancer caused by excessive exposure to ultra violet rays of the sun. The earth is getting hotter," said Abdul.

Three Days Later

Since US federal law requires that inmates work at least 40 hours per week, and earn at least $1 per hour of service, Abdul was sent to work in the bakery which is situated next to the kitchen. On his first week in the bakery, he was overheard a conversation going on between two inmates.

"Oh! How I hate that guy. There is this murderous urge that seizes me every time I see him. And on realizing that I cannot kill him because of the consequences, it makes me even more angry," said Joe.

"You need not kill him, he's not worth it. I feel like that whenever I see that Arab Islamist named Abdul. But I just took time to plot and get him out from the kitchen so that I would stop seeing him," said Edward.

"How?" asked Joe.

"Use Mr Bone and Mr Pattern against him. They are easy to use. Just tell them he is lazy. Put him to the defensive and launch your offensive incessantly. He wouldn't last a month here. He will be fired. It works. At least it worked on the Islamist," said Edward.

Abdul went back into the bakery.

CHAPTER 42

"What has this Islamic terrorist come to tell me that is so important?" thought the Prison director as Abdul crossed the doorway into his office.

"Have your seat," said the director, waving Abdul to a seat.

Abdul pulled the chair and sat down quietly.

"So?"

"What is it you want to tell me?" asked the director.

"I've come to let you know of an escape buzz I over-heard," said Abdul.

The director eyed him suspiciously over the rims of his half-moon spectacles held at the tip of his nose.

"Who is escaping?" asked the director.

"Joe, Edward and others I wouldn't know for now.

Joe and Edward are the leaders of the escape plot. It will be on Tuesday night at about 10.30pm. A helicopter will land in the prison patio," said Abdul.

"Good, if the buzz is authentic and they get busted eventually, you will receive your reward. Look out for more information," said the Director.

Abdul left the office. He obtained no further information about the escape plot before Tuesday – the D-day.

The patio was dimly lit on Tuesday night and warders lay ambush with their automatic riffles. At exactly 10.30pm, a helicopter noiselessly landed on the patio. Joe, Edward and four other inmates rushed out from their cells towards the helicopter, whose doors were held open. At that moment, the patio lights came brightly alit and security men rushed out from every corner, shooting and shouting orders.

"Freeze! Freeze! Your plot is foiled! Freeze!" shouted the security guards and warders shooting into the air - warning shoots.

The rotors of the helicopter got damaged with bullet shots, and it failed to hop back into the air.

The pilot, Joe, Edward and the rest of the group were

arrested, handcuffed, beaten and led away. The prisoners were taken to solitary confinement and the pilots were handed over to the police and appeared before a judge within the next 24 hours. They were charged with trespassing, invading a federal prison, aiding and abetting the escape of federal prisoners, kidnapping prisoners in federal custody.

Joe, Edward and others lost their chance of winning parole any time soon. They weren't charged with any crime because it is the right of any human being deprived of liberty to try to escape and regain freedom, as long as it is done without violence. It is a natural urge.

"Good, now we are on an even score," thought Abdul as he looked out the hatch of his cell door and saw Joe and Edward handcuffed, kicked, slapped and dragged away to solitary confinement.

Chapter 43
December, 30th 2006 (One Week Later)

"What a cold day," thought Abdul as the cell door squeaked open and colder air from the outside swept into the cell. The temperature in Washington was minus 10 degrees celcius. There had been a snowstorm the previous night, and the roads and streets of Washington were covered with snow.

"Good Morning sir," said Abdul.

"Morning," clipped the warder who had come to take him to go do some road work: clearing snow from the streets of Washington. It was a privilege given to prisoners who had demonstrated good conduct, and prisoners with short sentences or those who had a very short time left to serve. It was considered a privilege because the prisoner would see the outside world and take in some fresh air. It was the first time Abdul was invited to work outside the prison premises.

In the company of five other prisoners, Abdul got busy shovelling snow into the dump truck. Three warders were at some twenty meter distance, supervising them. Abdul's ears were aching from the cold. He ran the back of his hand across his nostrils and sniffed in, his mind at work. The dump truck got filled with snow and ready to drive off to dump the snow. Another truck was already positioning to be filled. The idea that was shaping up in Abdul's mind was desperate and dangerous. He'd heard and had thought of escape since he'd been in the prison, but his idea of escape had been in the night when nobody would be watching and all guards would be sleeping or weak and tired. Not an escape with the guards some twenty meters away, tightly clutching their semi-automatic riffles which they had orders to use. Abdul looked over his shoulder at the guard behind him, the only one that had a clear view of him at that moment. But he was not looking his way, and was not paying attention.

"He won't have any inhibition to use the rifle," a mind said to Abdul.

Everything in him, all his senses, his heartbeat, his blood pressure quickened. He knew what he would face if he got caught trying to escape. He would stay in solitary confinement for ninety days, lose his right to parole and will receive some beatings and humiliation and could even be gunned down in the process. He intoned a silent prayer and dropped into a crouch and disappeared under the truck, holding the back axle of the truck, and crossed his legs tightly over it at the other end and hung quietly as the truck rolled away. He waited for growling from the guards, ordering him to crawl out from under the truck, but none came. When the truck was at about 500 meters away from the site, he let go of his grip and dropped onto the chilly wet ground and lay still, the cold penetrating the fabric of his clothes and numbing his body. He waited on the snow until the truck moved off some distance before he crawled up to his feet. He crossed the road into an adjacent street. He wriggled out of his prison winter jacket and dumped it into a snow covered street trash bin, and continued down the street to the subway station.

"I must get away from the vicinity as quickly as possible," he thought as he boarded the train.

Chapter 44
The City Orphanage, Washington

Everything was fine in the city orphanage and the children developed healthily. Children above the age of seventeen were allowed to leave the orphanage and start a new life on their own, and new children were admitted into the thirty head capacity orphanage run with extreme efficiency by the astute Mrs Poet. Every day parents came from all walks of American life to the orphanage to adopt a child. Children chosen by prospective parents were invited into the director's office to meet the new parents. It was a sacred and happy moment for children in the home, because it meant a chance to have a family, a father, mother and possibly brothers, a chance to avert being dispensed into the wild open world at seventeen, to start a new life.

Hope, Nerry, Benneth, John and Omar stayed in the orphanage for years watching other children getting adopted and taken to their respective families, sometimes for good and at other times, when they were unfortunate, they were brought back to the homes for various reasons.

"Too stubborn."

"Sorry we can't stand him."

The five children refused all prospective parents for no apparent reasons and they were so close to themselves.

"I'm a Muslim right?" said Omar to Mrs Poet.

"Yes my son," replied Mrs Poet, studying him, wondering what was going on in his mind, what was making him wonder about being a Muslim.

She waited, expecting more questions.

"Why am I not a Christian?" asked Omar.

"Because your parents are Muslims," answered Mrs Poet.

"He has a father, and was brought here by the federal court. And Shariah law depicts death for anyone who converts from Islam to Christianity," she thought.

"But I'd rather you stay a Muslim, at least for now,

because in my honest opinion, both religions are one and the same, they are both monotheistic and ..." said Mrs Poet.

"What is monotheistic?" interrupted Omar.

It comes from the word monotheism, which means the belief that there is only one God, therefore both religions being monotheistic means that both believe that there is only one God," replied Mrs Poet.

"God?" asked Omar.

"It is the name given by the Christians to the supernatural being, the creator of heaven and earth. This same supernatural being, our creator, is referred to as Allah by the Islamic faith. The difference between the two religions lies in the medium through which each faith try to relate to this supernatural creator, and the position the faithful of the religion adopt when they communicate with the God or Allah through prayers. The Christians believe that Jesus Christ, the founder of the Christian religion, is the son of God and the gateway to heaven, to God's kingdom. And the Muslims believe that Prophet Mohammed the founder of the Islamic religion is the great prophet of God, sorry I mean the great prophet of Allah, and the only gateway to Allah and his kingdom.

The common thing between the two faiths is that neither of them believes in the present life, they both believe in the life after death, the next life, where there is no death, no disease, no sickness, needs, necessities, no struggle for dominance, no want and no ambition. A life where there is no hegemony, imperialism, terrorism and terrorists. The absolute ideal life where God, I mean Allah, Jesus Christ and Prophet Mohammed will be in bone and flesh blessing and caressing everybody," said Mrs Poet.

"God is Allah right?" asked Omar.

"And Allah is God," said Mrs Poet.

"But Jesus Christ is not Mohammed eh? And Mohammed is no Jesus Christ?" asked Omar.

"No, Jesus is not Mohammed and Mohammed is not Jesus but both of them know and believe in the same supernatural creator. They are both great prophets of the great creator. Both of them live in heaven, in the kingdom of the creator and they are great friends," said Mrs Poet..

"Interesting isn't it?" added Mrs Poet.

"Yes it is," said Omar.

"Now go and play with the other kids," said Mrs Poet dismissing the child.

* * *

Abdul felt light as he alighted from the subway station at the fifth stop the train made. All the fear of being hit by a warder's bullet disappeared. He was very far from the prison premises and the vicinity of the roadwork site. But apprehension abounded. He looked around him and at the people hurrying in and out of the station. The people were busy and headed to someplace, nobody seemed to care about the next or notice he is a fugitive, a prison escapee as he thought. Five years had passed and so much had changed in the world. The World seemed fresher and the people more beautiful and strong and the whole place lively quite unlike the dull stasis of the prison premises.

"Now what?" thought Abdul.

"I must find somewhere to hide."

"It's not the time or hour to hide, you've been hiding for long enough time in the prison, a terrible sanctuary. It's time to show up and use your abilities now. Find a way to disguise a little and get out of the state of

Washington. Soon they will be flashing your photo in the TV, broadcasting your description in the Radios," suggested a mind.

"The Washington police department, the CIA, FBI, the terrorist task force, the Homeland security and the whole lot of 365 million fear and terror stricken Americans will soon be looking for me," thought Abdul.

"Help me Oh Allah. Don't let me be recaptured, because it's been fine so long. I squealed on fellow prisoners and was granted an opportunity of an out of prison roadwork in compensation for my collaboration in foiling a massive prison escape attempt. While on roadwork, I made my own escape and there was no immediate chase. And it's nice to have achieved all these on my own. But right now oh Allah, I need to continue in this my new-found freedom and I will need all the good luck and guidance you could offer. I wouldn't need the usual Arab resentment from the people as I speak and wangle my way out of the state of Washington and the USA. So help me Allah.

Allahu Akbar," he intoned silently.

He paused to look at the poster across the street.

"Men's Barbing Salon

Come in and have a wonderful cut"

Abdul crossed the street and went into the barbing salon. While waiting for a turn to cut his hair, he picked up a newspaper from the table and held it up and as close to his face as possible and began to read. He read the story under the caption: 'Saddam Hussein Executed'.

'Officially, Saddam Hussein was hanged having been found guilty for his role in the 1982 killings of 148 Shiite Muslims. They were rounded up and executed summarily after a failed assassination attempt in the Iraqi city of Dujail. They attacked Saddam's motorcade aiming to assassinate the Iraqi president. Saddam survived.

The American President said thus about the execution:

"It is a testament to the Iraqi people's resolve to move forward after decades of oppression that, despite his terrible crimes against his own people, Saddam Hussein received a fair trial. This would not have been possible without the Iraqi people's determination to create a society governed by the rule of law. Bringing Saddam Hussein to justice will not end the violence in Iraq, but it is an important milestone on Iraq's course to becoming a democracy that can govern, sustain, and defend itself, and be an ally in the war on terror."

Saddam's defence was based on the fact that the 148 Shiites were killed according to Iraqi law, because they attempted to assassinate the president of Iraq," continued the report.

"Self defence," thought Abdul as his mind let loose into a deep rumination.

Sometime in the '90's, after the first gulf war – 'Operation Desert Storm', an ex-American president visited Kuwait, and there was a botched attempt to assassinate him. The ex-president survived.

Saddam Hussein survived an assassination attempt and killed all the 148 assailants. An ex American President survived an assassination attempt and...

There were 150,000 American military troops on Iraqi soil the day Saddam Hussein was executed.

Self defence.

Saddam Hussein seemed to be playing a dangerous game with self defence for a very long time. In the late '80's into 1990, after the Iran-Iraq war, Saddam Hussein was in dire need of capital to rebuild his country from the spoil of 8 years of war. Kuwait and Iraq are both members of the oligarchy named OPEC. Every member country of OPEC has a quota of oil output allocated to them. Like that, the oligarchy controlled the international crude oil market and price at a profitable rate for the members. The United States of America was fighting oil cartels round the world to bring down oil prices to sustain America's addiction to oil. In a behind the scene negotiation between the United States oil negotiators and Kuwaiti government, American oil refinery companies refined crude oil inside Kuwait and exported the refined petroleum to USA, thus beating down the world international oil prices because the USA was buying less crude oil from the international market. The price per barrel of crude oil obeyed the economic law of demand and supply. Iraq was loosing money, but Kuwait could not be nipped and reprimanded by OPEC, 'cause they were committing the economic crime with their hands well gloved. Iraq complained, but Kuwait argued it committed no crime or betrayal, that it wasn't putting out any more crude oil to the international market than its authorized quota. Kuwait was correct because OPEC oil quota referred to crude oil and what the Americans were ferrying across the oceans from Kuwait to the USA was refined petrol.

Smart eh? Very smart indeed.

Saddam Hussein couldn't stand the betrayal, the absurd daylight cheating any longer, especially as Kuwait began making repeated demands for Iraq to pay up debts owed to Kuwait, debt incurred during the long war with Iran. In his violent sense of justice, he invaded and annexed Kuwait to stem the economic haemorrhage. Saddam claimed that Kuwait was a part of Iraq, and the mainland Iraq wanted it to be integrated back to the Iraqi nation. America's interest and under the table oil racket was disrupted by Saddam's move and claims, and the hold down they had on the oil cartels threatened. In their diplomatic, intelligent and civilized sense of justice, the USA coalesced with the whole world under the UNO umbrella to fight Iraq and expel the Iraqi forces out of Kuwait in what was christened 'Operation Desert Storm'. This was Abdul's version of the details of the war.

Abdul never liked Saddam Hussein, especially for attacking and gassing the Kurds, disrupting Shiia religious celebrations and repressing Shiite Muslims of Iraq. Abdul was a Shiite Muslim. Besides, Saddam didn't entirely believe in Islam. He even had his own political religious group - Baath Party, which he'd meticulously turned into a somewhat religious group. And Saddam was a buddy of Washington. While the Iraq – Iran war reigned, Saddam was a tool used to punish Iran and the Ayatollahs for their stance in taking Americans hostages in Tehran in 1979. Once a friend, he later became an enemy that must be hunted down and hung.

Just like the Supreme Disciple, who was once a buddy of the USA, later he became an enemy and is now on the run for his life. But quite unlike Saddam-USA saga, in the USA- Jihadist Movement saga, both the hunter and the hunted are on the defensive and offensive at the same time.

But is it coincidence that he escaped from jail, the day Saddam was executed and the US President assured that the death of Saddam will help the war on terror? Why was Saddam executed during Hajj? Just before the start of Eid al-Adha. Could this pave the path for a stronger Arab nationalism and Islamic renaissance? This is a time of peace, not a period of vengeance, punishment and retribution. This is a slap on Islam. This is sin against Islam," he thought, as the barber beckoned to him to be seated and have his haircut.

Abdul took a seat, adjusted himself in the seat and the barber went to work.

"Saddam Hussein executed for crimes against humanity. Saddam Hussein was a bad man. He was a cruel man. But he was not worse than anybody," he thought and his mind waded into many atrocities that had happened around the global village and particularly in the Middle East.

He thought of his cousin Nadia, his only known relative, who died in the Palestinian refugee camp at Sabra, in 1982, killed by the Phallangists. In that year, in Sabra and Chatila, more than two thousand Palestinian civilian refugees were massacred by the Pallangists - a group of Lebanese Christian Militiamen. Israel had just invaded and occupied west Beirut, after Palestinian Guerrillas had assassinated an elected Lebanese leader – Bashir Jermayel, a Christian. This generated a hatred of the Phallangists over the Palestinians. On the orders of the then Israeli defence minister who led the invasion and occupation of Lebanon, the Phallangists went to hunt the Palestinian, and to massacre them till the last man, and they went to do so in the Palestinian civilian refugee camps. Abdul had never forgiven the Phallangists for their act, and till date, nobody has been held responsible for that crime against humanity – genocide.

Since the 1948 inception of the State on the so called 'land without a people for a people without a land', the Palestinian people and Arabs in general had been living in permanent state of fear and insecurity, fear for everything including their lives and property, including the massacre at Qibya in 1953, the Dier Yassin massacre in 1994, the Baruch Goldsteins massacre of Arab worshippers at Hebron in 1995. The bloodbath in that portion of the world, the Arab-Israel conflict has come to a point when the civilised world should dissect, reassemble and settle the issues without economic, cultural and political or electoral undertones. The free world and the UNO have all the economic, military and diplomatic muscle and ability to promote and establish order and legality in the middle-east and create the state of Palestine alongside the state of Israel. It is because of this quagmire that 'monster' like Saddam Hussein came to be," thought Abdul.

Salladin came to mind and Abdul smiled cruelly.

The barber looked somewhat quizzically at him and continued.

He was in nostalgic relish of the days of the legendary Islamic Commander Salladin, who fought and drove Christian crusaders out of Jerusalem in the 'Battle of Jerusalem', which started when Muslims conquered the then Roman Jerusalem in 638 and dominated it until the middle ages. In 1099, the European Christian crusaders waged a great battle and seized the control of Jerusalem, but around 1199, Salladin took it over from the crusaders after a bloody war. And from then on, the city of Jerusalem became a very important spring board for the then expanding Islamic empire that spread to Egypt, North Africa, Western Europe including Spain and Southern France, Vienna to the Balkans. In those days, the Islamic civilization was at per with the Western civilization.

"The Islamic civilization must be revived, the Islamic kingdom must reign. The infidels will lose, they are losing already. The future is against them, the children of Islam will celebrate the future. Palestine is Arab, Palestine is a State, and Palestinians need a home. The UNO resolutions 242 and 338 stipulated the establishment of the two independent sovereign national states – Israel and Palestine," thought Abdul as the barber signalled that he had finished.

He came out from the saloon twenty minutes later wearing a clean and cropped head, a clean-shaven chin, feeling strange, but safe.

Some thirty minutes later, he was riding in a Greyhound bus to Portland Oregon where there is the greatest concentration of Arabs in the US. Although he knew no particular person in Portland, he knew many people in Sao Jose, Detroit, but they were people he met in the Jihadist Movement. It would betray his alibi as a dead collaborator and spark off another manhunt.

He got to Oregon uneventfully and, after three weeks in Portland, he obtained a false US driver's licence and a fake US Passport. In possession of false documents and a stolen car, Abdul was speeding on interstate highway 35 to join the eight-lane world trade bridge that connects Texas with Nuevo Laredo Mexico. Thoughts fleeted down his mind as he sped along the highway to safety in Mexico. Nathan suddenly came to mind.

"If not for that son of a bitch named Nathan, I wouldn't be on this run today. He deceived and betrayed me big time. Who knows where and what he is doing with his life now"

CHAPTER 45
Nuevo Laredo, Mexico
July 2025

It was a bright and busy day in Nuevo Laredo, Mexico. Abdul was having a strong premonitory feeling. He had lived in a half dozen Mexican cities all these years, dodging the FBI agents and the USA Marshals services both agencies have a long established offices in Mexico cities and hosts websites which enlists mug shots of fugitives wanted in the USA. He'd come back to Nuevo Laredo not long ago, and taken a job as a receptionist in a four-star hotel west of Nuevo Laredo. He looked up towards the hotel entrance door and saw a young couple marching hand in hand behind a luggage-toting bell-hop.

"Beautiful, happy and educated looking couple,"

thought Abdul.

Omar and Hope were on prenuptial holiday to Mexico. They both recently received PhD degrees from George Washington University.

"Buenos vindos e Buenos tardes senhores," said Abdul, with a fixed professional smile as they approached the reception counter.

"Buenos tarde Senhore," replied Omar.

"Como vai?" he added.

"Mui bien," replied Abdul.

"Doble?" asked Abdul.

"Si," replied Omar.

"Cuanto tiempo ustedes se van a quedar?" asked Abdul.

"Yo no abla mui espanol," replies Omar.

"Disculpa mi senhor," said Abdul.

"How long are you staying?" asked Abdul, rephrasing the question in English.

"Two weeks," replied Omar with strictly American accent, though he looked unmistakably an Arab.

"Fill this please," said Abdul pushing a form to Omar.

Omar looked at the form before him and picked up

the pen beside it and began to write.

Name: Mr and Mrs Omar Allan

Nationality: American

Length of Stay: Two weeks

Heading to: Chicxulab, Yucatan Peninsula. He signed the form and pushed it back to the tall strong and healthy looking receptionist, that looked to be in his fifties, with an Arabian face and accent.

Abdul saw the ring on Omar's small finger as he pushed the form to him.

It was unmistakably his ring, the ring he inherited from his father Allan and gave to Omar at the Ronald Reagan National airport Washington as they parted, when he was taken into custody and eventually convicted and thrown into the federal prison in Washington. His pulse increase, his pupils dilated, his senses quickened. He picked the form up quickly and lifted it to his face, covering his face. He paused, swallowed and breathed deeply in to suppress any hint of anxiety and surprise in his facial expression and voice.

He read the form.

"Omar Allan?" he said, his heart pounding.

"Yes," beamed Omar.

"You are an Arab?" asked Abdul the receptionist.

"Arab American, Palestinian American to be precise," replied Omar.

"Your wife?" asked Abdul looking at Hope, his gaze lingered on her face for some moment and bounced back to Omar.

A heavy gleam of satisfaction and joy livened up his face, the satisfaction of a father who located a lost child. His lips curved into a pleasant smile.

Omar guessed and tried to explain the silent words in his looks and smile

"He is happy for seeing a fellow Arab in this part of the world," thought Omar..

"Yes, she is my fiancé," replied Omar with a smile.

Abdul selected the key to the best suite in the fifteen-floor hotel and handed it to the bellhop who had been standing quietly beside the counter at a distance from the guests. It is a suite that's often reserved for the hotel's special guests. "Enjoy your stay," said Abdul the receptionist.

"Thank you," replied Omar.

Abdul looked on as the bellhop led the couple to the elevator and they disappeared into the elevator car. He was surprised at his emotional control - that he didn't shout out loud, jump up, hug him and say "oh son, my son!, how I missed you".

As the elevator car started on its ascent, his lips drew back firstly with a suggestive smile, then to a sob, hearty and joyful sob of emotion, a pure unalloyed emotion of a father for a son.

A pause.

Pictures and memories of events came fleeting through Abdul's mind, his life all those years in Mexico, his escape from prison, his stay in jail, giving Omar the ring at the airport, his arrest, the flight from Cairo to Washington, his life in Cairo Egypt, Amina's death, Bahrian Island, Saudi Arabia, the Royal Saudi guest hotel, the failed attempt and Nathan the Jew.

"The Supreme Disciple?"

"They will never catch him."

"And Zuba?"

"He was ready to forgive me, ready to give me a second chance."

"Allah be with you wherever you are, comrade Zuba," mused Abdul.

Chapter 46
Lalibela, Ethiopia
January, 2025

"This is where I belong," murmured Nathan as he stopped to kiss the mossy moist sacred wall of the cave. Dressed in a flowing white robe and in the company of two other priests and a deacon as they clumped up the slippery steps of the winding tunnel to the worship hall, one of the eleven stone hewn churches the Ethiopian orthodox church built by King Lalibela some 800 years ago, and this cloudy northern Ethiopian town was named after him. The priests nodded religiously to the hermits sitting in reddish walled tombs as they went from one church to another to worship and preach. The atmosphere was serene in the Bet Medhane Alem church, the largest Orthodox Church in Ethiopia. Worshippers knelt in quietude on the clean stone floor as the priests padded across. It was the first day Nathan was preaching and conducting worship as a priest after years as a deacon during which period he learnt and upgraded his eloquence in Geez language – the language of worship in Lalibela churches. He felt an inherent peace and happiness as he looked across the faces of the worshippers in the sanctuary and bent to read a message from an old book of the New Testament.

He paused to let what he'd read sink in. Nathan was happy that at least he was accepted whole heartedly and respected among the folks of this town, that he was helping to resuscitate the church and its rituals that appeared to have been lost in the mist of time since the advent of Christianity in Ethiopia in the fourth century.

"I belong to the people that respect me and listen to me. I wasn't a good enough Jew. I wasn't Jewish enough to have a good and descent living in Israel or marry a white Jewish girl – Askhenazic Jew. But I was Jewish enough to suffer the odds associated with Semitism. I belong to the Ethiopian people. I'm a good Orthodox," he thought, his heart blossoming with happiness.

Nathan dejewified while serving time in a Riyahd prison predominated by Arabs and Muslims. Today, the celebration of the Orthodox Christimas, he had no regrets.

CHAPTER 47
Guantanamo Bay, Cuba

Zuba recited the common Jihadist Movement hate passage against the infidels by mind, his gaze distant and fixed on the American flag behind the table as Captain Caldwell, an American interrogator tried to coax him into confessing. He'd been trying hard two times a day, every day for the past ninety days.

"America doesn't hate the Arabs, Islam, Muslims and not even the Jihadist Movement, because the USA harbours no hate for anyone and it's in the most sincere interest of the United States to institute a free uni-po-lar world devoid of hate, partiality and terrorism. The United States prays for her enemies to change, that they will someday not only live the American dream but will become part of it, for it's forever been the American dream to spread liberal democracy, abundance of food, health and lots of human freedom and dignity to all corners of the globe. That the enemies of America understand the good and progress that the United States is bringing to the free world. It's not in the least interest of the USA to keep you a prison for the rest of your life here in Guantanamo or put you and your likes to the electric chair," said Captain Caldwell pausing for a moment to study Zuba before continuing.

"America the righteous," adjoined a split mind of Zuba's that was listening to Caldwell's oratory.

"Oh Allah don't hide thy mercy from the Arabs, from the Muslims. Allah of Mohammed and Islam cast thy wrath on the infidel, because the infidel's deceitful propaganda and despotism have spoken against Islam and the Jihadist Movement with a lying tongue. For our love, devotion and dedication to thee, the infidel is our adversary," prayed Zuba.

"Look at what America and the US justice department wants to do for you in exchange for the truth and all relevant information on the Jihadist Movement and the whereabouts of the Supreme Disciple," continued Captain Caldwell.

"Let the infidel be clothed with shame and let her be enshrouded with her own confusion and thy wrath as with a mantle. Let Satan, destruction and downfall besiege the Infidel. Let her days as a hegemon, imperialist and as a despot be few and let the Islamic Renaissance reign so that the children of Islam will celebrate the future. And let the infidel's generations be continually powerless and despised like the children and widow of a fallen tyrant. Let the greatest of hurricanes and earthquake besiege the despotic infidel, spoil her labour and cut off her prosperity," continued Zuba in his prayer.

"You will have your sentence reduced to 10 years with no hard labour," crooned Captain Caldwell.

"But oh Allah, deliver and exult me and Islam, because we Muslims are pure and humble and have been humiliated so much by the infidel, our hearts wounded hugely within us. Help the children of Islam and the Islamic civilization and ambitions according to thy mercy so that the infidels may know that you are a living Allah, the Allah of Mohammed," prayed Zuba.

"At the end of your sentence, you will receive a $20 million reward to start a new life in the United States or any country of your choice," said Captain Caldwell.

"Shake up the world oh Allah and bring the infidel to her knees, let the infidel grow old, let her memories engulf her dreams and let her wither so that the Islamic civilization and kingdom may reign," intoned Zuba.

"A new document, identity and nationality will be arranged for you. Use your brain, it's all about benefits for you and your future, it's far better for you," said the Captain.

"Allahu Akbar!.," intoned Zuba.

"What do you have to tell us eh Mr Zuba? Where is the Supreme Disciple? When, where and what is the next target of the Jihadist Movement?" quizzed Captain Caldwell.

"I've nothing to tell you. I don't know nothing" hissed Zuba, looking over the captain's shoulder into the open at the electrified barbwire fence that separated the famous mined field from the high walls of the Guatanamo prison, the walls that separated him from the seas, freedom and civilization. It had been three and a half months since he was scooped off the streets by a joint team of FBI and CIA terrorist task force agents as he alighted from the AL- Makdum University theatre in Zambounga, a city north of Basilan Islands south of

Philippines. The city was shrouded by thick jungles and mangrove swamp. Basilan Island is the base of Abu Sayyaf, a Filipino Muslim group who'd been fighting for a separate Islamic state in the predominantly Roman Catholic Christian Philippine nation. Abu Sayyaf is an ally group of the Jihadist Movement whose leader Janjlani also fought on the side of the USA during the Afghan – Soviet war, as did the Supreme Disciple of the Jihadist Movement.

Zuba spent two days in 'Clark', an American air-force base in the Philippines which was reactivated after the 9/11 attacks on the WTC and defence department of the Pentagon, and the increased sharing of intelligence on the Abu Sayyaf group between the US government and the Philippines government.

"You're playing too tough son, and..." said captain Caldwell as he rose and left the interrogation room in frustration.

"The son of a bitch is not cooperating. This has lasted for 90 days and we don't have the all the time in the world, the homeland, America, is on a red alert warning of a terrorist attacks. I mean the earlier we get the information from him the better. Let's get it from him willy-nilly," said Captain Caldwell to the Naval Base Commander.

"Torture and pressure tactics, you mean?" asked the Base Commander.

"Yes," replied Captain Caldwell sternly.

"Won't that be violating the civil liberties rights?" asked Mr Patterson, a former attaché to the state department.

"Information obtained by pressure and torture tactics cannot be used in the court and he, I mean the victim can sue, and even the US government can charge you for battery," he added.

"The information we want most are the whereabouts of the Supreme Disciple of the Jihadist Movement, about the nature and targets of future attacks on the homeland. The Supreme Disciple is already condemned, taking him to court when captured will be for mere formalities," said Captain Caldwell.

"Here is not the USA, it is Guantanamo Naval Base Cuba, a piece of the United States in Cuba, a US protected territory. An Islet conquered by the United States in 1898 during the Pan American war. And in 1934, an American-Cuban accord warrants its indefinite occupation by the USA until a new accord to the contrary is signed. Yes we can torture him, this is Cuba, torture and repression is allowed here. It is Fidel's trademark," said the Base Commander.

"That's why they were brought here, because resistance and Ometta were anticipated. Here is like a hand gloves for us. Torture, pressure and drugs could be used to break their resistance and Ometta code, and extract the needed information to save the free world. They can't sue in the US courts because it wasn't committed on the US soil and they are not US citizens or permanent residents," he added.

Mr Patterson made a resigned shrug of his shoulders and said nothing.

"Do your job Captain," said the Naval Commander.

"I'd rather we use the truth serum," Captain Caldwell suggested.

"Good," obliged the Naval Commander.

"Thank you Commander," said Captain Caldwell and turned to leave for the forensic Science department of the Naval Base.

Dr Goodluck, a short balding man, was in the balcony of the laboratory complex when Captain Caldwell approached him. Goodluck was in one of his most lucid moments, wearing beige Jeans and a T-shirt, one of the rare moments he was not in a laboratory coat. He was crouching over the balcony rail as captain Caldwell made his request.

He listened carefully and hurried into the laboratory when Caldwell finished. It was another twenty five minutes before he came out clinching a bottle in his right hand.

"This is an absolute dose," he said as he handed Captain Caldwell a bottle of the truth serum.

"Thanks doc," said Captain Caldwell.

"It depresses a guy to a point he cannot coordinate any lie, he only says the truth as he knows it," said Doctor Goodluck.

"Even a guy who's taken a vaccine against all depressive drugs?" Joked Captain Caldwell.

"Even depression itself," indulged the doctor.

"What's this one called?" probed Captain Caldwell.

"It's Sodium Pentothal."

"A good one, we'd once used it," said Captain Caldwell, and turned to leave.

Two hours later Captain Caldwell was back in the interrogation room with Zuba. He allowed some time to give the serum enough time to ready Zuba.

"So what have you got to tell me Mr Zuba?" Began Captain Caldwell.

"About what?" said Zuba.

"The attacks in Riyahd Royal Palace and at the government guest house?"

"Oh those attacks, they were wasted opportunities, they were planned and executed by us, but all the Jahadists involved are dead now," said Zuba.

"Us who?" quizzed Captain Caldwell.

"Why did all the Jihadists involved died?"

"Because they failed the Jihadist Movement, the Movement supports no failure, no comedy," replied Zuba.

"Any new attacks coming soon against the USA and her interests?"

"A lot," answered Zuba.

"Like...?"

"Anything American is a target," replied Zuba.

"Anything?"

"Yes, anything," replied Zuba.

"Operation Destroy the Infidel will never end until

the infidel hegemon is brought to her knees and the Islamic Kingdom is established. I want to strangle you and set this whole base ablaze," yeaned Zuba.

"Do the Jihadist Movement have nukes?"

"Yes we do, and they will be used at an opportune time."

"Where are the nukes?" asked Captain Caldwell.

"Everything is in Tora Bora."

"Where in Tora Bora?"

"In the caves, only the good one knows the exact location," said Zuba.

"Who is the good one?" asked Captain Caldwell.

"You joking right? Of course you know the good one. Everyone knows him and his goodness."

"The Supreme Disciple?"

"Allah bless him," replied Zuba.

"The Supreme Disciple is safe in his sanctuary."

"Where?" probed Captain Caldwell.

"In Tora Bora caves."

"In which of the Caves?"

"I don't know, there are so many of them in Tora Bora".

"Do you think he is still alive?" probed the Captain.

"Very much alive. He got healthier after the Shamshaad swindle. He communicates with the elite disciples every forth-night. He will never die. He will be the last Arab, the last Muslim to die. Allah will forever protect and guide him," extolled Zuba

"When is the next attack coming?" asked the Captain.

"Any time it is convenient for foot soldiers of the Movement, and any time it is politically significant for the Movement, at the time most damage will be inflicted on the infidels," replied Zuba.

Captain Caldwell sighed and looked murderously at Zuba.

"You will pay for all this hate. You son of a bitch," hissed the Captain and rose to leave the room.

"You sound very silly and unintelligent like that. Do you think I give a damn how much and for how long I pay? No I don't care provided the infidel hegemon pays even more. We are already in hell. Think we are afraid of the devil? Now, we can embrace the devil," said Zuba.

"Sergent!" the Captain called out.

A warder appeared by the doorway.

"Take him to his cell," ordered the Captain.

* * *

Behind the reception counters of the hotel Dos Amigos in Nuevo Laredo Mexico, Abdul was going through the stock of his life. Rodrigue suddenly came to mind.

CHAPTER 48
Caqueta, Southern Columbia

In an alley in Brooklyn New York, a junkie unfolded a piece of white paper and carefully took out a rock of cocaine and fed it into her pipe. She lit it nervously and took a long drag and held it inside her lungs.

"It is alright," she thought.

"Good stuff, I love Columbia," she mused as she breathed out, letting some of the smoke out.

"Mui bien, mui bien.

Mui guena marca Americano.

Vamos a achar pelo meno diez Helicoptero de ellos esta mes," said Rodrigue with enthusiasm as he inspected a stinger, an American made land-to-air missile launcher, American made Bazookas and semi-automatic riffles heaped in the warehouse in southern Columbia.

It was one of the inspection sessions of new weapons shipment to FARC – Forcas Armadas Revolucionarios Columbiano, from their American suppliers. The weapons used by the 15th Batallion of FARC to protect the 300,000 acres of coca cultivated land in Caqueta southern Columbia against the US aerial pesticide spraying campaign. In exchange to the protection to the farmers, FARC received five percent of the market value of the coca crop from the farmers. They use the money to finance their war that had lasted for decades and killed about 42,000 people in their effort to turn Columbia into a socialist state.

Rodrigue had joined FARC since he returned from the US jail. He was the Commander of the 15th Battalion of FARC.

CHAPTER 49
Hotel dos Amigos
Nuevo Laredo, Mexico

The thought of the hotel receptionist kept intruding into Omar's train of thought. And he thought of him with a peculiar fondness.

"He is a good man," he murmured as the Salsa music from the music system petered out.

A faint rap on the door interrupted his thought. He lifted his gaze to the door as its handle made a downward arc and it slowly opened. The receptionist came into view and into the suite carrying a tray with three cups of ice cream.

"But I didn't order any ice creams," objected Omar.

"Yes I know, it is complementary from the hotel management," replied Abdul.

"Your wife?" inquired Abdul.

"Did she order it?" asked Omar.

"No, like I said, it's complimentary."

"Is she in?" asked Abdul.

"She is in the swimming pool," said Omar.

Abdul put the tray on the table and walked towards Omar.

"It's for you Omar."

"You're my son," he said tearfully and stretched out his hands to embrace him.

At that moment it occurred to Omar. The face.

"Daddy!? Dad!?" He said out loud as they embraced warmly.

Sniffs.

"I've always known I will find you one day. Thank thee Oh great Allah," said Omar looking skywards, tears streaming down his cheeks.

"You changed so much. I had never thought I will not recognize you at sight," said Omar.

"You changed even more son. I recognized the ring, and when you gave me the guest form, I became sure it's you, my Omar, my son" said Abdul.

"Why didn't you tell me at that moment?" asked

Omar.

"Because of the lady with you and the bellhop. I'm still a fugitive," said Abdul.

"Fugitive, an ugly word," thought Omar.

Omar hates to remember the times when he had to walk away from the TV room of the Orphanage whenever his father's photo was flashed on the TV screen with the caption:

"Wanted by the FBI terrorist task force, the CIA, Homeland security and the federal prisons authority".

Silence.

"You are looking younger than I'd imagined you'd be looking," said Omar.

"I would've been looking even younger than this if not for the worries of my fate, your fate and all that happened. But thanks for the compliments anyways," said Abdul.

"I was waiting to regain full sensitivity in my hands before I could come to the USA safely to search for you," said Abdul.

"What has your hands' sensitivity got to do with coming to the USA and finding me?" asked Omar.

"When I was caught, tried and imprisoned, my finger prints and mug shots from different angles were taken and stored. Now, to come to the USA safely, I had a hand transplant.

The surgeons spent about twenty hours cutting and connecting nerves, tendons, veins and arteries from the donor to my hands. Since then, I have been on heavy medication of anti-rejection drugs. And the nerves have regenerated fully well. It remains to regain full sensitivities and now I have new fingerprints. I also had a little facial surgery to add a cleft, this little cleft," he said touching the cleft on his chin.

"And..." he continued.

"....diminished the length of my upper lip. I mean the length between the nostril and the upper lip, it increases as one gets older. Just to make a little facial difference," said Abdul.

"Probably because of this little difference I failed to recognize you at sight," said Omar, with a bit of elation.

"Probably," said Abdul.

"Sometimes, I feel numb in my hands so I'm waiting and I 'm still seeing the surgeon to have a total recovery," added Abdul.

"But what really happened Dad?" asked Omar.

"You were caught in possession of a controlled substance?" said Omar.

A pause.

"Uranuim 235 they said. And after you escaped, the police, the FBI said that you are a suspected member of a terrorist organization. True?" asked Omar.

"Son…" began Abdul.

Omar listened attentively as Abdul went into minute details of why and how he became a terrorist and enemy of the infidel, and an American prisoner.

"Son, the Jihadist Movement will destroy the Infidel hegemon," said Abdul.

"You mean you were once a member of the Jihadist Movement and even know the now troglodyte Jihadist Supreme Disciple in person and still share his values and principles? A man that ordered your assassination? Oh Dad!" said Omar.

"Son, he ordered my assassination because he believed I trusted an infidel to the detriment of the Jihadist Movement on such an important mission. But he erred because he refused to see that I never knew that son of a bitch called Nathan, never trusted him, I just tried to use him to get to the target because there was no other alternative. But I forgive him — the Supreme Disciple because it is an unpardonable sin in the Movement for any Arab, a fadeyin and especially a Palestinian to trust an infidel," said Abdul

"Trusting an infidel is equal to collaborating with Zionism. It's being a collaborator. I should've known that the man Nathan is an infidel. He slipped twice. He said Yiddish words when we were talking. I messed up big time," said Abdul, his gaze distant.

"Unpardonable…?" said Omar.

"Of course, son. How can you trust an infidel, we are at war with them. You don't trust your enemy. You've been in America all these years, thanks to Allah you never converted to Christianity. You proved yourself a true Muslim, a true Arab at that," said Abdul.

""I didn't convert to Christianity because of the free thinking of America and Americans. The chairperson of the Orphanage, Mrs Poet, wouldn't allow me to convert, she said they are all the same thing, Christianity or Islam, because they all believe in one God. She told me to stick to the religion of my parents until I get to the age of majority to decide what is good for me. It is America.

America made it possible," said Omar.

"If you think it's good I didn't convert, then say thanks to America," he added.

"She said that?" said Abdul.

"Yes," replied Omar.

Silence.

"But Dad, I have always believed that the Arabs and the Palestinian people should particularly resent, despise and resist the Israelis because they occupy their lands, and not because they are Jews. Despising them and resisting them because of incursion to the Palestinian territories is one thing – a civic exercise – but resisting and despising them simply because they are Jews is a hate crime, evil.

Remember, the Arabs had once showed hospitality to the Jews, saved and gave them refuge from Christian invaders during the conquest of Spain when many Jews fled Spain and the crusaders, to take refuge in Arab countries of North Africa. And it has often been the interest of the USA to see Israel and Palestine live in peace and side by side. I'm still bullish on an eventual peace accord between the Israel and the Palestine," said Omar.

"Son, every Arab should join in the struggle and pray that the infidel hegemon be brought to her knees so that the Islamic kingdom and civilization to reign," said Abdul.

"Dad, don't hate and curse America. Cursing and hating America is cursing humanity. America is an indispensable member of the global community and civilization," said Omar.

"America is a hegemon," said Abdul.

"Dad, America is not a hegemon, America is rather the only surviving superpower. They find themselves in that position, what do you expect them to do?" said Omar.

"That is a honorific name for imperialism, hegemony and the imperialist America," replied Abdul.

"And America is ambitious," he added.

"Most nations and people are ambitious, fact is that some are more than others, and the weak should not blame the strong for being strong. The weak should blame themselves for being weak," replied Omar. "Besides, America is not ambitious in itself, ambition is an inherent part of human nature and being America."

"How not, when they maintain strong military presence in all parts of the globe. Twenty thousand troops in the gulf area and in the Middle East, in Europe, East Asia. Thirty seven thousand troops in South Korea, and they are putting the rise of China in check, and you said America is not ambitious," said Abdul.

"Being strong doesn't mean being ambitious," said Omar.

"How?" inquired Abdul.

"Well, I love America," said Omar.

"But America is not doing anything new and out-landish in their reign, as you said in their hegemonic dominance. Remember the Egyptians, the Pharaohs and their Israeli slaves? Egyptians are Arabs and Mus-lims right? Do you remember the Greeks of the ancient times, the Romans of the Middle Ages, when all roads led to Rome?

Today, all roads lead to Washington. Do you re-member the great British Empire and their Colonies, one of them being the USA? They all came and went. It's America's turn and I think the world must allow America to reign. If you believe in nature, in God, in Allah and all natural laws, then you must believe in the natural code that says: 'What goes up must come down'.

As for me, I will help America in any way I could to become even stronger and better. Don't border yourself Dad. Let the natural order of things take its toll. America falls if it ever will. It is better to get along with America than spend a whole lifetime and generation trying to bring America to her knees for the Islamic renaissance to reign. I I've often prayed that the Arabs get rich enough to give themselves decent education and standard of living to wipe out ignorance, and religious intolerance. I have never prayed for the Islamic dominance and civilization to reign. It is no good business dominating other people, nor bringing other people to their knees," said Omar.

"But they are so arrogant and hectorial son," said Abdul.

"That's part of it. It is part of being America, being at the top, it is part of being the global economic and political trouble-shooter. If one wouldn't exhibit a bit of arrogance, be despotic, hated and have a couple of sycophantic following. What's the need of being at the top, having a veto power without being a little arrogant sometimes, without being able to use it? It's the confirmation of your superiority. It's all natural, Dad. Don't border with America," advised Omar.

Abdul gazed up at Omar, a younger version of himself that didn't know nor understand America in the manner Arabs and Palestinians do. Life is no linear progression. He's taken the opposite direction.

"It's all the fault of America," thought Abdul.

Omar glanced at his father.

"Poor Dad, he hates America so much. He's chosen the easier course, because it is easier to hate than to love, easier to be brutal and violent. It takes courage to embrace the pacific and diplomatic course. As for me I love progress and I love America. And above all, I love the planet earth and the earth I'm out to salvage and the earth I will save," thought Omar.

Silence.

"How did you feel all these years?" asked Abdul, breaking the long pause.

"It's not been easy but I managed to obtain a PhD in Nuclear Engineering from the George Washington University," said Omar.

"Nuclear Engineering?" asked Abdul.

"It has been my dream for you son. It is for that we left Egypt so that you would be educated," said Abdul.

"America did it for us Dad," said Omar.

Omar noticed a flicker of discomfort in his father's face.

"Do you have a good job?" asked Abdul.

"Yes I like my job, especially the new project I'm developing," replied Omar.

"A project? What project?" asked Abdul.

"A type of an Anti-ballistic missile defence system, just like the one that is already in existence, but with some new features and capabilities," said Omar.

"Who will you give it to?"

"To the American government," replied Omar.

"Oh son, don't, please don't, bring your project, your discovery and give it to PLO, to Hamas, to Hezbollah, to the Jihadist Movement, to the Supreme Disciple. Give it to the needy. You can change the world political scenery with your discovery," said Abdul

"Look Dad, we Americans..." said Omar.

"Don't say that, you are not an American. Don't say you are because the Movement is at war with America and all the inhabitants of the Land," said Abdul.

"No matter the nation the project is given to or developed in, it belongs and will protect the entire global village, the entire human abode, the mother earth from extra- terrestrial invasion," said Omar.

"But where the control centre is stationed matters, doesn't it?" asked Abdul.

"Yes it does because it could be programmed not to protect a certain part of the globe, but that will be stupid because when any part of the global village is adversely destroyed by a heavy tonnage of extra-terrestrial blast, all other parts of the earth will feel the effect. I will work for America. America gave me the knowledge, in America I learnt the magic of discovery and project management," said Omar.

"Omar I lived my life fighting the infidel and now you say you will protect America. It is good if you know that America and the entire West, and Israel are known not for their kindness, peaceful intents and humility, but for their technological conquest, especially military technology and military might."

Come and prop up the Islamic civilization. It is the break we need most. Don't feed the American ego with your project. They have boasted of everything, including creating humans in the laboratory. And now you want to give them this new might of protecting the entire Universe from interplanetary attacks and invasion, with the ability to exclude any part of the universe from protection? Please don't empower them against the Islamic states," pleaded Abdul.

"Dad, when interplanetary terrorists attack the earth, they know no America, Europe, Asia, Arabs, Jews, Oceania or Africa. They will hit the mother earth from whichever angle they deem fit. The mother earth waits for and deserves our help, after all, it welcomed us all to life with air to breath and water to drink and hydrate our system. The earth waits for our rescue. I'm happy I've found a way to protect the mother earth from extra terrestrial terrorists. And I conceived it in America," said Omar.

"Extra-terrestrial terrorists? He is a catastrophist," thought Abdul, gazing at Omar.

His mind got busy on some concepts of catastrophe. Abdul knew that catastrophists had deduced that extra terrestrial life had been identified outside the atmosphere, and that microbes were found in the air samples trapped by balloon flying some 400km above the earth surface. And have suggested that diseases like influenza, that torment the inhabitants of the earth, might have arrived from space. And that black death of the 14th century that killed more than one third of the European population had much to do with asteroids and comets from outer space. Asteroids and comets are constantly bombarding the earth, sometimes small ones and at other times by big ones like the big one about six miles in diameter that catastrophists believe extinguished the dinosaurs from the face of the earth.

Abdul once heard of a big asteroid that bombarded the earth on the Siberian coast in 1908.

"And Omar is going to Yucatan Peninsula from here, something has been said about the peninsula and asteroids," thought Abdul.

"You will be going to the Yucatan Peninsula from here, eh?" asked Abdul

"Yes, to make some observations on the 180km diameter Chic-Xulub crater in the Peninsula. And bigger ones are yet to hit the earth. Remember the 1994 enormous fragments from the shoemaker comet, and the monstrous fireballs, some as big or bigger than the earth itself, thrown up when it plunged into the surface of Jupiter? Imagine such fireballs hitting the earth surface. It will set the earth ablaze and melt it into nothingness. That's a bit of the disaster from interplanetary strikes that the earth will witness anytime from now. And we must all work together to stop it, to save and protect the mother earth and preserve our common humanity," said Omar.

"With such a defence system, it becomes difficult to destroy the Infidel," said a mind to Abdul.

"America is vulnerable as long as volunteer suicide bombers are available on the Islamic soil. The infidel is there to be attacked. Just think it up and it's done. Nothing gives security and immunity to attacks more than common political and economic goals," thought Abdul.

Omar was studying his father, and from his expression he could see that Abdul was still very unrepentant.

"How could he spend an entire life in hate and anarchy?" thought Omar.

"But thank God I'm alive and I will get my children to live a life of integration and inclusion. Hate kills."

"Don't bother him too much. He is lost to the American system. Besides you were not there all these years to prune him into the struggle. To indicate the Islamic and Arabic values into him," thought Abdul.

"What of your childhood friends in the Orphanage? Hope, Nerry, Benett, John and ehmm…?" asked Abdul.

"You still remember their names, wonderful. Hope is the lady with me. She is my wife. We are here on pre-nuptial holidays. She is wonderful," said Omar.

"She is American," said Abdul.

"Yes," answered Omar.

"And we will get married in the next three months," added Omar.

"The Arab and American from the ashes of hatred," thought Abdul.

"Do you love her?" asked Abdul.

"She is marvellous. She has a large expanse of personality. You meet a differently sweet and lovely woman in her everyday. She arouses me every moment. You know she is that woman you never get tired of discovering. She is a person you will want and struggle to know, and explore, and she never ends. She can be a sophisticated American lady at one time and can change to the submissive Arab wife, ready to wear the veil at the next moment. She is very flexible. She is the ultimate. My ultimate love," said Omar.

A pause.

"As for Benett, he's getting married to Nerry on the same day I and Hope are getting married," said Omar.

"Benett is the German or Jew?" asked Abdul.

"Nerry is Jewish and Ben is German," replied Omar.

"The German and the Jew from the ashes of holocaust," thought Abdul.

"At first Nerry seemed not to like Benett. But Benett proved his self indispensable in her life. He helped her in academic works, acted as her body guard, protecting her against bullying from other children and students and was always on her side on any issue, and kept her company. Benett showered her with presents. He really loves and won her over," said Omar.

"Good! And John?" asked Abdul.

"John is African, eh?" he added.

"Yes, John is of African descent," answered Omar.

"Poor Johnny, only John is not getting married and it is not all well with him. It's really very unfair. Johnny is a good guy. He tried to date Vivian the British girl, but she seemed not to have interest in him. He tried to win her over but no ways. He tried mademoiselle Angelica the French girl, but she slipped away. Erica the American girl dumped him some five months back after a two years platonic relationship. And he lost a litigation law suit he filed against a New York aristocratic family whom he claimed had enslaved his great grand parents.

The court though recognized that it was a blight on the family's history and image, but ruled that the present generation were not responsible for enslaving John's ancestors.

Poor Johnny," added Omar.

"But the present generation inherited the wealth from the past generation. Wealth generated from enslaving Johnny's ancestors," said Abdul.

"Problem is that John is such a low budget guy. But he appealed the case to the Supreme Court. He once told me that if he wins the suit in the Supreme Court, he will use the indemnity to upgrade his standard of living and enhance his public relations and persona," said Omar.

"Poor Johnny I hope he wins," said Omar.

"Being poor and low budget is the more reason why he should have to use the only legitimate tactic available to the poor and the language that calls the master's attention − terror language. You don't negotiate with the master, because he as the master gives orders, he doesn't negotiate. Terrorise him and he gives you attention," said Abdul.

"Do you only think and talk of terror Dad?" asked Omar.

"You won't believe how much it works," replied Abdul.

"In life, people respond most in fear or hurt. Terror instils fear or hurt," said Abdul.

A pause.

"The wedding, your wedding is in the next three months right?" said Abdul.

"Yes the last day of the month," replied Omar.

"I will be in Washington to witness your wedding son," promised Abdul, his gaze crawling into the distance, chasing and knitting a malicious plot.

Omar saw the mischief in his father's gaze.

"I hope you are not coming to Washington with any hidden agenda, to unleash terror. If you have such plans, you better desist, Dad, because in the first place you and your likes have no more good and justifiable reason to be making terror on the American soil or American interests anywhere in the globe again, because you will all be easily nabbed. America is so strong, and just. You and your group cannot destroy America. Sometimes you can scratch America, when its security system is caught off guard. I doubt if you can carry out any more successful terror attacks in America. America has all sorts of defensive and security systems in place now and ..." said Omar.

"Propaganda. The American invisibility," thought Abdul.

Omar paused on seeing impugn on his fathers expression.

The phone thrilled with a call on the table.

"Excuse me," said Omar, and reached to get the receiver from its cradle.

"Good one," said Omar into the receiver.

"Good one," thought Abdul a curious frown creasing his brows.

"Hope, my wife," said Omar after replacing the receiver.

"You call her good one?" said Abdul

"Yes, and she is really good. It is most befitting to her. She has all the delicacy of goodness. She is very tolerant, religiously and otherwise. She is flexible. She gets along with people and never tries to dominate her friends and neighbours. She is kind and reasonable. She harbours no hate and rancour in her. She loves everybody, and loves the German, the Jew, the Israeli, the Palestinian, African and European. She hates terror and she loves to live life and loves the mother earth immensely," said Omar.

"You are in love son," said Abdul.

Omar smiled broadly.

"What will you tell Hope about me?" asked Abdul.

"How do you mean?' asked Omar.

"Will you tell her you found me, you found your father?"

"I've not thought of that. But of course I will tell her, why?" inquired Omar.

"She is so good and innocent she might want to do her country a favour and turn me over to the FBI, Federal prison authority, Homeland security, CIA or the Marshals. I'm still a fugitive you know. You wouldn't like to see me back in Jail, will you?" said Abdul.

Omar became thoughtful.

"But I can't lie to her," said Omar.

"You don't have to lie to your wife. Just don't tell her

anything. Omit the topic. Omission is not lying. I mean it is better than lying to her," advised Abdul.

"What if she finds out?" asked Omar.

"How can she find out if you don't tell her, you are the only person on earth today who knows about this? She's got no crystal ball, does she?"

"Dad!" said Omar thoughtfully.

"I will do it for you Dad, but you must promise me one thing," said Omar.

"What?" asked Abdul.

"You must desist from hating and cursing America," said Omar.

"Son, no sin, no terror," said Abdul.

"Hate and terror breed sins," replied Omar.

"Sins breeds terror, hate and curses," argued Abdul.

"Promise me Dad," urged Omar.

"I will think about it and while I think, you keep our secrets a secret, right?" said Abdul.

"Sure Dad," replied Omar.

"I will have to leave now, there is nobody in the reception," said Abdul and rose to leave.

Chapter 50
October 2025

American mediators in the middle-east peace talks had successfully got Israel and Palestine to implement the UN Security Council resolutions 242 and 338 that call for two separate sovereign national states with capitals in Jerusalem and Haran-al Sherif on the Palestine side of Jerusalem. American emissaries witnessed the unconditional withdrawal of Israel from the occupied territories though Israel refused to use the word 'withdrawal', but instead announced that she was giving Palestine some lands and autonomous territories. A week later, a general democratic election was held in Saudi Arabia, compliments of the new American foreign policy and avowed task of spreading liberal democracy to all corners of the world.

The Pentagon announced the withdrawal of the American troops scattered all over the global village to be replaced by an efficient minuscule satellite monitor of the global village that also enhanced military communications, and, compliments of the advanced American military technology, unmanned military jet fighters and bombers that could reach any part of the globe in less than five minutes, cruising at the speed of sound and at an altitude out of reach of any country's radar watch, thus violating no nations airspace to reach their targets from American bases in the Americas and intercontinental waters.

The Supreme Disciple hailed the new developments from his sanctuary in Tora Bora.

"We trust but will proceed with caution on the angelic moves made by the Infidel," he told TVAl Jazeera .

A member of the political arm of the Jihadist Movement won the mayoral election in the maritime city of Jeda.

The CIA, FBI and the Marshal services keep busy nosing around the caves and valleys around the global village in search of the most wanted and elusive fugitive and enemy America had ever known. The American enigma.

CHAPTER 51
Washington DC, USA
October 31, 2025

Abdul arrive in Washington by train from Portland Oregon on the Eve of Omar's wedding. He checked into a hotel west of the city. Omar met him in the hotel three hours later.

"You are welcome to America Dad," said Omar hugging him.

"Have you heard, Dad?" asked Omar.

"What?"

"The new American foreign policy and effort in the Middle East and the Arab Peninsula, the election in Saudi Arabia?" asked Omar.

"I heard the full details just this evening," replied Abdul.

"And what do you say to it?" probed Omar.

"It's good for America, for Palestine, For Arabs, for Islam, for Israel and Jews," replied Abdul.

"No sin, no terror. Dad say it with me," urged Omar

"Okay."

"No sin, no terror," father and son said in tandem.

Omar shot futile glance at the bag under the table. The bag was laden with germ bombs and germ grenades, but Omar didn't know it. The next morning, Abdul dressed in a western style three-piece suit to avoid calling attention. He crossed the street on his way to the wedding arena. He glanced back and forth to make sure nobody was looking at him before dropping the bag laden with germ bombs into a street bin.

"Hope they find it, deactivate and dispose of it. Hope it doesn't hurt nobody," he said.

In the wedding hall, Abdul, Rev. Robert and Sister Agnes looked on as the Judge declared Omar and Hope 'Husband and Wife'. He prayed for them.

"...and God bless America," prayed the Judge.

"God bless America," echoed the congregation.

"She is so beautiful," whispered Sister Agnes into Rev. Robert's ear.

"I hope they make the best of couples," said Robert.

"They will," replied Sister Agnes.

"We wish you a happy married life daughter," they said.

"God bless America," Abdul found himself saying.

"And bless Islam too," he added.

He closed his eyes and turned his face east towards Mecca and read his new creed:

Shake up the world oh Allah, and bring awareness to the entire human population to acknowledge that all races are indispensable members of the human community and civilization and should rather respect our differences and honour our common humanity for the entire human race to celebrate the future.

Oh Allah bless the German and the Jew.

Bless the Palestinian and the Israeli.

In thy great and omnipotent might Allah never allow the assemblage of the type of genes and how they interact with each other, as seen in the hate and terror trove named Herr Hitler. Let his genes and likes be forever wiped out from the face of the earth for thy peace and kingdom to reign.

And in thy tender and abundant mercy, do bless
America and let her dreams engulf her strong and ador-
able memories, so that the entire human race will celebrate the future, and live not only the American dream
but also the dream as spelt out in article one of the UN
charter and article one of the European court of human
rights:

'All human are born free and equal in rights and
dignity'.

Allahu Akbar

Allahu Akbar."

The End

About the Author

Obi Orakwue is a Biochemist, Research Associate and President of Obrake Corporation. Presently he's busy pruning his latest work entitled "Career Spouse".

His other works include:

Fiction
- Overqualified Labourer
- Corrupted Ambition
- Comedy of Time
- The Lost Gene
- Victim of Want

Non-fiction
- A Complete Guide to Overcome 'No Canadian Experience': How and Where to Obtain 'Canadian Experience'
- Two-Dozen Businesses You Can Start and Run in Canada, The USA and Elsewhere
- Immigrate, Live, Work, Study and do Business in Canada

He lives in Toronto, Canada.